SHADOWRUN:
THE JOHNSON RUN

KAI O'CONNAL

SHADOWRUN: THE JOHNSON RUN
Cover art by Ian King
Design by Matt Heerdt and David Kerber

Published by Catalyst Game Labs,
an imprint of InMediaRes Productions, LLC
7108 S. Pheasant Ridge Drive • Spokane, WA 99224

ONE

"I told you this would be easy."

It was practically a law that those words were guaranteed to be a curse, bringing down all the misfortune possible and then some. Keandra regretted them the moment they passed her lips.

As if reading her mind, E-jekt snapped his attention to her rather than the AR display in the air. She shrugged in response. He returned to hacking the alarm system for the next room with an exaggerated sigh and mumbling. If not for their current activities, he could have fit the stereotypical old ork sitting on his porch, scratching at his frizzy white beard, complaining about the kids. She imagined him screaming for her to get off his lawn and claiming to have clothes older than she was. Judging by the state of his tattered jacket, it didn't seem like too much of a leap.

Keandra looked down the hall, trying to catch any sign of the rest of their team. The white-tiled floor and brightly painted walls reflected the little light available to let her see all the way to the elevators. The hall was empty, which was both a good and a bad sign.

The good news was the guard on patrol was nowhere in sight. Her sole consolation rested on the fact she'd see him the moment he stepped into the hall. But the only tool at her disposal to deal with him was the Beretta tucked under her arm. If her responsibilities included being the muscle, things would've progressed so far past south they'd have looped around the world.

The bad news was Lance and Paz hadn't finished their rounds. She had no way of knowing if they found trouble. This floor of the tower was small, and shouldn't take more than ten minutes to do a sweep. Keandra glanced down at the display mounted on the inside of her wrist and winced. They'd been gone for almost twelve.

Closing her eyes, she strained to listen for any sound of the other runners. She heard the steady rattling hum of the HVAC system in the background and E-jekt's ever-present wheeze; the ork really was getting on in years. But she couldn't hear anything she could attribute to her teammates.

When she opened her eyes, Keandra jumped and put a hand against the wall behind her as her breath caught. Lance stood at the intersection only a few meters away, flashing a smile that would be menacing if she didn't know him better. He looked like a shadow, sleek and covered in black except for his shaved head. With his dark skin, he merged with the shadows to the point where she worried about finding him again if she took her eyes away. Not for the first time, Keandra appreciated having him as an ally.

His sword rested in its scabbard under his long coat, so he hadn't found any trouble. Experience taught Keandra that if he'd run into any disturbance, he'd still be armed. Despite their history, he continued to impress her with his stealth. Even watching him strut toward her, she couldn't hear his footfalls.

Paz was another story altogether. The sounds of the sturdy dwarf tromping down the corridor preceded her long before she turned the corner. Then again, it was expected of walking tanks with short metal legs and one unskinned cyberarm. Paz looked more machine than dwarf. Even the tight braids of her short hair added to her android impersonation, looking like thick, dark wires coming out of her head.

Unlike Lance, she held her assault rifle out and ready, moving with military precision as she swung into view, her gun barrel leading the turn. When she recognized the rest of the team at the end of the hall, she pointed her gun at the ceiling and marched toward them.

"All's clear on the east side of the tower. Looks like everyone cleared out for the day. How's the west side, Meat-sack?"

"Dark and empty, like your soul." Lance said the words with a grin that reached his eyes as he gave Paz a deferential nod.

"Somebody must've messed with his brain. We both know I don't got a soul."

Lance was quick to continue the verbal sparring. "I thought it was a heart you didn't have. I swore you had it replaced with a mechanical pump last year."

E-jekt let out a low growl, a cue to Keandra the banter distracted him. She hushed the other two and they quieted with professional precision. Paz spun around to watch the elevators, her gun lowered and ready to react at the slightest movement. Lance slid across the floor, moving like a whisper as he took up position behind E-jekt, ready to burst through the door if need be.

Several seconds of tense silence followed, straining Keandra's optimism. The security here should not take this long for E-jekt to dismantle. Perhaps his age reached the point where it affected his abilities. It wouldn't be surprising. But she couldn't picture going on a run with another decker. They'd been together since her first run, over twenty years ago. She glanced at him and opened her mouth to say something, but shut it before uttering a sound. Anything she said would add stress and make him take longer. Besides, she reminded herself, E-jekt was one of the best hackers she'd ever met.

The ork closed his eyes and pinched the bridge of his nose. He waved at the door with one hand, gesturing they should proceed. Lance opened the door, his leather jacket creaking as he slid through the narrow gap. Keandra waited, counting in her head until she reached twenty. Then she opened the door all the way and stepped into the room beyond. E-jekt crept in behind her, closing the door and leaving a small crack visible to the hallway beyond. Paz maintained a lookout position to secure their exit route. Everything moved as planned.

The room was a private office, with various fine art pieces decorating its walls and corners. Just one of those statues or portraits could fetch over twenty thousand nuyen to the right buyer. Keandra couldn't tell for sure, but she'd bet the glass decanters on the small table next to the desk were filled with real alcohol – and top-shelf stuff at that. The temptation rose in her to open one and waft the mouth to get a subtle taste of the rare beverage, but she tore her attention away. They had a specific target and the mission came before anything else. Besides, she had a bottle of her own at home. With what this job paid, she'd be able to afford another two or three.

Lance walked around the edge of the room, lifting the corners of the portraits away from the wall with a gloved hand to peer behind them. Three quarters of the way around, he stopped and waved the other two over. As they reached him, he lifted the nearest painting from its hook to reveal a safe embedded in the wall.

"I'll never understand the obsession with being old-fashioned and hiding your valuables behind pieces of art," he said. "It's such a trite custom, observed in most cases by those with far more wealth than sense. Still, their predictability makes our jobs easier."

Keandra pressed her lips into a thin line and glared at her verbose companion. Now was not the time for foolish witticisms. When he saw her stare, Lance offered a slight bow before moving out of the way, carrying the painting with him. He rested it against the wall, tilting his head to study the abstract shapes from a different perspective. It made the tattoo on the back of his head look comical as the angry dragon's gaze tilted to the side.

E-jekt fiddled with the keypad of the safe, alternating between it and his AR interface before giving her the thumbs-up to let her know he had it under control. Keandra turned away and investigated the rest of the room while she waited. The desk had a full holographic display, but she didn't dare turn it on. She kept her distance in case it was motion-activated. There was no telling what kind of security measures might be layered on top of it. Any unsanctioned activity could alert the corporate executive who worked here.

One of the walls in the room stood bare of any decorations or furnishings. Wandering over to it, Keandra noticed it wasn't a normal wall at all, but a large projection screen. Based on similar offices she'd been in, she guessed it displayed an outdoor scene when powered on. Having a large window would be a liability, but you couldn't deny the successful businessman his window office. That had been a representation of power ever since offices existed, and Keandra knew that these white-collars valued their status symbols more than any tangible success. She'd seen enough of them in her time and knew how to use them to her advantage.

"Problem."

Paz's voice snapped Lance and Keandra to attention, both turning toward the door to the hallway. Lance sprinted across the carpeted floor, but the sound of heavy gunfire erupted before he crossed halfway across the room. Keandra saw staccato flashes of light through the small crack in the doorway. Above the noise she heard a distinct deep thrum followed by a brief clatter.

Paz burst through the door and slammed it shut behind her as an explosion shook Keandra's knees.

"We've got company."

Several people shouted in the hallway, too jumbled and distorted for Keandra to make decipher any words, but it was clear they didn't have much time. Lance took up position behind the door as Paz stood near the edge, gun pointed at the opening. She gave a nod and Lance slid the door open enough for the dwarf to fire a burst down the hall. She and Lance moved in unison: she stopped firing and pinned her back to the wall as Lance slammed the door shut with his foot. The return fire ripped into the metal portal and echoed in the office like heavy rain on a tin roof.

Keandra rushed over to E-jekt, checking how he was coming with the safe. Sweat streamed down his face, running down the heavy wrinkles etched into his skin. His hands shook as he worked with his sprites. The entire scene proved impossible for her to decode.

"E-jekt, we need it open ten minutes ago."

For a moment, she wondered if he heard her, or more accurately, if it registered. He paused to take a deep breath, and then his entire body went slack. Now, more than ever, he needed to be protected. Keandra crouched in front of him, shielding him with her body. Nothing in the room looked usable as portable cover. The desk might stop a bullet, but the weight of it made it an impossibility for her to move on her own.

Across the room, Paz and Lance continued to work together to fill the hall outside with a deadly rain of bullets and explosions. A few return shots made it through their defense and bit into Paz's armor. More than once, a bullet sparked off her arm or leg before ricocheting and embedding itself in one of the walls. If it affected Paz in any way, she didn't show it.

Time was critical. Reinforcements would arrive soon. Those would be the heavy troops, maybe even Knight Errant. They needed to get out, even if it meant abandoning the mission. Keandra turned, grabbing E-jekt's shoulder and getting ready to force him back to the physical world if need be. Before she had the opportunity, the safe whirred as gears turned inside and the door swung open. Keandra stood and flung the door open the rest of the way, reaching inside and dumping most of the contents on the floor. At this point, secrecy was pointless.

In the back of the safe was their objective, some type of BTL chip in a glass case. She snatched it and held it to the light from her commlink, verifying the part number etched into the main processing chip. Their intel had proven valuable—this was the one they needed.

Shoving it into one of the pockets of her coat, Keandra grabbed E-jekt by the arm and dragged him up. "Target acquired. We need an exit, now."

Paz dumped the magazine from her assault rifle and slammed a fresh one into place. She also loaded a couple of grenades. "Next burst, Lance take point. I'll keep 'em pinned down. My hallway, second office on the right. Taking the express."

E-jekt's arm tensed in Keandra's grip before he yanked it free. Keandra knew he wouldn't be happy with the plan, but it was better than fighting through the entire security team and their reinforcements. Besides, it was Paz's call. When things went south, she got them out in one piece.

When there was a brief lull in the clatter of bullets against the door, Lance jerked it open and Paz fired into the smoky hall. This time, instead of slamming the door shut, Lance ducked low and slipped through the opening, skirting to the far wall as he drew his blades and tapped into supernatural speed.

He shifted one shoulder, dodging a bullet that would have pierced his chest, and then he stood in the middle of three security guards. His blade slashed the throat of the first man within reach and then he spun, driving the tip deep into the chest of the second. He dropped to the ground, yanking his blade free with the motion and taking cover as Paz burst out of the room and sprayed rounds with a beastly roar. The final guard in the advance group fell, her body ripped to shreds by the hail of bullets. The rest of the security team ducked behind the far corners and didn't dare peek around and expose themselves.

Paz held the trigger down until the magazine emptied and she reloaded once again. Keandra sprinted, steering around her dwarf companion and following Lance as he turned and made for their exit point. Her feet slipped in the blood and she stumbled forward. Rather than catch herself, she went with the momentum, turning her shoulder to slam it into the wall and bounce back toward the office serving as their contingency plan. Once out of the line of fire, she turned around to take stock of her team while Lance broke the window. A sudden rush of air breezed past her as the wind howled through the makeshift opening, drowning out the crystal rain sound of fractured glass.

Turning the corner, E-jekt lurched to the side and his eyes widened. He stretched a hand toward Keandra as he collapsed, his other hand clutched to his bleeding side. Time slowed as he hit the ground, and Keandra couldn't move, couldn't even force herself to breathe. Then everything snapped back to normal speed fast enough to cause her head to spin.

Paz's weapon roared to life once again, drowning out the other noise as she laid down suppressive fire. She came into view, holding her gun in one hand as she reached down with the other to grab E-jekt's belt. Walking backward, she half-dragged, half-carried him to the office before kicking the door shut. Keandra's muscles listened to her brain once again and she rushed to one of the tables, sliding it across the floor to bar the door.

"Come take the old man, Beanpole. Don't get squished on the way down."

Lance didn't respond except to pick up E-jekt's limp body. The old hacker groaned and his eyes fluttered. He was alive, but how long he stayed that way depended on them getting off corporate property in a hurry. Lance cinched a strap around his and E-jekt's waists, connecting the two of them. He hobbled over to the window, looking like some strange bi-meta conjoined twin, while the two women braced the table against the solid thudding of a portable battering ram. Lance fell out of the window, and Keandra hoped he got enough distance from the tower.

"You next. I got this." Paz's legs and arms let out soft *whirr*s as they locked into place.

The wood door splintered, making Keandra flinch as she stood up, ready to follow Paz's order. She sprinted to the hole in the window and dove through, spreading her arms out to slow her fall as much as possible so she could get her bearings. Below her and almost half a block away was Lance; he had already deployed his chute and looked close to touching down. Keandra angled herself in his direction and pressed her arms against her body, plummeting through the sky to gain speed and distance. If she knew Paz, there would be a significant surprise left behind for those who broke down the door.

Sure enough, a loud explosion went off behind her, followed by the sound of splintering glass. Her distance saved her from the heat and shockwave of the blast, so she pulled the cord to deploy her chute. She came down hard, rolling when she hit the pavement to keep from breaking an ankle or a leg.

A few people on the street ran away as Keandra and her team dropped into their midst. The explosion gathered a bit of a crowd, but none wanted to be around when the authorities showed up. Or else they didn't want to be caught in the crossfire. Either way, the street became deserted except for her and Lance cutting himself free from the tangled mess of his chute. Already she heard DocWagon's sirens; E-jekt would be in good hands soon. It cost a fortune, but she never doubted the worth of it. Few runners did.

With the *thud* behind her that she felt as much as heard, Keandra knew Paz escaped. The pavement cracked from the force of the dwarf's impact, but it didn't slow her. She sprinted to the van, already using her connection to bring it online and get the engine started. Keandra hurried to the other two members of her team.

She took E-jekt from Lance and laid him gently at the edge of the street while Lance collected and coiled up their chutes. They were generic, but any proof left behind could lead back to them in ways they never considered. They left nothing to chance.

E-jekt's breathing was steady, but his eyes refused to focus. One hand still pressed tight to the wound in his side. It looked like the bleeding slowed, but a small trickle continued to run and the copper odor permeated the air.

E-jekt squeezed Keandra's shoulder with his other hand; its lack of strength concerned her. "Easy, huh? We're getting too old for this."

"I know, friend. Take it easy. DocWagon's almost here."

The lights of the emergency vehicle reflected off the buildings across the street. Tires squealed as the medivac took a sharp corner. Keandra gave E-jekt's hand a final tight squeeze before resting it against his chest.

"We'll meet you at the safehouse. They'll have you patched up in no time."

He smiled and Keandra turned away, rushing to the van. Lance stood in the back next to their collected gear. One hand rested on the door handle, ready to slam it shut as soon as she got inside. Keandra vaulted the small step and rolled in the tangle of chutes as Paz took off. Lance closed the door, and for a few moments, Keandra allowed herself to rest in the darkness with her eyes closed, taking deep breaths. When she felt her heart slow its erratic rate, she crawled out of the fabric and up to the passenger's seat.

By now, Paz drove through the streets of Seattle with deliberation. They were far enough from the towers for normal traffic to resume, giving them the opportunity to blend in with the regular Friday night commuters. Keandra pulled down the visor and fixed her appearance. They weren't scheduled to meet with the Johnson for hours, but she believed in being prepared at all times. They had a reputation to maintain, and even a casual glance from a passing vehicle could ruin that for them. If anyone recognized her, she needed to look presentable and professional.

Once satisfied, Keandra checked E-jekt's commlink. It pinged from Group Health Central Hospital. She let out another deep sigh and collapsed into her seat, sinking in as much as the stiff leather would allow. "He's at the hospital, still in one piece."

"You know, I bitch whenever that bill comes up, but I gotta hand it to those DocWagon suits. They got some damn good drivers and are worth every nuyen. Glad the old man's gonna be fine. Sticking with the original plan?" Paz glanced at Keandra without turning her head.

"Yes. I can't meet our Johnson smelling like gunpowder and blood, so I need a change of clothes. There's only so much I can do from here."

"He's gonna be pissed every suit and his brother's gonna hear about what we did tonight. Didn't he say he wanted it quiet?"

"You let me handle that."

From the back of the van, Lance chuckled just loud enough to be heard.

TWO

The clock read 8:20 pm as Keandra pulled into the parking lot of Elliot's. The meeting wasn't scheduled to start until eight forty-five, but Keandra wanted to set the scene to her advantage. She was thankful that at this point in her career, she had her beautification routine down to a science. It was her specialty, no different than Paz going to the gun range. Tonight she scrubbed her pale skin clean and smoothed over any wrinkles. She had pulled her wavy black hair into a tight braid and rested it over one shoulder. Her dress was modest and modern, an indirect sign of one who could afford to pay attention to fashion for those who were knowledgeable about such things. She doctored her appearance to showcase her professionalism and class with even a glance. Thankfully, she aged more gracefully than E-jekt.

She took a moment to do a final review while waiting for the valet to reach her car door. When he opened it, she extended a hand and slid out with the grace of a dancer. On the passenger's side, Lance exited and walked around the rear to meet her. She took the lead, with him following just half a step behind, the human socialite and her elf bodyguard. It was a role they played well, and served them better.

As she climbed the half set of stairs, she took a quick glance around to survey her surroundings. Granted, she wouldn't pick up as much intel as usual, since E-jekt was still out of commission. Paz should be with him by now, making sure everything was okay. Keandra blinked and fought the urge to shake her head as she forced herself to focus on the surroundings and not be distracted. Everything was taken care of to the best of their abilities.

The crowd waiting in front of the maître d' consisted of the standard selection of the population she'd anticipated: mid-level corporate workers, a state judge with an escort, and a young elf couple who reeked of excess. The corporate group occupied the entire center of the hallway leading up to the maître d's stand, and Keandra stopped just before reaching their group. She wouldn't maneuver her way through them. She had time to spare. One of the human men turned to her and offered a smile that would have made her skin crawl if she bothered to notice it. Instead, she kept her gaze focused through the group, looking past them.

Her presence made the man shift his weight from one foot to the other, and the smile faded from his face. He looked back to his friends and they chuckled behind upraised hands. Clenching his jaw, he whirled back to her and opened his mouth to say something. Before he got a word out, the well-dressed ork maître d' appeared behind him and forced him out of the way with a shove that knocked him into a few of his companions. The small tangle collided with the wall next to the elven couple.

"I apologize for making you wait, Miss Tiernay. If you'll come this way, your table has been prepared. It is a pleasure to see you again."

Keandra took the ork's offered hand, giving a small dip of her head as she did so. The smile on her face was genuine.

"Think nothing of it, Francis. I only just arrived. Your service is, as always, impeccable."

He smiled and seemed to blush a little at her compliment, but with orks it was always difficult to tell. The limited lighting didn't make it any easier. As soon he opened the doors to the restaurant proper, a wave of heat and sound washed over Keandra; she felt herself flush and her body threatened to start sweating.

As her gaze meandered around the tables, a flood of information about the other diners assaulted Keandra's cybereyes. Her programs still ran, collecting data about every person she saw. Without E-jekt's sprites filtering the data and collecting it in a database, it was too much for her brain to process. She forced herself to ignore the information, and focused only on what was physically around her. She also made a mental note she'd need to turn off the information scrubbers before the Johnson arrived.

Francis led them to the far side of the restaurant and opened one of the glass doors to a patio overlooking the Sound. The gust of cool air felt great on her skin even as it raised goosebumps on her exposed arms. They both stepped outside and Keandra saw that only one table was set on the patio. Even without her special reservation, the patio no longer appeared a popular choice among regular diners. The dropping temperatures did make certain aspects of her job easier.

"The waiter will be along presently. If you need anything, please don't hesitate to notify the front desk. We are at your service."

"Of course. Thank you, Francis."

He gave a final smile and a bow, closing the door behind him as he returned to the heated room. Once the door was shut, all the noise cut off abruptly. The only sounds were the wind and the lapping of water as it splashed against the hulls of a few boats moored nearby. Keandra walked to the railing and took a deep breath, appreciating the heavy salt smell on the air. She stared at the lights of several ships in the Sound, each one reflected in the dark water below.

After a few moments enjoying the view, she returned to the table and took her seat. She chose the chair that put her back to the only door leading to the patio. Mr. Johnson would want to keep the entrance and exit in view at all times. If he had his back to it, he would be uncomfortable and suspicious, which would make him harder to negotiate with. He was already bound to be disappointed with their performance. In order to smooth out the situation, Keandra needed him as comfortable as possible.

Lance took up a position on the far side of the door, standing straight and crossing his arms but not leaning against the wall. Keandra knew he would stand like that all night if he wasn't needed. His body control was thorough enough for him to remain as still as a statue for hours at a time. His position was deliberate. Far enough away that Mr. Johnson would know Keandra was protected, but not so close to threaten their employer.

A waiter came out on the patio carrying a standing bucket filled with ice and a bottle tucked under his arm. He placed the stand next to Keandra's table and presented the bottle so she could read the label. A natural Chardonnay with no synthetic modifications or additions. It was pricey, but it was also Mr. Johnson's favorite. She nodded and the waiter slipped the bottle back into the bucket, twisting it until half the label sat submerged under the ice. The staff at Elliot's knew better than to open the bottle until her guest arrived. He would make a show of inspecting it like a connoisseur, even if the only thing he was checking was that it had not been tampered with.

"Is there anything else you need?"

Keandra smiled and shook her head. "That's all for now. Thank you."

The waiter bowed and left, closing the door behind him and once more shutting out the restaurant noise. For a few seconds, Keandra enjoyed the peaceful night and forced herself to relax. The tension from their earlier run continued to creep through her entire body like a contagion. All she had to do was handle one small negotiation and then it would be time to move on.

But move on to what was the question. Another job? Another run where they dodged gunfire and barely managed to get out by jumping out of a window? While it was true that they were an accomplished runner team, sooner or later everyone's card came up. Security was always improving while their bodies were degrading, except perhaps for Paz— her body might technically be improving. Nonetheless, the weight of her forty-four years burdened Keandra like a stone collar, and she felt an exhaustion extending beyond their recent adventure.

While she waited, she accessed her commlink and connected to the private network shared by her team. She needed an update from Paz.

<*How is he?*> she texted.

<*He's doing fine. Tough old bastard. It'll take more than just a random bullet to take him out. Doc's already removed it and got him patched up. He's just sleeping it off. They'll be kicking him out soon. I'll take him back to primary. How you holding up? Suit show up yet?*>

<*Not yet. But the meeting doesn't start for another five minutes. He never shows up early; likes to make sure he's never kept waiting.*>

<*Meat-sack keeping an eye on you?*>

<*At least I have the wherewithal to know how to dress appropriately for the occasion.*> Lance replied. <*There's a reason

*you never get to attend these dinners. I believe it is called class? It's
a shame really, since the alcohol is to die for.>*

<Real alcohol? Not synthahol? Bring some back!>

Keandra's commlink pinged an alert that her guest arrived
and was being escorted to her table. She silently thanked
Francis for his diligence. It was one of the many reasons she
loved using the venue.

<Enough, you two. Our employer just arrived.>

Keandra put her commlink away and folded her hands
on the table, forming the perfect picture of etiquette and
form. She heard the door open behind her, but did not turn
around at the sound. She waited until Mr. Johnson came into
her field of view before she acknowledged him. He was an
older human, easily in his fifties, but possessed a strength and
vitality of someone still in his early twenties. Working for a
AAA company certainly came with its benefits.

She stood up and extended her hand. He took it in both of
his and offered a small bow while his bodyguard maneuvered
around them to pull out his boss's chair. Keandra didn't know
his name, but she did know it was the same bodyguard who
always accompanied Mr. Johnson on these transactions. She
detected the slight bulge of a firearm underneath the human's
jacket, also no different than she expected.

"A pleasure to see you again, Miss Tiernay. It is always
enjoyable to have these chats with you."

Keandra scanned his face as he spoke, searching for any
sign of how he really felt. There was a slight twitch to his cheek
that made the skin around his eyes tighten when he said the
word 'pleasure,' but other than that, he gave her nothing to go
on. He was good at this game, as she both expected and knew
from personal experience. Otherwise, he never would've
reached the status he currently held.

"The pleasure is all mine, Mr. Johnson. I've ordered your
favorite."

She gestured toward the bottle chilling in the ice bucket.
As he picked it up to examine it, she took her seat. Out of the
corner of her eye, Keandra saw a faint shimmer on the other
side of the glass separating them from the rest of the diners.
The AR screen shielded their conversation from any prying
eyes. For the moment, they had their privacy.

Mr. Johnson finished his inspection of the wine bottle
and handed it behind him without looking at his bodyguard.

Then he sat down, folding his hands on the table and staring at Keandra. She refused to yield under the scrutiny of his stare as he attempted to ferret out her secrets just as she had done moments before. She smiled and held out her glass once the bodyguard opened the bottle. He served her first, and then his employer. Keandra raised her glass.

"To good business."

She took a sip, noticing that Mr. Johnson waited until she swallowed and put her glass on the table before lifting his own to his lips. It was nice to know she had earned so much trust over their years of working together. Then again, it wasn't a surprise. If he behaved any differently, it would have made her nervous. Up to this point, everything proceeded according to her expectations.

"Speaking of business, I heard there were some difficulties."

Keandra kept her smile consistent and easy without forcing it. She wouldn't give him any indication of how ugly things had gotten.

"Nothing we couldn't handle. After all, you specifically requested our services because of our ability to handle difficulties."

"The report I received indicated a violent response and some trespassers dealt with. Nothing was stolen and the company suffered a minimal amount of collateral damage."

"Since when have you ever known a security company to confess to an utter failure on their part?"

Keandra deepened her smile and cocked an eyebrow before picking up her glass and taking another sip. It was cool and smooth, with just a hint of fruity acidity as it slid down her throat.

Mr. Johnson leaned forward in his chair. The motion was subtle, and Keandra noticed it by the tightening of his suit coat around his elbows.

"You were able to complete your objective?"

For a few seconds, Keandra stalled by savoring the wine. It wasn't completely an act—it really was an excellent vintage. But she wanted to enjoy the moment a bit longer as well. She couldn't let the bait hang out for too long, but even the brief second of holding the upper hand brought her no small amount of glee. She let her glass hang from her fingertips and swirled it in front of her, dropping her gaze to focus on the liquid climbing its walls. From this viewpoint she could still make out every detail of Mr. Johnson, but it gave the appearance of inferiority. He was not a man who dealt well with being in a weaker position and assuaging his discomfort mattered.

"Of course," she said at last. "I would not have handled our meeting with the original arrangements if it was only going to lead to disappointment."

Now that the moment had passed, Mr. Johnson eased back and picked up his own glass, once again resuming the aloof air feeding his sense of superiority. It was his turn to savor the alcohol while buying time and forcing Keandra to wait for his response. This was the game they played, and one Keandra enjoyed. She looked up to match his gaze and refused to speak before him.

The silence stretched on long enough that the waiter came out carrying a couple of plates of steaming food. They had come here often enough that the waitstaff no longer bothered to take their orders. Mr. Johnson never touched the dish, but he appeared to relish the aroma of the spices. Keandra refused to let the food go to waste, so she'd gotten used to her fish growing cold. She wouldn't eat in front of her employer if he refused to partake. It was still good, even if it had to sit for several minutes.

Mr. Johnson waited until the waiter departed before he spoke again. "I do believe my instructions specified no one was to know of your presence. It seems as if you have done quite the opposite."

He tilted his head to the side. Again, it was almost imperceptible and most people would never notice. Most people did not have Keandra's levels of scrutiny.

"Sometimes such encounters are inevitable. Even the best of plans can run into unexpected obstacles."

"Were any of your resources damaged?"

His words cut her off before she had a chance to justify the encounter with security, and caught her off balance. Did he know about E-jekt? Or at the least, did he know that one of them had been injured? Keandra took precautions to make sure most of her team remained hidden and never known about. Being too well—known could be a hazard. The only faces and false identities they ever shared publicly were hers and Lance's.

Too late, Keandra realized she gave him information. This time the smile crept around his face and reached up to his eyes with a brief sparkle letting her know he was only plying her for information. Even if he did know about her team, he clearly didn't have the facts relating to E-jekt's injury. But now he knew someone was hurt. She cursed herself for slipping up with so easy a trap.

"Nothing you need to worry about. After all, the resources at our disposal are not what you're really interested in, are they? You are more interested in our results."

Lance stepped forward as if summoned, pulling the BTL chip out of his pocket and resting it on the table before resuming his sentry position. With two fingers, Keandra slid it across the tablecloth, leaving it halfway between the two of them. He reached out and picked up the chip, handing it over his shoulder without glancing back. The bodyguard removed it from its case and plugged it into a scanner on his watch. Both negotiators waited until the bodyguard performed his analysis.

"It checks out. The chip is valid and undamaged."

The bodyguard placed the chip back on the table in front of his employer. Mr. Johnson drummed his fingers on the table next to the chip. The motion was light, and the impact with the hard surface made little sound.

"Your team performed adequately, and I am glad to see you have in fact recovered your objective. However, I still maintain issue with your methods."

"Clearly you don't have that much of a problem with our methods, or you wouldn't keep us in your employ. This is the tenth time we've been of service to you in the last six months, I believe. If you had a problem with our methods, surely there would be others who would take your money."

"True enough, which is why it is such a disappointment that you did not rise to the usual level of excellence I have come to expect. Perhaps your reputation is catching up with you and you have hit the limits of what you can accomplish. All things start to fade with time."

"Even corporations?"

Mr. Johnson chuckled, something Keandra had never seen before.

"Especially corporations."

Mr. Johnson pushed his chair back and stood up from the table, scooping up the BTL chip and dropping it into his jacket pocket. He extended a hand palm-up to Keandra. She placed her hand on top of his and he nodded.

"You will find your usual fee deposited into your accounts. I'm sorry to say that your performance means there will be no additional bonus. However, I do hope this is not the last time I will be able to count on your services."

Keandra smiled and returned the nod. "Of course. I understand completely, Mr. Johnson. Have a wonderful evening. I look forward to our next endeavor."

"I'll be in touch."

With those words, he took his leave, the bodyguard close on his heels as he left the patio. Keandra waited until she received the notification that his vehicle had left the parking lot before picking up her fork and digging in to her food. She was glad to have the opportunity, since her mouth wouldn't stop watering at the scent of poached sturgeon with lemon. Lance took that as his cue and sat down in Mr. Johnson's chair, helping himself to the food left behind.

"That seemed to go smoothly, all things considered," he said between bites.

"Something he said has me uneasy. Did you see how he reacted when I made that crack about corporations? Something big is going on." Keandra shrugged and devoured another bite of fish. "At least we'll have more work ahead of us. I suppose that's the most we can hope for. That and not catching any bullets on our next run. Speaking of, let's finish up and get back to the primary. I want to check on E-jekt."

"Paz will be less than pleased if we come back empty-handed."

"Then take the bottle. We've already paid for the whole thing."

THREE

Their primary safehouse was a secured apartment on the twelfth floor in downtown Seattle. Keandra owned the place, purchasing it using certified credsticks years ago when they started to hit their successful stride as shadowrunners. It wasn't perfect, but it had everything they needed to plan their excursions. Keandra was proud of it, and thankful to have it considering how many times they'd needed to lie low over the years. The building owner made a point not to determine his tenant's identities, and even removed all cameras in the building. Plus, the location was convenient right in the middle of downtown with restaurants, clubs, and corporate sectors all within easy walking distance. Keandra wondered if they were an anomaly, or if the location was popular with other shadowrunners. She'd seen several members of high society in the hallways, so it was clear the apartments catered to the wealthy with a desire for anonymity.

By the time she and Lance arrived at the apartment, E-jekt and Paz were already there. The older ork rested on the couch, splayed out with his head propped up on the arm. He had the distant stare of someone fully in the Matrix. Paz sat on the floor, cleaning a small collection of her armaments she kept at the safe house. She must have stopped when the door opened as Keandra stared at the barrel of an Uzi. Paz put it back down and clicked the safety on when she recognized the new arrivals.

"You better have brought me back some of that good stuff."

Lance hurled the bottle at her as soon as Keandra was out of the way, and Paz snapped her arm up to catch it before it smashed against her shoulder. She grinned, pulling out the cork and taking a long swig before putting it down next to her, now smudged with black grease. Keandra went to the kitchen and turned on the air filters. Hopefully they'd help clear out the gun-oil smell pervading the air. When she returned, she dropped on the couch next to E-jekt and looked him over. His body was limp as she lifted his arm and examined the wounds on his side. The hospital did a good job patching him up, and only a little bit of redness had bled through the bandage, so he looked like he'd be fine. Probably hurt like hell, though.

She let his arm go and sent him a quick message.

<Care to join us? It's time to debrief.>

E-jekt blinked a few times as he came back to reality and shifted on the couch, wincing in response to the motion. Keandra patted his leg before standing up so he could have the entire space to himself. She moved to the center of the room where everyone could see her. The rest of the team gave her their undivided attention, Paz even putting down the gun she worked on.

"I met with Mr. Johnson and he transferred our fee into our team account. On the way back from the restaurant I verified it's all there. There was no bonus, so after taking out expenses and overhead, we'll each get about five thousand nuyen. Nothing weird there, and the scrubbers are already siphoning the money through to our accounts. It should all be there in about two days."

"What did the suit have to say? Was he pissed things got loud and messy?" Paz asked.

"He was less than pleased. That's why there was no bonus. But at least he didn't try to cut our fee. He also said he'd be willing to work with us again, so we didn't burn that bridge."

"That's a good thing, right? I mean, of all the suits we've worked for over the years, this one pays the best. Usually gives us a bonus too, when things don't get all messed up. Still wish you'd let me go try the fancy food for once."

E-jekt pushed himself to a sitting position, swinging his legs around. He put his hand on his side and pulled it away, checking the palm.

"So I guess it's on to the next job, right, boss?"

"How do you feel?"

"Dead tired and like my skin's hanging loose around me. I might need to be out for a bit and running remote support. I don't think I'm up for pushing that limit."

Keandra began to pace, a nervous habit she made sure not to demonstrate when meeting clients. It was one of the reasons she preferred a sit-down meeting when engaging in business. However, in front of her team, she didn't bother to hide her habits. She paused, an idea coming to mind. It was crazy, but it could work.

"She's getting that look again. I don't like when she gets that look. At least let me stock up on ammo first." To accentuate her point, Paz picked up one of her handguns and slammed a magazine into place.

Keandra snapped her attention back to her team.

"I've got an idea. Look, we have a reputation, right? We always get the job done, no matter the risks. We've earned that reputation, and more than one Johnson out there knows we can handle ourselves. Hell, we get more offers for work than we could take on even if we cloned ourselves. I only tell you about the best offers we get. I literally turn down at least ten every week. But you know who doesn't know us? Or at least doesn't know our faces?"

"Knight Errant?"

"Anyone, hopefully."

"Corporate security?"

"UCAS?"

Keandra shook her head and waved a hand to stop the stream of guesses.

"Other runners. Hell, we don't even know the faces of most other runners. All we know are their aliases and their reputations. Granted, there's a few who like to showboat, but most runners know getting too popular paints a big target on your back."

Keandra paused, waiting to see if anyone else would jump to the same conclusion she had. She glanced from one team member to the next, but they were all silent and waiting for her to finish. Just before she gave up and continued, she saw the light of an idea on E-jekt's face as his eyes went wide and he shook his head.

"You can't be serious."

"Yes I am! Think about it. It could totally work!"

Paz frowned. "Someone mind filling in the rest of us who aren't as quick? Your nice loveable enforcers are kinda in the dark here. No offense, skinny."

Lance just waved a hand, brushing aside Paz's comment.

E-jekt spoke up. "Well, our illustrious leader wants us to hire other runners to do the work while we get paid."

The room became so quiet Keandra heard faint snatches of music from the club across the street through their soundproofed windows. Paz stared at E-jekt and turned slowly toward Keandra, her eyebrows raised all the way up. Lance tilted his head and scrunched his face.

"It isn't as crazy as it sounds," Keandra said. "If other runners don't know who we are, we claim to be a Johnson. I'll handle the negotiations. It won't be anything different than what I'm currently doing, I'll just be sitting on the other side of the table."

"But you don't work for a corp!" Paz slammed her gun down on the floor.

"But *they* don't know that, do they? We take a job and then farm it out to a team we know can get the job done, at a reduced rate. We take the payscale that our reputation earns, and subcontract the work to someone else, letting us collect a small portion of it. Think of it like a finder's fee. The job still gets done, the Johnson still gets what he wants, the runners still get paid, and so do we. Everyone wins. The best part is, no risk for us. We don't go into the hot zones."

"This is absolutely fucking insane—" Paz began

Lucas's eyebrows lifted. "In a rare show of solidarity, I find I have to agree with our mechanized infantry."

"—and I love it!" the dwarf finished.

Lucas rolled his head back until he struck the wall and spoke to the ceiling. "So much for harmonious unification."

Keandra turned to face E-jekt directly. His opinion would be more than enough to sway Lance to her way of thinking. "What do you think, E-jekt? We're all getting a little long in the tooth. Maybe it would be best to leave the grunt work to someone else and ride on the reputation we've earned. We'll start small, something easy, and see how it goes."

All eyes in the room turned to the ork as he deliberated. He took a deep breath and winced, bringing his hand once again to his side. After a few more gentle breaths, he opened his eyes and looked at Keandra.

"You do have a point."

Keandra turned to Lance, but she already knew the battle was won. He appeared to know it too, as he held up both hands in supplication. "If everyone wants to go down this crazy road,

I am more than willing to participate and learn what trouble I need to save you from."

She nodded. "All right, it's decided, then. The first thing we need to do is find a good job, and then start looking for runners who could take it on. E-jekt, I want you to start compiling a list of runner teams in the area looking for work. Try to find someone who has a decent track record, but is either new to the scene or at least hasn't taken on any big jobs. I'll start filtering through our backlog and see what we can try that wouldn't be too large of a task: probably something normally beneath our paygrade. I'll come up with an excuse for why we're taking the job. Lance, you'll need to take on the most dangerous part of this."

"What would that be?"

"You need to help Paz look presentable as a bodyguard for a Johnson."

For what may have been the first time Keandra had ever seen, Lance was speechless. No pithy comeback rolled of his tongue. All he managed to do was stare at Paz. She offered him a toothy smile promising a future filled with difficulty.

"But that's tomorrow. For tonight, let's get some rest. We've certainly earned it."

With those words, the meeting ended. Lance and Paz gathered their belongings and prepared to leave. When E-jekt stood up from the couch, Keandra put a hand on his shoulder. "Crash here. I'll get you a blanket and a pillow."

"I can make it back to my place just fine."

Keandra didn't bother responding. She knew the more she argued, the more he would dig in his heels. Instead, she went to the linen closet and pulled out some extra bedding. By the time she came back into the living room, the other two had left. Keandra tossed the bedding on the couch next to E-jekt. She turned around and walked down the hall to her bedroom. Behind her, she heard him grumbling, but also making himself comfortable. Yes, he could handle the trip back, but she felt better this way.

As she crawled into her own bed and arranged the pillows around her to form a nest, her mind wandered over the proposed plan. Doubts crept in past the false confidence she'd displayed to her team. She mentally worked through the potential problems multiple times, convincing herself as much as she had the others. It took over an hour, but she eventually managed to fall into a restless sleep.

She woke at five in the morning, sweat covering her body, and jerked to a sitting position. Keandra rubbed her face, shaking off any last vestiges of sleep. Out of habit, she checked the proximity sensors, but none had been tripped. As she started her morning routine, she called up a list of the possible jobs archived on her commlink.

By the time the sun rose and she didn't feel quite so guilty about disturbing her guest, she'd identified the job they'd use for their trial run. She'd even sent a message to the Johnson, requesting more details and negotiating the fee. The initial communication with his secretary had gone well, and everything appeared to be going according to plan. He was grateful they found time to take on his task. It was a straightforward wetwork gig for a target with a very predictable schedule. Discretion was not required, which made Keandra more comfortable handing it off to runners who might possess less finesse. It wasn't her favorite type of job, but they had taken a few over the years and this was the best option to use as a trial.

When Keandra entered the living room, E-jekt was awake and already plugged into the Matrix, given the distant look in his eyes. She sent him a message. *<Any luck finding us a team?>*

<Going through the potentials right now, actually. Do you know what kind of job it is?>

<Wetwork, so make sure they've got a track record for that.>

<I've got a team that'll work. Not too famous, but they have some prime jobs under their belt. They've got a rep for being hotheads, though.>

<Set it up.>

Keandra closed the display and went back to her room to pick out an outfit. She probably wouldn't need to meet with Mr. Johnson to finalize the arrangements. They had worked together before, and this job was simple enough that they already had enough details to go on. So she needed to make sure she looked the part of a corporate employer. Something strong and commanding, intimidating without being over the top or trying too hard.

She was perusing her options when her commlink pinged with a message from E-jekt. <*Lance and Paz are on their way. Our meeting is scheduled for three hours from now. I don't like this plan.*>

<*Starting to have doubts, my old friend?*>

<*Barely older than you.*>

Keandra paused, waiting for his next message. She knew he was mulling over his exact words.

<*I'll still go along with it. Let's just be careful.*>

<*We always are.*>

<*And yet I still got shot.*>

<*Maybe you should wear some armor. We'll pick you up some on the way to the restaurant. Besides, you need to look your part as well. As for your worries, what's the worst that could happen? They realize I'm not a Johnson and decide to open fire in the middle of a public venue? This'll be easy.*>

<*I hate when you say that.*>

FOUR

Keandra looked around the small room of the restaurant they were using for the meet. She didn't want to use Elliot's, because she didn't want to risk being recognized. While she trusted the staff there, trust only went so far. She was taking on a completely different persona, so it made sense to use a completely different location. They had decided on an upscale sushi restaurant only a few blocks from Pike's Place market. It was close enough that the scent of saltwater and fish was strong every time the door opened.

The room was dimly lit, which suited Keandra's purposes. If it was harder for anyone to see her face clearly, she could use that to her advantage. They had decided that E-jekt and Lance would stay with her in the room, while Paz took on the role of external guard, limiting who gained access to the meeting. Just in case things did go poorly, Keandra wanted the entire team around for an easier escape.

She set up the chairs so she faced the only entrance. It made a quick getaway more difficult, but it granted her the power seat. And even if she was nervous about the meeting, she wanted to project the appearance of complete control and confidence. After all, it was the seat she would have given to a Johnson if she were the one seeking a job. Lance stood just behind her right shoulder, while E-jekt took the chair to her left and pulled up his AR interface. He shifted in his seat, grunting and shrugging his shoulders as he tried to get used to the new armored vest. As far as Keandra knew, this was the first time he had ever worn anything protective enough to be restricting.

"It would be trivial to code up a simple sprite to hide your face and alter your voice."

Keandra's jaw clenched and she resisted the urge to sigh, instead taking a slow measured breath. "Stop and think for a second about what you're suggesting. Have you ever known a Johnson to be afraid to show her face or hide her voice? They'd know we were faking it in a second."

"Not if I made your voice sound like someone else."

"And not be in complete control and work my magic? No. We've been over this. It's a bad plan. No disguises and no filters. We'll play it out and it will work."

<We got company. All five of them showed up. The staff pointed them in our direction.>

The message from Paz made Keandra sit up straighter and lift her chin so she was looking down her nose when she stared at the doorway. She fired off a quick message before tucking her commlink away.

<Only let two of them enter. I want them outnumbered for the negotiation.>

<Roger.>

The three in the room waited in silence as the other group confronted Paz. The room's soundproofing made it impossible to make out the words, but they heard voices increasing in volume. Apparently the team's reputation for being a bit hotheaded was well earned. Through it all, the door handle didn't budge until the voices died down and it was clear some type of agreement had been reached.

The door slid open, and a human walked in with a large, angry female troll behind him. The troll sneered as she stomped into the room and pulled her shoulders back, letting her jacket part a little to display the arsenal she carried. Keandra was not impressed and also not surprised. The human took a seat at the table directly across from Keandra. The troll in turn glared at Lance, who kept his face impassive, not even making eye contact.

"You must be our Johnson. Name's Graham. I heard you got a job for me and my team."

Graham extended a hand, but Keandra kept hers folded in front of her. After a brief moment of tension, he withdrew it and hid it under the table. At least he was being professional, even if he didn't have quite the level of sophistication she was used to. She offered a brief nod as greeting before she spoke.

"Indeed, we do have work that may appeal to those of your talents. You received the dossier?"

Graham nodded, sliding forward in his seat so he could lean back more easily. The leather of his coat creaked as he made himself comfortable. He looked up, staring into the space above Keandra's head for a moment. His gaze flicked over to the troll before returning to her. Keandra's legs tensed. Clearly he was reading or sending a message. She kept her arms still, willing her nervous energy not to creep up past her waist.

"Although I do have a bit of a problem with the fee. I think that for what you're asking, we should be looking at fifteen thousand. Ten seems too low a bid when you're buying services of our caliber."

Keandra relaxed and let the corner of her mouth creep up into a smile. Price negotiation was something she could handle. It was also something she should have expected, especially for a first contact. They'd want to see how much they could squeeze out of their new Johnson, and how much of a stickler she would be for the proposed arrangement.

"I do not think your reputation precedes you as much, or as favorably, as you expect. If you'd like, my associate here would be more than willing to provide some recordings that clearly demonstrate your caliber. Three weeks ago, a convoy heist, I believe?"

E-jekt pulled up a video feed for everyone in the room. It was a recording from a series of traffic cams catching the entire heist from start to finish. There was no sound, but the resolution was high enough that E-jekt ran a facial recognition program at the same time, identifying three of the members of the team. As the video progressed, Graham's mouth tightened and he looked away, glancing toward an empty corner. Keandra nudged E-jekt under the table with her boot, and he cut the display.

"As you see, we do our due diligence when looking for the services that your kind provides."

Keandra watched Graham as she pressed her superiority. His eyes flashed and his gaze shot back to her, so she decided to ease off for the moment. Right now he was still willing to do the job. If she pushed too far, she would lose him.

"However, I do appreciate your candor and dedication to making sure the job gets done. Your team has shown a persistence and determination that are worth paying a premium. I'll raise your fee to twelve thousand, with an additional three thousand as a bonus if you handle the matter discreetly."

Keandra sat back, letting her posture ease. She could see him recognize the gesture, and some tension seeped out of his neck. That was the effect she wanted, and at the perfect time. She waited as he debated her offer. Most likely, he was conferring with his team and making sure they agreed to the terms. She was tempted to ask E-jekt to poke into their conversations and see if he could relay the messages to her, but it wasn't worth the risk. A corporate Johnson wouldn't bother with such tactics because the Johnson would have all the power. She needed to be the Johnson and think like one.

"Well, Ms. Johnson, it looks like you have yourself a team," Graham said. "We'll take care of your problem within the next twenty-four hours. and report in when it's done."

This time when he stuck his hand forward, Keandra grasped it. His grip was strong, and he offered a single solid shake before letting go and turning his back to her to leave the room. His companion backed out, facing forward until the door was shut. Keandra and her crew waited in silence, the entire group staring at the door until Paz messaged them.

<They're gone. Got in a car and turned the corner.>

The dwarf walked into the room so they could have some privacy without needing to resort to messaging. She dropped into the chair vacated by Graham and the simple wooden structure groaned in response to her sudden weight. E-jekt let out a sigh that matched the furniture's complaint.

"It actually worked." His tone indicated his surprise.

Keandra nodded and smiled. "Of course it worked. I told you this would be simple enough. I've certainly met with enough Johnsons over the years that impersonating one wouldn't be a problem. I'm just glad you were able to add the facial recognition program to the recording. I think that bit tipped him over the edge. Now we need to make sure they actually do the job.

"Lance, go keep an eye on them. I want you in position in case they fail to take out the target. If they handle it on their own, don't be seen. They've seen our faces and I don't want them thinking we're keeping tabs on them. But for this to work, they need to succeed. Otherwise, we'll need to pick up the slack."

Paz smacked the table with a bark of laughter. "Looks like I get to be stuffing my face this time while you're doing the heavy lifting."

"Sorry, Paz. We won't be staying," Keandra said. "We'll be in the van a few blocks away in case he needs backup. I don't want to take any chances."

Despite some heavy grumbling, Paz agreed and left to go get the limo they'd rented in case anyone watched their movements too closely. It was a bit much, even for a Johnson, but Keandra figured it would be better to go over the top than too subtle. They didn't want anyone looking too hard into their past, and would rather have an aura that radiated wealth and influence. A little bit of wealth made you a target. A lot of wealth made you a force to avoid.

As they passed back through the restaurant, Keandra paid close attention to the people who looked at their group. She made mental notes of anyone who showed more than a passing interest. Most of the diners paid attention to their food, ignoring them as much as they did the waitstaff.

One elf sitting at a table by himself caught her attention. She recognized him from when they'd first entered. He still didn't have any food in front of him, and the only beverage on the table was water. Their meeting hadn't taken that long, but his presence still seemed odd. He looked at her, but as soon as he recognized her scrutiny, his gaze snapped back to the space in front of him. Keandra didn't know if she was being paranoid, but the interaction made the hairs on her neck stand on end. She'd need to ask E-jekt to investigate this person later. For now, they had a job to do and an image to maintain.

Within minutes, they'd left the restaurant, dropped off the car, and retrieved their van. Lance was in pursuit of the runner team they hired, close by but staying out of sight. Apparently the team wasn't too careful about making sure they weren't tracked. They had settled into a building, possibly one of their safehouses. Keandra and her team likewise got settled, ready to wait all day and night if need be. They slept in shifts, getting rest while they could in case they'd need to be up all night. Lance had the unfortunate reality of needing to stay awake the entire time, but with his abilities, one night wouldn't be a problem.

The sun had long since set when Paz shook Keandra's shoulder to wake her. They were still parked on the edge of the same side street in downtown Ballard, but now the continuous roar and rumble of passing cars had faded to the occasional hum. Few people were out on the street at this time. The display on the windshield said it was 2:20 in the morning.

"They're on the move. Meat-sack has a feed," the dwarf said.

While Paz navigated through the streets, Keandra watched the feed playing on the interior wall of the van. It showed an empty intersection, dark with a flickering light overhead. The view panned around the corner until they saw a single car on the road, brake lights coming on before it turned. Lance drove out of the side street to the next corner, and then continued to watch. He drove without lights and crept up to each intersection, taking all the precautions he could to not be detected. Keandra was amazed that he didn't lose the other team, but he knew how to do his job.

Eventually the car came to a stop and the team climbed out of the vehicle. Lance parked his bike against a wall, then scaled the surface so fast that the feed was a shaky blur. Keandra closed her eyes to keep from getting motion sickness. When she opened them, Lance was at the front corner of the building, looking down at the runners across the street and just over a block away.

Another car met them at the location and a couple of other people joined the small group. They gathered in a knot and talked as they unloaded and prepped their weapons. All told, there were five people in the group. That was their entire team.

<It appears our employees are ready to hit the target.> Lance sent a message over their network.

<Maintain watch, but keep out of sight.> Keandra wanted to see if this would work, and the only way to test that was to pretend as if they weren't there.

Two of the team members stayed near the vehicles, leaning against them and passing a bottle back and forth. The other three crossed the street and walked up to the front door of an apartment building. Two kept watch while the third took a knee and manipulated the lock. After a few moments, the area was suddenly bathed in light, making all the runners jump.

The liquor bottle smashed against the ground and shattered. The troll grabbed the guy working on the door and yanked him back so hard he fell on his ass in the street. Then she charged the door, breaking it down with her sheer size and strength.

<Guess they won't be able to claim that bonus you proposed.>

Keandra didn't bother to respond; she was transfixed by the feed. Secrecy was never part of their arrangement, but she needed to make sure the team at least pulled off the job. If they failed now, the target would be aware and any future attempts would be much more difficult, if not impossible. She turned to E-jekt, crouched up against the van's back doors.

"Can you see if that building has any security cameras? We need eyes inside."

The area in front of the building was still bathed in light, but at least the three runners were inside the building now. The other two ducked behind the vehicles, taking cover and holding up their weapons. A few seconds later, a couple of Knight Errant vehicles skidded around the corner, lights flashing.

"They have cameras, but I'd need a local bug. There should be access on the roof."

<Our local, incorruptible law enforcement has arrived.> Lance texted. <If I need to intervene to finish the contract, I should enter now.>

Paz revved the van's engine and glanced at Keandra. "Time for some backup action?"

FIVE

Kendra shook her head. "We're staying here. They may be amateurs and hotheads, but they've got three people on the inside, and I'm not ready to blow our cover yet. Plus, we don't have a good support plan now that the Knights are involved."

She texted Lance. <*Get to the roof and install a remote access uplink for E-jekt. That'll give us access to the cameras. Then I want you to hold your position. Keep an eye on the street, but don't be seen.*>

As soon as she sent the message, Lance burst into motion. The feed blurred until it came to a sudden stop at the building's network hub. It had a physical lock, a decent indicator of the building's age. Lance picked it and planted the portable bug into the broadcaster. The bugs were a useful gadget E-jekt invented, a way to let him get access without being in the physical location as long as it wasn't a dead zone. As soon as the bug was placed, the grizzled ork went to work on cracking the building's security.

Once that was done, Lance returned to the edge of the roof to check on the scene below. He paused, not peeking over the top immediately.

<*Lots of gunfire. I am certain this will garner more legal attention. Are you sure you don't want me to interfere?*>

<*Maintain position and get us eyes on the street.*>

Lance did as he was told, and the camera slid up until Keandra and the rest of the crew could see the gun battle going on several stories below his position. Both the runners retreated behind the second car, keeping both vehicles between them and the Knight Errant squad. The cops angled their cars to form a V and took shelter between the fronts of both vehicles. One of them lay bleeding in the street, his leg still in the car but the rest of his body hanging outside the open door. The other three took turns firing on the runners' position. While they were working together, they lacked the precision of a well-trained unit.

At least that was something in their favor: these weren't the best the Knights had to offer. Keandra had seen the top officers responding to high-priority crimes before, and they moved like something out of a posh nightclub, their precision and coordination bearing all the elegance of a squad of dancers who spent months training together. These officers were more like the hobby performers taking night classes. Still, Lance was right—time was not their friend.

A series of camera feeds popped up on the van wall next to Lance's view. They flipped past, one after another, showing different floors and stairwells. The halls were empty. The feed paused on a scene where one of the doors was open, but it was just an older woman poking her head into the hallway to look around before jerking back and slamming the door shut.

After scanning through more feeds, the display stopped on one where a panting troll paused in front of a door. The other two members of her team came into view behind her, also out of breath. They took a moment to collect themselves, and then the troll kicked the door.

The first impact sent the wooden structure flying open in a spray of wood splinters. A rush of bullets drove the troll back as they cut through the hallway and embedded in the wall. A few slipped past the troll's armor, and blood trailed from her wounds. The runners flanked the opening, guns up and ready. When the flashes of gunfire stopped, the troll reached around the corner and fired blindly into the room.

<E-jekt...>

<Trying.>

A couple more rounds of ammunition were exchanged. By now, the wall across the hall from the doorway was more holes than substance. The troll got unlucky and took a bullet to the arm that made her drop her gun in the middle of the entrance. Rather than try to recover it, she pulled another from under her jacket, but her right arm now hung limp at her side.

Another camera feed popped up, this one showing the interior of the apartment. Their target—an older dwarf with a distinctive Celtic knot tattoo covering most of his forehead—was crouched behind a counter, the sides of which had been chewed up from the firearm exchange. He fired another burst of bullets and then dropped back behind the counter, reaching up to one of the shelves for something Keandra couldn't see. When he pulled his hand back, he held some kind of grenade.

He tossed it around the corner into the hallway. Keandra shifted her attention to the hallway monitor and saw the small metal cylinder bounce near the troll's feet. She kicked it away, back into the apartment. A flash of light filled both screens, forcing Keandra to rub her eyes to clear them of spots.

When she could see again, the troll was in the room, lifting the dwarf by the neck. She put her gun barrel against his forehead and pulled the trigger a single time. Keandra looked away from the ensuing graphic display. After a few seconds, she realized E-jekt turned off the other monitors. There was no need to see any more. They got what they needed.

<The mission was a success. Pull back. Their exit strategy is their problem, not ours. Let's go collect our fee so we can be ready to pay up if they survive.>

Lance cut his feed immediately. The mission had been a success, even if the job had been handled with a lot less finesse than her team would normally employ. But that was to be expected, since they'd hired a team barely above amateur status. She looked at this as more of a proof of concept than anything else, and they had proved it would work. As she crawled into the passenger seat, a grin creased her face.

While Paz navigated back to their base of operations, Keandra drafted a message to their Johnson, letting him know that the mission was a success and requesting payment to be transferred to her account as soon as it was convenient. To her surprise, she received a transfer notification before they'd reached the safe house. It was the fee they'd agreed on, with no bonus or additional commentary. In other words, business as usual. If the Johnson had a problem with their methods or was curious about the uncharacteristic nature, he didn't appear to think it was worth bringing up.

"Looks like we got paid, gang. And without anyone taking a shot at any of us. I told you this would work, and it'd be worth it."

"Sweet. Nuyen is nice, but easy nuyen is even better. So are we going to do it again?" Paz asked, the excitement strong in her voice.

"I think we should. It isn't as much as we'd normally make, but it still seems to be a profitable endeavor. What are your thoughts?"

Keandra leaned back and looked over her shoulder to make eye contact with E-jekt. He was out of the Matrix now and looking at the front cabin. He shrugged, but Keandra knew he'd have no issue with voicing a problem if he saw one.

"I'll admit, I had my doubts," the decker said. "But you're right. We got paid, and I do like the not-getting-shot-at bit."

"It's settled, then. I'll start going through our job backlog and see what else we have that we could farm out. I might want to take on something a little bit bigger now that we know it can be done. E-jekt, you'll need to keep working on assembling team dossiers so I can make the right connections between team and job."

Paz parked in the garage and used her commlink to check her accounts. She grunted, which caught Keandra's attention.

"What is it?"

"It's just..." she paused. "It's less than I was expecting. That's barely enough to keep things running."

"That's why we need to take on bigger jobs. I figure we'll be keeping about the same percentage. So the bigger the run, the better payday we'll get. Of course, it'll never be as much as if we did the run ourselves. Think of it as a safety fee. That's the price we pay for not being in the line of fire."

"Then we better take on a hell of a lot bigger jobs, safety fee or not."

SIX

The next several months were good to Keandra and her team. True to the plan, they decided to tackle larger jobs with better payouts. This necessitated hiring more professional teams, but as time went on, things started to fall into a groove. They even had access to a couple of teams they used multiple times. The runs started to achieve the professional level that Keandra and her team were known for, which emboldened them to take on ever higher profile jobs. The percentages were still low, requiring them to tap into their reserves and drain them almost to nonexistence.

That just meant they needed to make a big score.

Currently, Keandra sat at her patio table at Elliot's, waiting for Mr. Johnson to arrive to begin negotiations. Based on the preliminary information, this run would be at the top tier of what she could commandeer if they were performing it directly. The percentage for their finder's fee should be enough to get each of her team comfortably through the rest of the month, assuming all went according to plan.

Her commlink got a ping from the front desk. Francis let her know Mr. Johnson had arrived, and was on his way back to see her. She nodded at Lance, who stood in his customary position at attention, ever the ready guardsman.

When Mr. Johnson stepped onto the patio, Keandra waited until he came around to stand and extend her hand by way of greeting. She had to remind herself that she was in the subservient position now, after spending so long as the social dominator.

"Mr. Johnson, it's a pleasure to see you once again. I'm glad our business ventures can continue."

"Ms. Tiernay, it is a pleasure to see you again as well. I was wondering when we might have reason to meet, and was hoping to continue our mutually beneficial relationship."

"I must say that you have the ability to make an offer too tempting to refuse. As is the nature of these kinds of problems, if you throw enough nuyen at it, a solution will present itself. I'm hoping we can be the solution to your current predicament."

Mr. Johnson pulled a small, disposable commlink from inside his jacket. He placed it on the table and slid it halfway across before removing his hand. Keandra picked it up, placing it on her edge of the table and folding the napkin over it.

"That contains the digital imprint of a certain file we need liberated from some servers. The server is, of course, located in a secure facility that has no remote access to the Matrix, otherwise we would not need a team with your unique talents. To facilitate your success, you also have a copy of the blueprint of the structure, as well as some preliminary reconnaissance as to the security you might encounter. In short, we have done as much as we can to lead you down the path of success. I trust you realize the importance of this package, if we have gone to these lengths to assist you."

"Of course. I'm also honored and privileged you accepted our bid. We won't let you down."

"See that you don't, Ms. Tiernay."

There was no need for overt threats. Keandra knew how important this mysterious data file was, considering how much Mr. Johnson had already put on the line. Normally, the team would be responsible for their own surveillance and attempting to scrounge up information such as blueprints. If the company was throwing around weight to pull some strings, this was bigger than the latest simsense encoding software. Things that important were not left to chance.

She uncovered the commlink and turned it on to check the data stored on it. The first thing she noticed was that it was isolated, and had no hardware to connect it to the Matrix. That was odd, but she brushed it aside. Based on the information she'd already received, this commlink wouldn't need Matrix access to accomplish their mission. The rest of the data was there, as he promised. Keandra turned it off.

Then Mr. Johnson pulled out a gold credstick and slid it toward Keandra. Despite her rigorous control, she couldn't help but raise an eyebrow in response. This was unusual, and not part of their initial negotiations.

"Given the importance of this endeavor, a limited down payment was approved to procure your services. I trust you will find this satisfactory. That amount will be deducted from your final payment, of course."

Keandra recovered as quickly as she could and palmed the credstick, sliding it up her sleeve where it would not be obvious if anyone caught a glimpse. The windows looking into the restaurant were screened as usual, but she didn't want to take any chances.

"I thank you for your generosity in this matter. Is there anything else we need to discuss?"

"I believe not. I look forward to reconvening with you three evenings from now."

With those words, he stood up and walked to the door, his bodyguard following close behind.

Keandra waited until she received a message that he had left before she pulled out the credstick to check it. It contained a certified balance of twenty-five thousand nuyen. She tried to keep her expression blasé as she texted the team. <He must really want that data file, whatever it is. He just paid half our fee up front.>

<What the ever-loving hell? Suit never pays up front. That's not good, is it? What's that mean?>

<I don't know. I'd love to say it's a sign of our growing trust and business relations, but I know better. This means we need top-of-the-line runners, and we need to meet them tonight. E-jekt?>

<Already set up the meeting with the alpha team you selected. They agreed to meet in an hour.>

<Looks like Skinny won't get any fancy food this time. Chop chop, let's get a move on!>

Paz was right: they needed to get going now. Keandra paid their bill and rushed out of the restaurant, leaving the food cooling on the table. It was a waste, but there was nothing for it. They needed to make sure to arrive at Japonessa in time to set the scene. They had used the establishment enough that the staff would have prepared the room correctly, but much more needed to be done now.

Traffic was not on their side, and Keandra grew restless as they crawled down the street on the way to pick up the limo. She drummed her thumbs on the dash until Paz glared at her, then folded her hands in her lap and forced herself to sit still. As she stared at the brake lights of the car in front of her, she chastised herself for her restlessness. She was nervous. This was one of the largest jobs they'd ever taken, not just the largest one they'd handed off. Still, they'd picked a solid team, one she believed would get the task done. And they needed this.

If only they could get to the restaurant and start the ball rolling. The sitting still was the maddening effect.

By the time they reached the restaurant, Keandra managed to rein in her emotions. Lance opened the door for her and she slid out, the picture of grace and power as she unfolded her legs and took the lead to the front door, the rest of her crew close behind her. The staff at the front of the building recognized her immediately and waved her through. As she entered the meeting room, she cursed herself for setting the meetings too close together. The runners were already here.

Meritus, the team's human leader, sat in the power seat directly opposite the entrance. He had two other members standing behind him: Kylie, their elf decker, and Tors, their ork street samurai. As soon as Keandra saw their faces, lines from their dossiers danced through her mind. She was well familiar with their skills, strengths, exploits, and weaknesses.

Meritus smiled and held up a glass in salute when Keandra entered. He gestured across from him, instructing her to take a seat. They'd obviously arrived early, attempting to play the position of power. A dangerous move for a group of runners to try with a Johnson. Keandra swallowed her pride and took the offered seat, not wanting to make a scene. After all, the role she was playing would portray a persona of not care about such a slight.

Meritus grinned, clearly pleased with his initial victory. "Thank you for reaching out to us, Ms. Johnson. I'm glad that our resume caught your attention. Seems like you have a rather urgent need for our services."

"I do, and I see no point in wasting time going over preliminary details. You've already read the pertinent information about the task and agreed to the fee. I am here simply to provide some assistance."

Keandra pulled out the disposable commlink she'd acquired only an hour ago. Following the same motions as the Johnson she'd received it from, she placed it on the table and slid it toward Meritus. He picked it up and immediately handed it over his shoulder to Kylie so she could scan it. As she went to work, Meritus spoke.

"I think the fee is fair. A good day's pay for a good day of work. However, that's the issue, isn't it?"

"What do you mean?"

"You want this job done over the next twenty-four hours. That's a very tight window. While I'm sure you have other teams you could reach out to, I wonder how many would be of sufficient caliber to accomplish this task."

"I assure you, Mr. Meritus, that while your services would be helpful, they are by no means required. There are many skilled in your profession who would jump at this opportunity. Do not make me regret presenting this offer to you in an attempt to blackmail me for a higher fee than what was agreed upon."

Meritus held up his hands in a placating gesture. Keandra narrowed her eyes, but waited to see what he offered as a response.

"I was not suggesting an increase in pay, but merely that perhaps it would be worth a significant prepayment. If we could have, say, twenty-five percent up front, it could go a long way toward helping us succeed. Bribes, extra equipment, and the like."

Keandra leaned back and lifted a hand to her chin as she considered the offer. They could easily afford it, especially considering they'd received half of their fee up front. And it seemed like it would appease Meritus and his crew. Despite what she said, he was their only option right now, especially if they left with the commlink. Then their only option would be to go in themselves, and they would be blind while doing it. She analyzed the possibilities, looking for downsides.

"Very well, Mr. Meritus. We agree to your terms." She glanced over her shoulder and nodded at E-jekt. "You should find the funds transferred to your account shortly. Now, if we are done here, I have other business to attend to."

"We are. I'll see you tomorrow night."

"I look forward to concluding our business."

Keandra stood and held out her hand to Meritus, forcing him to rise and accept it. It was a way she could salvage some of the power lost due to their late arrival. Then she turned and left, letting the rest of her team follow behind her. None of them said a word until they were safely in the limo and on the way back to pick up the van.

Keandra shared the thought they were all thinking. "Now we wait. And pray they succeed."

SEVEN

"Keandra, you're going to want to take a look at this."

Keandra shut down her commlink and rushed over to E-jekt's place on the couch. Paz and Lance circled around him, getting close so they could see what he was about to show. He gestured, pulling up a traffic camera and displaying it in the center of the room. The view showed a parking lot surrounded by an electric fence and connected to a three-story building. Through the first-floor windows, they saw the telltale staccato flash of gunfire.

"I thought it might be a good idea to check on our runners since there's so much riding on this one. This is the parking lot, and I think there might be a problem."

Everyone grew silent as they focused on the video feed, waiting for any sign of how things played out. Keandra took a breath and gasped, not realizing she'd been holding it the entire time. She smelled the musty odor of E-jekt's sweat as the gunfire continued, but no team emerged from the facility.

Finally, one of the windows crashed outward, glass shattering across the pavement. Meritus jumped through the opening, sprinting and firing a gun wildly behind him. Keandra was impressed that he managed to avoid hitting his own team in his mad dash. Shortly behind him, Kylie jumped through the window, followed by Tors. Even with the limited resolution of the traffic cam, it was clear all three were injured.

A large blast knocked Tors down on his face, shredding the back of his armor and leaving him stunned. Kylie and Meritus both turned. Meritus rushed back to help his teammate, but Kylie grabbed his arm as she passed him, jerking him along with her. Tors struggled to push himself up on his arms, but it was futile. An unseen force picked him up and hurled him back toward the building, sending his hulking form flying through another row of windows and out of sight.

"Do you think they got it?"

Keandra and E-jekt both shushed Paz as they watched the scene. It looked like the they had already cut a hole in the fence and were aiming for it. Kylie slid through first while Meritus provided cover fire. As soon as she was past the barrier, she stood up and returned the favor so Meritus could escape. They climbed into a waiting car and took off down the street so quickly that E-jekt had trouble hopping traffic cams fast enough to follow them.

"Let it go. They got out and we'll be hearing from them sooner or later. Wherever they go from here is irrelevant."

"So I'll ask again: do you think they got it? 'Cause if not, that means we gotta go in there and get it ourselves, which is gonna be insane. After this, they'll be clamping down tight. Something tells me the suit won't be too happy if we tell him we're empty-handed, especially since we can't even pay back his deposit!"

"We know, Paz! There's not really anything we can do but wait. What else do you want us to do right now?" Keandra snapped.

"I don't know, maybe figure out how we're gonna break into a high-security compound to steal something we don't even have the blueprints for, since we gave away our only copy?"

Lance took a breath and held up a hand. All eyes turned toward him as he spoke in his soft, even voice. "I'd like to remind you that we tried cloning the information off the commlink, but E-jekt wasn't able to crack the encryption in the time we had. I doubt any of us could have done better."

"Well, then maybe we should've scheduled the second meeting a little bit later and not jammed 'em together like that. I thought the whole point of this insanity was to avoid getting shot at, not make it all worse!"

"Hindsight, my vertically-challenged associate. That is of little help to us now. What we need to do is remain calm and wait until Meritus attempts to contact our Ms. Johnson. His team might have still succeeded. We don't know. All we do know is that Meritus and Kylie escaped, and Tors didn't. Anything beyond that is speculation."

"And how long do you think we're gonna have to wait for that?"

As if in mocking response to Paz's question, Keandra's commlink beeped to indicate an incoming call. She pulled up the display and saw it was from Meritus. She didn't need to ask for silence; all conversation in the room stopped. Keandra let the call page her a couple extra times before she answered—despite their current circumstances, there was no need to appear too hasty.

"Mr. Meritus. I was not expecting a call from you. I thought we had agreed to meet at the restaurant."

"I know that was the original deal, but I need to know if you might alter the arrangement. There was a slight problem."

Keandra's breath caught for a fraction of a second. If he was wanting to alter the deal, that meant he had to have at least acquired the data file. Only with severe effort did the keep the relief from creeping into her voice.

"And what alterations would you suggest?"

"I hoping that we might be able to meet now, or at least in the near future. There appears to be some—" He paused, and Keandra heard tires screeching in the background combined with a curse. "As I was saying, there appears to be some difficulty maintaining control of the package. It would be very helpful if we could arrange a more immediate exchange. Look at it this way: you'll get your data hours ahead of your original plan, and I'm not even asking for a bonus for that."

Keandra fired off a quick message while she listened to Meritus.

<See if you can get a private room at Syberspace. Meritus wants to meet now, and we need a place.>

"I appreciate your initiative, Mr. Meritus. However, it does seem like your delivery might pose a significant risk if I were to meet with you right at this moment. As I am sure you can appreciate, discretion is of critical importance in this matter."

<WHAT ARE YOU DOING?> Paz shouted on her screen. <WE NEED THAT DATA! YOU'RE GONNA SCARE HIM OFF!>

<Trust me.>

"I understand that, Ms. Johnson. But I do feel the need to point out one tiny detail. The script we ran didn't copy the data file—it moved it. If we're unable to deliver it in the near future, it might be lost. Permanently."

"Is that a threat?"

Keandra kept her voice icy, even though sweat formed at the base of her skull and dripped down her spine. If he destroyed the data, they would have to face their Johnson's disappointment. Unlike her, he wasn't pretending to have the full strength of a megacorp behind him.

"More like an advisory or update on the status. You see, it is rather urgent that we arrange a meetup as soon as possible."

"This is most...unusual. I expected something more from a man of your reputation, Mr. Meritus."

<I have a private room. Reservation starts in twenty minutes, and we have it for an hour.>

"However, as you so eloquently put it, I would be able to receive the data sooner than expected. Provided you can lose any additional attention in your current activities, I suppose we could arrange a rendezvous. I will be at Syberspace shortly. Meet me there within the next sixty minutes—discreetly—and we can verify you have the necessary data."

"A pleasure doing business with you, Ms. Johnson. I look forward to the conclusion of our agreement."

Keandra cut the connection and rushed to her room to get ready for the meeting, confident that the rest of the team would be scurrying about collecting what they would need as well. They didn't have much time. Even if they avoided the traffic, it would be at least thirty minutes before they could get to the club. There wouldn't be time to reserve the limo. Hopefully the charade would last long enough for them to get the data.

Even though she hurried, Keandra took care to look every part the professional. She finished her preparations and then returned to the main room to find E-jekt still shrugging into his suit.

As he rushed to put the jacket on, a ripping sound broke the silence when the shoulder seam gave way. He froze, and Keandra rushed over to help him pull it on the rest of the way.

"It's fine. We'll get it fixed after this meeting. As long as you don't shrug your shoulders or roll your arms, it shouldn't get worse or be noticeable."

"This is cutting it too close. I don't like this."

"We can talk about that later. Right now we need to get down there and get the data. If Meritus doesn't show or doesn't deliver, we're screwed."

With a final flurry of activity, the group hustled out of the apartment and down to the ground floor where Paz's van was parked. They piled in, and Paz started driving before the doors were shut.

"What do you want to do when we get there? My beat-up armored van doesn't scream suit transport."

"Park a block away and wait for my signal. I'll go in with Lance and E-jekt. If anyone sees us, we'll look like an executive with her bodyguard and technical advisor. Nothing unusual about that. I doubt they'll ask questions. And besides, they might not even be there yet. They had quite a bit of heat to lose first."

Keandra took a deep breath and looked out the window. She hoped they did lose the heat. If they didn't, and that data was lost, there would be no way to recover it. And then they'd need to figure out how to deal with Mr. Johnson. They could scrounge up the funds to return his advance, but something told her that wouldn't be an acceptable trade. There was no way they had the resources necessary to go on the run from someone with his reach and influence.

But now was not the time to think about that. She had to portray the successful businesswoman—the person who had the power and influence to be feared. She could only focus on one problem at a time, and the current obstacle involved getting the data from Meritus. Luckily, she had already gotten the necessary certified credsticks for the rest of his payment.

As soon as Paz turned down a side street and slammed on the brakes, Lance opened the side door and jumped out, running as he hit the pavement to keep from falling. Keandra waited until the vehicle came to a complete stop. Running in heels at all was a difficult venture; doing it while jumping out of a moving vehicle was foolishness. She strode to the club's front entrance, her "advisor" walking next to her while her "bodyguard" stayed a few steps behind. E-jekt pinged the staff as they walked.

<Club manager says no one's asked for us yet, so looks like you get to set the stage.>

Keandra let out a relieved sigh. Finally, something was going their way. With any luck, they'd shortly be walking out of the club with the necessary data in hand.

When they got to the front entrance, the bouncer waved them through with only a passing glance at her SIN to verify her identity. They passed through a small foyer with another set of double doors before entering the club proper. As soon as the second doors in the airlock-style atrium were open, a combination of sights, sounds, and smells blasted Keandra and almost sent her reeling.

The main floor of the club had a bar and several tables scattered around the border, but the vast majority of space was completely open. These open areas had some walls as physical barriers to divide one AR simulation from another and prevent them from overlapping. The individual scenes ranged from wild, seizure-inducing raves to a dungeon area where clubgoers engaged in a heated battle against a virtual dragon. At the far end was a stage where some tribute band belted out the latest hit at a volume making Keandra want to cover her ears. She didn't think she'd be able to hear E-jekt if he shouted at her, and he was within an arm's reach. The air was filled with a mix of sweat, perfume, cologne, and the unmistakable scent of pot for those who preferred to get their rush the retro way.

E-jekt tugged on her arm and said something, but she couldn't make out his words. He pointed to the left side of the club, where a darkened doorway led deeper into the shadows. She strode through the crowd, stepping over a couple of BTL users passed out on the floor, oblivious to the world around them.

Once in the hallway, the sound dropped from overpowering to simply loud. Keandra looked to E-jekt, and he nodded at the third door. It was locked; the digital keypad read *OCCUPIED.* E-jekt punched in a code and the indicator light turned green as the door swung into the room beyond. Keandra and her entourage stepped through, Lance closing the door behind him.

As soon as it swung shut, a silence so sudden that it created a rush in Keandra's ears settled over her. It took a moment to realize that the sound she was hearing was her own blood coursing through her veins. It was as if they stepped into a different world, completely isolated from the one outside. At least they wouldn't need to worry about an observer trying to spy on them through the door. Keandra wagered a gunshot wouldn't be heard outside the room as long as the music was still playing.

The chamber was well-furnished, with a large table against one wall, three chairs, and two small but expensive-looking couches covered in probably-fake leather. She headed to the table and Lance moved to help her without a word. He had watched her set the scene enough times to know what she wanted. She put the table in the center of the room and put her seat directly opposite the door. Then they pushed the couches to the walls on either side. E-jekt took the chair next to Keandra's. The remaining chair was meant for Meritus once he arrived. If he brought anyone with him, they could stand or use the couches.

Once the room was set to her liking, Keandra gave it another sweep, looking for anything out of the ordinary. She found a small camera in the back corner where the walls met the ceiling. It was small enough that she'd missed it on her first cursory pass, and only caught it when she gave the room a thorough check. She tagged it and pointed it out to E-jekt, who was already wired into the Matrix.

<Simple camera drone. It's wireless, so I can put up a firewall. Not currently on, but I'd rather be safe than sorry. That way if anyone tries to break through and see what's going on, I'll know.>

<Good. Also check the security system and see if there are any other drones or anything I might have missed.>

<Not seeing anything. If it's here, it's not on and doesn't have an active connection. I think we're secure.>

<Monitor that camera and let me know the second Meritus arrives.>

<Front desk says someone just asked about our room and is coming back.>

<Show time, people. Lance, go out and make sure it's Meritus. If he has an escort, they can all come in. But I want you staying in the hall to keep an eye on what's going on out there. Security doors are nice and all, but they go both ways.>

Lance did as he was instructed as Keandra arranged herself in her seat. Next to her, she felt E-jekt's leg tremoring as he bounced it up and down on the ball of his foot. She put a hand on his thigh and gave it a quick sharp squeeze before folding her hands on the table in front of her. He got the message and planted both feet flat on the ground.

The door swung open, and both Meritus and Kylie entered the meeting room. Even if she hadn't watched their narrow escape, Keandra would have known their operation hadn't gone as smoothly as they hoped. Pain, exhaustion, and fear left obvious marks on their faces.

Meritus held it together better than his companion, but it was telling that he hadn't stopped to take the time to clean up before coming to meet his employer. He kept his decorum as he slid the chair away from the table and eased into it. By contrast, Kylie collapsed onto a couch hard enough to make it slide a short distance across the floor.

Meritus pulled out the disposable commlink she had given him at their last meeting. He placed it on the table in front of him and kept two fingers resting on the top of it.

"This is what you're looking for. All of the data, just like you requested." Meritus offered an easy smile that said he was just there to do business as usual. The only thing off about him was his ragged appearance.

Keandra risked a quick glance at his associate. The couple beads of sweat running down the side of her face appeared since they entered the room, and she seemed unwilling to meet Keandra's gaze, even briefly. It could just be the narrow escape, but it made Keandra nervous.

"I'll need to verify the package is complete, of course."

"Of course."

Meritus slid it across the table and lifted his fingers from it so Keandra could inspect it. She passed it to E-jekt, who connected it to his commlink. He began running commands on it while Keandra and Meritus stared at each other with matching expressions of stone.

<The data checks out, but there's something odd->

With a crack like thunder, the lights in the room exploded in a shower of sparks. Meritus was on his feet in a flash, drawing a gun from under his coat. Keandra kept her hands on the table in plain view, not wanting to startle the runner. His hand shook as he held the gun out in front of him, the first time she'd seen him visibly shaken.

"Pay up! Now!"

EIGHT

"Mr. Meritus, there's no need to be rash."

Kylie rose and drew her gun, keeping it trained on E-jekt as she walked over to stand behind Meritus. Even in the limited light available from the floor's emergency strips, Kylie's skin had visibly paled.

"I'm going to reach into my pocket and retrieve your payment." Keandra kept her voice calm and moved slowly, not wanting to accidentally push Meritus over the edge.

While she retrieved the payment, a message came in from Lance. <*I hate to disturb you, but something's going on out here. A few explosions, some electrical overload, the music stopped, and a lot of screaming. It sounds like a raid. You might want to conclude your business so we can make an expeditious retreat.*>

Keandra hoped E-jekt would respond, but he was quiet. She didn't dare look in his direction while under watch, let alone try to access her commlink. She nudged his foot and it slid across the floor with no resistance. Keandra sucked in air, making both Meritus and Kylie twitch. She opened her suit jacket so they both could watch as she reached into an inner pocket with two fingers and pulled out the credstick stashed there. She put it in the center of the table.

<*Keandra? E-jekt? Did you receive my message?*>

<*What's going on, Meat-sack?*>

<*If you can read this, I'm coming in.*>

"Here is the rest of your payment. Thank you for your services and for delivering the package."

Meritus snatched the credstick just as the door started to open. Kylie whirled around, aiming at the opening. When Keandra spoke, it was loud enough she hoped Lance would hear.

"Now that our business is concluded, my associate will see you out."

The door opened enough to show Lance standing in his suit with his hands at his sides. The sounds of panicked chaos echoed down the hall just past him. It sounded like a stampede, and Keandra was surprised they couldn't feel the vibrations through the floor. Meritus and Kylie bolted into the hall and out of sight without checking the credstick or a word of thanks. Lance watched them go and then stepped inside, slamming the door shut.

"What happened?"

Keandra rose from her chair hard enough to send it crashing to the floor. Sheknelt at E-jekt's side and grabbed his wrist to check for a pulse. He sat slack with a hand pressed against his chest. His eyes were open, but distant and not tracking anything. A bit of drool leaked from one corner of his mouth. At least his pulse was strong. Whatever happened, it hadn't killed him.

"I don't know. I had E-jekt check the data package. He said everything was there, and then the lights went out and he got like this. I didn't see it happen; my attention was focused on Meritus."

"Whatever made the lights spontaneously explode, it didn't just happen in here. I heard a couple of cracks from the main room, about the same time the music terminated. If I had to guess, I'd wager the club's entire network was attacked."

E-jekt groaned, a sound that had never sounded so good to Keandra. He closed his eyes and refused to open them, but at least he seemed cognizant. His limbs were still weak, and he offered no resistance as Keandra attempted to move him. She hunched forward, draping one of his thick arms across her shoulders, and heaved him up, trying to stand—*frag, he's heavy!* He was small for an ork, but still outweighed her by half again. She lifted him a couple of centimeters before her legs gave out and she dropped him back into the seat.

"Lance!"

"I'll take care of it." Lance rushed over and took her position, hefting E-jekt out of the chair. Once they were standing, hee gave a little shrug, rebalancing the weight. His face strained with the effort, but at least he could move.

Keandra snatched the disposable commlink off the table and shoved it into her pocket as she headed toward the door.

She opened it and peeked into the hallway before stepping out and waving her companions forward.

<Paz, we're coming out hot.>

<Got it. Make for the back. Front's too crowded. I can see 'em from here.>

Keandra ran to the doorway connecting the private rooms to the main club. The scene was worse than she anticipated. Several people writhed on the floor in various states of injury. It looked like most of them had been trampled, and more than a few were unconscious. There were a few scorch marks, both on people's skin and on the wall near some of the projectors. The heavy odors of ozone and crisped flesh filled the air. Sparks flashed and electricity crackled.

Luckily, most of the crowd had already fled out the front entrance. A few stragglers sprinted down the steps, taking two or three at a time in their haste. An ork man in a smoking sport coat misjudged the distance to the last step and caught the edge of it under his heel. He tumbled forward, flattening a dwarf and a human under him before scrambling off them in his hurry to escape. Keandra moved toward the back exit, swerving around the two on the floor as she blazed a path for Lance and E-jekt.

Once she got around the edge of the stage, she saw the open doorway leading outside. The light was blinding in its intensity after the darkened room; she squinted and raised a hand in front of her face to help filter the brightness. Pushing through the confused throng near the exit, she heard Paz shouting curses at people as she forced a way to the exit from outside.

"Let's get the frag out of here!" Paz pushed an elf couple holding each other, shoving both of them aside to create an opening for Keandra and the others.

Keandra saw a clear path to the nearby van and picked up speed, the sight giving her a burst of energy. She jerked the door open and turned to help Lance load E-jekt while Paz climbed into the driver's seat.

Paz took off as they slammed the door shut, swerving back and forth to avoid the clubgoers standing in the back alley. She made liberal use of her horn to shock some back into awareness enough so they didn't get run over. Keandra tried not to think about the thumps against the side of the van as they barreled out to the main street.

Once they'd reached it, Paz eased up and merged into regular traffic. Keandra opened and closed her fists several times, shaking out her arms to loosen her tight shoulders. E-jekt propped himself up in the back, his eyes open and clearing. He looked sleepy and confused, and he winced whenever the van hit a bump, but otherwise appeared uninjured.

Keandra moved over to sit next to him. "Do you know what happened?"

E-jekt took a deep breath before responding. "Not for sure. The key checked out, but I thought I saw a glitch. I wanted to open the file for a peek and run some integrity checks." His brow furrowed and he squinted as he tried to remember the details. "When I opened it up, my entire system went haywire. It was like a hacker got hold of my DNI. Whatever it was, it hit harder than some black ice I've seen. I dumped myself out as soon as I could. Didn't want to stay for that ride."

E-jekt stared straight ahead, obviously not seeing anything. Keandra glanced at Lance. The worried expression etched on his face matched her own feelings about this scenario.

She pulled out the disposable commlink and looked it over. The small piece of technology sported scorch marks that looked like they'd originated from inside the casing. The device wouldn't turn on, and it was clear even to her untrained eye that it was damaged beyond repair. E-jekt might be able to salvage something from it, but she doubted it.

While the ork stared at the wall of the van, Keandra tried to do a quick assessment. She'd love to give him some time to relax and recover, especially after the shock he'd just gone through, but that wasn't an option. Every second that passed made it that much harder to track what happened and follow any breadcrumbs to the data they needed. They couldn't trust anyone else with this, so even if it was painful, she needed his expertise. She touched his arm to get his attention before speaking.

"Right now I need your complete focus. I need to check any traces at the club to see who hacked us. I also need to see if you can figure out anything from this."

She handed him the charred commlink. To her surprise, his grip was strong when he took it from her. The muscles around his jaw tightened as he nodded and then sat up, crossing his legs in front of him. He opened his virtual display and went to work with an intensity Keandra appreciated. She didn't need to tell him how serious this was; in all reality, he probably knew better than she did.

Lance gestured for her to come over. When she did, he crouched close enough that she could smell the faint traces of his home-brewed herbal tea on his breath as he whispered into her ear.

"I don't mean to sound overly dramatic, but unless he's able to find that data quick, our life expectancy will take a sharp and sudden decline."

"I know that, and so does he," she replied "It does no good to remind him of it when he needs to be focused on doing something we can't. All that will do is add stress, which I think he's had enough of for the moment."

"I merely wanted to remind you of the severity of the problem."

Keandra almost snapped at him, but held back before the words escaped her lips. He was nervous, just like the rest of them. Turning on each other wouldn't do them any favors either.

"He'll find it. You know he will. He always comes through in the end. We just need to give him some time and stay under the radar until we know what we're going to do."

The drive back to the safehouse was devoid of conversation, everyone focusing on their own thoughts. Every few seconds, Keandra glanced back at E-jekt to see if he had moved. He wasn't dropped in completely, so he was still aware of his surroundings. His eyes twitched, scanning code and images that only he could see while his fingers were a blur.

When they arrived at home, E-jekt stayed in his AR world, keeping his head bowed as Keandra and Lance served as escorts, guiding him to the elevators and keeping anyone from getting too close. The decker was aware enough to avoid static obstacles like walls and pillars, but moving obstacles were another matter altogether. Just because he wasn't in VR didn't mean he wasn't distracted.

They got to their apartment and E-jekt made a beeline for the couch, lying down and letting his body go slack as he jumped into the Matrix completely.

Keandra kept busy while she waited for news. She made a pot of soykaf for the team, but Paz was the only one to join her. At least it kept her moving, and the smell and warmth of the caffeinated beverage helped soothe her nerves.

A page on her commlink interrupted that serenity. It was her business line, but managed to bypass her filters and be classified as high priority even though it came from a restricted contact. Curious, she opened up a private chat with the caller.

<Greetings, Miss Tiernay. I represent a certain Mr. Johnson by whom you are employed. They were hoping that there might be a status update regarding your objective?>

Keandra's heart skipped a beat. She dropped her cup, its crash making Paz and Lance snap their attention to her. Hot soykaf splashed over her legs, and she jumped back, then snatched a towel off the rack and wiped at her calves. Even after she'd mopped up the liquid, individual pricks of heat stung where drops struck her.

"I'm fine. Just got a message from our Johnson wanting an update."

Paz's eyed widened. "That can't be a coincidence. No. No fucking way. The suit just *happens* to call right when all this goes down? What are you going to tell 'im?"

"My thoughts exactly. I just got rattled for a moment— caught me off guard. I can handle this. I'm going to stall. We need to give E-jekt time to find something, find anything, before we can come up with a plan. In the meantime, I'll run damage control."

<I don't know who you are or why you might be contacting me. Even if I were under the employ of someone you claim to be working for, it would be far too risky to communicate in this manner about any arrangements that may or may not have been made.>

The response was nearly instant. <I understand your precautions, and my employer expected no less from someone with your level of professionalism. In truth, they would prefer if such communication were not transmitted in such an easily recorded medium. However, they instructed me to let you know that they will be attending your usual restaurant for an early dinner in a short while. The reservations have already been handled and start promptly at four-thirty. They look forward to your progress report at that time.>

Before Keandra could process the message, let alone think of a response, the connection was severed. That meant this wasn't a negotiation or a request; it was an order. And one Mr. Johnson expected her to comply with.

"Well, I guess I won't be able to stall as much as I hoped."

Paz's surprised look morphed into a scowl. "I don't like that look on your face. It's the one when something bad's about to happen, and you're gonna tell us it isn't that bad, and you've got a plan. 'Course, the plan doesn't always work. But that's why I always carry extra ammo."

"You're right, something bad is going to happen. Mr. Johnson wants a meeting and a progress report, and has already arranged a reservation at Elliot's. He's never wanted to meet during the day before, and he's never set the meeting time out of the blue like this. Everything's always been planned well in advance and fit into a nice little package. Hell, he's never actually called me before. We've only ever met in person or through anonymous one-way postings on the Matrix. They have to know about what happened with the job. There's no other explanation."

E-jekt sat up and rubbed his gnarled hands over his face, stretching the skin and digging in with his fingernails. Keandra dropped the towel on the counter and came over to him. Out of the corner of her eye, she saw Lance drift over and start picking up the pieces of the shattered cup, using the towel to clean up the rest of the soykaf puddle.

"What'd you find out?" she asked, trying to keep the urgency out of her voice.

"Not much, I'm afraid. Looks like the damage done to the commlink, the club, and me all came from the busted commlink."

Keandrea frowned. "You think it was trapped? Some new type of data bomb or something?"

E-jekt shook his head and dropped his hands to his legs. He took a deep breath before continuing. Lance poured him a cup of soykaf and held it out. E-jekt took it with a nod of thanks as he sank back into the couch cushions with the steaming cup cradled in his hands.

"Not a data bomb. Something in the file itself. Some sprite was attached to it, and as soon as it got a valid network connection, it jumped through that and torched everything in the immediate vicinity. Whoever wrote it probably hoped that would make it difficult to track and figure out where it went. Kind of like escaping in the confusion. It would have fried my commlink too, if it weren't for all my failsafe mechanisms. Still, I'm going to be feeling this one for days. Like I told you, I've met nicer black ice than this thing. Whoever coded it is an absolute genius."

"But can you track it?"

"I think so. It won't be easy, though. It literally fried the circuits at Syberspace. They'll have to spend a fortune to bring the club back online. But I managed to piece together part of a digital signature. There's still a few pieces left, and once I have that I can start scouring the Matrix, looking for the data. It has to be somewhere. Something with a sprite that powerful isn't going to just disappear. We just need to find where it's programmed to go."

Keandra nodded. "Good. I need you to stay here and work on that. Paz will keep you company."

"Where are you going?"

"Mr. Johnson called. He wants an update."

NINE

Keandra couldn't remember the last time she'd felt this nervous before a meeting. Even when she had to deliver bad news or deal with an angry employer, she always had an ace up her sleeve—something she could use as a bargaining chip to help turn things in her favor. But right now she had nothing, and she was about to ask for more time from a very dangerous man without letting him know his data might be lost forever. It was not an exciting prospect.

Nonetheless, the meeting was going to happen—the only thing worse than delivering bad news was not showing up to deliver it at all. Keandra dressed well, using her physical appearance as a shield to hide her misgivings and insecurity. Lance accompanied her as always, equal parts to maintain the persona and be security. His presence made her feel safe, even if the current battlefield had very little to do with physical confrontation.

As they approached the restaurant, a nervous twitch raced down Keandra's spine. Glancing around and taking in all the details, she realized why. Francis wasn't working the front desk. She had grown accustomed to seeing his face here whenever she arranged a meeting. While it was a few hours earlier than her usual arrival, it still seemed odd. She doubted the restaurant had one maître d' for the early diners and another for the later arrivals. That would be excessive, even for Elliot's.

"Miss Tiernay, thank you for joining us. If you'll follow me—your host has already arrived." The current maître d' was a small elf who exuded slipperiness from his oiled hair to his guarded body language. His demeanor was discomforting, and she didn't trust him in the slightest.

The man led her up the steps into the restaurant, where several groups of people were enjoying their meals. As she followed her escort, she looked him over, taking in every detail. A few displays popped up in her AR as E-jekt analyzed the data. It was nice having him active once again for these meetings. Everything about the host looked normal, except for his shoes. Judging from the information E-jekt scrounged up, they were a hand-tooled cut of a designer print, easily costing well several thousand nuyen—and well out of the price range of a maître d', even for an upscale restaurant like this one.

Armed with this information, Keandra surreptitiously scanned the crowd, letting E-jekt take some time to process the data. The waitstaff all checked out, all of them broadcasting legal SINs that were easy to identify and process. That, plus nothing seemed out of the ordinary in their attire or presentation. So it was just the maître d', then. Why would that be important, and why would Mr. Johnson want to replace him?

To her surprise, several groups were dining on the patio. Four tables were spaced out, three occupied by diners in the middle of their meals. Mr. Johnson was nowhere to be seen. When she hesitated, her escort turned around and gestured for her to follow him.

"This way, Miss Tiernay. Your host has reserved the private club room for the evening."

If her nerves were on edge before, the elf's words set them on fire. She managed to keep her breathing normal and flashed a smile as she dipped her head, indicating he should lead on. She fell into step behind him, trying to process this new information.

Perhaps the reservation on the patio wasn't fesaible because of previous obligations, but Keandra doubted it. That wasn't something that bothered people like Mr. Johnson. He had more than enough resources and sway to have arranged the restaurant exactly to his liking. Was this just a show of his power, then? A move to demonstrate how insignificant she was in comparison, and remind her how much backing he had? That was the most logical conclusion. Regardless, it didn't change the game she had to play, nor her goals.

At the stairs leading up to the second floor, a large troll stepped to the side and unhooked the velvet rope to let them access the upper loft. She'd never been up here before, and this was the first time she'd seen it roped off in all of her business appointments over the years. The maître d' left her here, indicating with a wave of his hand for her to go up the stairs. Keandra took the first two, and then stopped and turned when she heard a quiet tussle behind her.

The troll held his arm in front of Lance, blocking him at chest level as he climbed up after Keandra. The burly guard shook his head and moved to put the velvet rope back in place.

Lance tensed and glanced up at Keandra, looking for some sort of sign. She gave a subtle shake of her head and he backed down, removing his foot from the step. Starting a fight now would give away her fear and discomfort. Keandra climbed the stairs alone, not sure what exactly would be waiting for her at the top.

The stairs ended at a single door, beyond which was the private dining chamber. It was an expansive area, designed to host parties of up to fifty people comfortably. One entire wall was made of glass, looking out over the Sound and the docks. A large table dominated the center of the room, with chairs spaced evenly along both sides. Another wall was dedicated to a wine rack, the bottles angled so the labels could be read. Each bottle was stored behind glass designed to keep the treasures inside safe from the ravages of time or sunlight. Small tables dotted the lengths of the other walls.

Mr. Johnson sat at the center of the table, on the side facing the door so Keandra was looking at him as she entered. With the exception of his regular bodyguard, the room was otherwise empty. As the door closed behind her, it drowned out the sounds of the restaurant below, and a moment of utter stillness filled the air before Mr. Johnson stood.

"Welcome, Miss Tiernay. I appreciate your being able to meet me on such short notice. I hope you will forgive me for the imposition, since I realize it is highly unusual, given our normal arrangements."

He gestured to the seat across from him, and Keandra walked to it. Three opened wine bottles sat on the table in front of her place, all the labels turned so she could read them. When Mr. Johnson took his seat, she turned her attention toward the labels, pretending to study them. Display of power it was, then.

"I agree. This situation has been most unusual. When dealing with people in my line of work, sudden shifts in schedule and expectations can put one on edge and cause suspicion. Plus, there is normal protocol to observe. I notice we are not alone, but my bodyguard was not allowed to accompany me. Should I be concerned?"

Keandra looked Mr. Johnson in the eye and raised a single eyebrow. She held the gesture for the space of a heartbeat, then turned back to the wine, selecting one at random and pouring it into the glass in front of her rather than waiting for a member of the waitstaff to come along and handle it for her. She picked up the glass and swirled it gently, taking a sniff as she stared over it at her employer. The bouquet was heady, with a hint of plum.

"I assure you, there is no need for concern. The policy of the restaurant, I am afraid–not my own. No weapons are allowed within this room, and I would not suggest to your bodyguard that he leave his armament behind. My associate agreed to forego the tools of his trade so he could be present. A security measure, nothing more."

Keandra wanted to call him on his lies. Even if that was a company policy, it was something he could easily overrule, and besides, she had no doubt that like Lance, the Johnson's bodyguard would be equally capable unarmed. But there would be no point in mentioning any of that.

She put her glass down without taking a sip. "If you don't mind my being so bold, why did you request this unconventional meeting? I do not want to take up more of your time than is necessary to conduct our business."

He nodded minutely. "I appreciate your candor, so I'll be equally frank in return. As I mentioned during our initial negotiation, this objective is of critical importance. Those whom I work for want to make sure everything is going according to plan. You've had some time now, so I wanted to check on the status of your efforts."

"Everything is going according to plan."

"I'm pleased to hear that. I've heard troubling reports, but it is comforting to know you have it all under control."

Keandra debated how much to share. It was a given that he knew about the break-in. Anyone as connected as he was would have to know about it by now, even if it wasn't public knowledge. Would he have known they farmed out the job, or about the incident at Syberspace? Those were less likely. In her experience, most Johnsons kept their hands scrupulously clean of the incident once the contract had been agreed to. The less connecting them to the actual incidents, the better.

"There was an incident, but nothing my team couldn't handle. We will deliver your package by the original timeline."

Silence once again reigned supreme as Mr. Johnson stared at her, eyes slightly narrowed as he took in every detail. The scrutiny made sweat appear at the base of Keandra's neck, but she ignored it as best she could, meeting his stare.

It only lasted a few seconds, but it felt as if much more time passed before he put his hands on the edge of the table and stood. He buttoned his suit jacket and turned to look out the window. The bodyguard continued to watch her, probably armed despite Mr. Johnson's claims.

"See that you do, Miss Tiernay. It would be most unpleasant if I had to inform my employers about your failure to perform. I'm sure you would understand that people would need to be held accountable for such a transgression. In the meantime, I suggest you ensure that you keep up your end of the bargain and perhaps spend less time at clubs. After all, such locations can be very destructive. That is all."

Keandra took the dismissal in stride and kept her composure as she nodded, stood, and walked out of the room. It felt as if every muscle in her body were tensed to the snapping point, even when she heard the door close behind her and was halfway down the stairs. Seeing Lance perk up at the bottom when he caught sight of her brought some relief. The stairwell guard dropped the velvet rope for her again, hooking it back into place after she passed.

Lance glided into position at her side, rather than behind her, but she didn't speak to him. Not yet. Not until they were outside and away from easily prying eyes and ears. Mr. Johnson made it clear that he knew more than she realized, but she wasn't about to give him any more information if she could help it. There was nothing veiled in his threat. With luck, by the time they got back to the safehouse, E-jekt will have solved this problem for them.

When they reached the front of the restaurant, Keandra noticed that a crowd had formed, and the maître d' was nowhere to be found. The crowd appeared just as confused as she was. Just as they left, she spotted the elf running up, pushing through the crowd without any sense of decorum or poise.

Keandra grabbed Lance and pulled him to the side, ducking behind a small group of elderly diners wearing more jewelry than her net worth. Lance didn't ask questions, but fell in line next to her, presenting his back to the maître d'. They waited until he'd headed off, escorting a couple there for a romantic dinner. Only then did Keandra leave the restaurant.

<Check the car. I'm pretty sure the host isn't employed by the restaurant, and he came from the direction where we parked.>

Lance pulled out a scanner and held it in the palm of his hand while he opened the door for Keandra. He casually draped his arm over the roof and walked around the car, appearing casual as he swept the scanner over the entire vehicle. Before climbing in, he took a knee and retied a shoe as he passed the scanner underneath the vehicle. He got in, sliding his device back into his pocket so deftly that Keandra couldn't say for sure when he'd tucked it away, even though she knew what to look for.

<Two bugs. One recording sound and the other just a tracker. How do you want to handle this?>

"That meeting didn't take as long as I anticipated. Since we have some time, let's get the car cleaned. We keep putting it off. We have a few minutes before we're needed back, so let's take advantage of it."

At least that would give them a justifiable reason for the bugs being removed or destroyed. It was a thin excuse, but it would have to do. In the meantime, she needed to figure out what they were going to do about the missing data. Mr. Johnson was invested in this, more than she realized at first, and the hiccups in the operation had forced him to take action. If he decided to bring the might of his corporation to bear against them, they'd need to run. And to do that, they'd need nuyen, something they were dangerously low on right now.

Hopefully, E-jekt had what they needed and this would all be behind them soon enough. But Keandra hadn't survived this long without having multiple backup plans in place.

At least now she knew why Mr. Johnson had gone to such great lengths for this meeting. He was scared—and that frightened her.

TEN

"Gone? What do you mean, gone?"

Keandra's hands clenched so tight at her sides that her nails dug into her palms and threatened to draw blood. Paz sat in the corner, chewing her bottom lip as she watched Keandra react to E-jekt's less-than-pleasant news.

"I mean the data has disappeared. I tracked the sprite to CalFree, where it hopped around a couple of labs and corporate offices. Had to hack their security, but I followed the trail from there to a couple other megacorps across UCAS and even a couple overseas. I was in the middle of trying to break through a firewall when the sprite spotted me and ejected me from the system. When I went back, it changed its signature. There's no way I can find it now. It's gone."

"How the hell can a sprite boot you from the system? Couldn't you stop it?"

"Maybe, if I wasn't dealing with ice *and* trying to breach a corporate firewall at the time." He shrugged. "It caught me off guard, and I couldn't split myself well enough to handle it. But once it changed signatures, it's pointless."

Keandra closed her eyes and forced herself to take deep breaths. Everyone else in the room was quiet, waiting for her to speak. She was always the one with the plan and she could feel their stares, heavy with expectation. They were counting on her to know how to get out of this.

When she opened her eyes, she knew what to do. "All right, so we've lost the data file. That means we can't finish the job, and after my meeting with Mr. Johnson today, he's not going to accept us returning the initial deposit and just calling this off."

"The suit was that pissed?"

"He bugged us. Actually had someone go out and bug the car. Not only that, but he made a definite show of power. He knew about our meeting at the club, though I don't think he knew any specifics other than that we were there. Whatever this data is, he's going to be very unhappy when we tell him it's gone. He specifically said someone would need to be held accountable for our failure. I'm pretty sure he wasn't planning on taking the blame himself."

Paz grinned the feral smile she got whenever she was ready for a fight, even one that was probably hopeless and had no way for her to win. To her, the idea of risk assessment started and stopped with making sure her gun didn't overheat and explode in her hands. On the other side of the fence, E-jekt and Lance wore expressions that matched her own concern.

"We need to face the fact that Mr. Johnson will come after us if we tell him we failed. And if that happens, there's nothing we can do here. He clearly has contacts all over the city, and enough influence and wealth to make anything happen just by throwing his weight around. If we want to survive, we would have to leave."

She waited for the news to sink in. While the others were digesting what she'd laid out, Keandra moved to the couch and perched on its arm, her hands on her knees.

Lance pressed his lips together and nodded, whereas Paz looked disappointed. E-jekt ran his fingers through his hair several times, but remained silent.

"You don't mean this place, or even just Seattle, do you?" Paz asked.

"I was thinking out of the UCAS entirely. Mr. Johnson might have global contacts, but anywhere overseas would require a lot more paperwork before he could get his hands on us. I also think we should refund his deposit. If he hasn't lost any nuyen, it will be a little bit harder for him to convince the rest of his corp to hold us liable."

"If we do that, there's no way we can jump ship. Getting new SINs, traveling under the radar, crossing international borders..." E-jekt waved his hand in small circles. After a heavy sigh, he continued. "All these things cost money. And if we want to get out before our deadline, we don't really have time to sell property. Refunding him will drain almost all our reserves and whatever we can scrounge up on short notice."

"I've thought of that. There's only one solution I can think of. We take another job."

She paused again, after delivering the second silence-inducing shock in such a short time.

"I went through our potential bids, and there's a structure hit this evening we could run. Not our specialty, but one of the few types of missions I'd be comfortable running on that short a timeline without all of our necessary preparation. We don't even need to be quiet, just successful."

Paz perked up at that, her feral grin a break from the heavy expressions around the room. "Even if we don't decide to cut and run, I'm in. Been far too long since I've had the chance to blow something up."

Lance began pacing, his gaze focused on the floor in front of him as he walked from one end of the room to the other. The entire time, his expression never changed.

After a few laps, he glanced at Keandra. "You've thought this through, like always, haven't you?"

Keandra nodded. "I don't see any other options. If we can't get that data, we need to jet, and then figure out what we're going to do from somewhere safe."

"I trust your judgment. I'm in."

As usual, E-jekt was the last to speak. He always took the most time to come to a conclusion, but Keandra appreciated his tendency to analyze all the information thoroughly before committing to a course of action. It served as a nice sounding board, and reaffirmed her own considerations. She watched as he deliberated; his brow furrowed. He would sit still for a few seconds and then shake his head, all the while muttering under his breath. It was barely a whisper, sounding more like wind through the trees than actual words.

With a long exhalation, he collapsed onto the couch, shoulders slumped. He looked up at everyone else, then held up both hands, shrugged wearily, then let his hands drop to his sides.

"There's really not another option, is there?"

"I'm afraid not. If any of you has an idea, I'd love to hear it."

E-Jekt looked around again, finding only head shakes. "I don't either. I just feel like we've painted ourselves into a corner, and are scrambling to find a way out before it's too late. And part of me wonders if it already is."

Keandra made sure her voice was firm when she replied. "Nonsense. We have a plan and we can make it work. We've gotten through tough jams before, ones we probably shouldn't have survived. This is no different. We'll do this quick run, and in a couple days we'll be sitting somewhere new planning our next venture. It's what we do—we survive." Keandra wasn't sure she believed her own words, but just the act of saying them made her feel better.

She nodded at Paz and Lance. "Go get equipped, get some rest, and meet back here by three. I'm going to handle the job negotiations remotely. It should be pretty effortless, since it's a straightforward task. It should give us enough to get set up with new identities and prepped for international travel. I'll also put out word to our fixer to get the balls rolling there. It'll all come together."

After reviewing notes to finalize the details of the job and what gear would be required, Lance and Paz left to get prepared.

Once they were gone, Keandra got up from the couch and sat down on the floor in front of E-jekt so she could look at him without twisting her body. She took one of his hands and clasped it on both of hers.

"What's going on? I know you're worried about how things are going, but there's something more than that. Is it because we're going to need you in the field? I know it'll be your first time out there in a while, but we'll keep you safe. Plus, we got you that new armor. With how much you wear it, it has to be broken in by now."

"Nah, it's not that. It's just..." He trailed off, so Keandra sat and waited, never letting go of his hand. He would share when he was ready, and she wasn't about to push him into it. After a while, he rewarded her patience.

"It's all my fault."

That response surprised her and she cocked her head as she looked at him.

"What's your fault?"

"This. Everything. Having to leave the country. It's all because I lost the data. First the sprite blasts through my defenses and scrambles my brain. Then while I was trying to track it down, I get ambushed, losing the trail for good. If I hadn't screwed that up, we wouldn't be in this position and need to flee the country."

Keandra rose from the floor and moved to sit next to the ork. She rested her arm on top of his and patted it. "It's as much my fault as yours. More so, even. I'm the one who came up with this idea in the first place. I'm the one who insisted we try something different and put us in Mr. Johnson's crosshairs for taking on something too big. I'm the one who had you check the data file, rather than just passing it off as we should have done. If there's any blame going around, I think I deserve far more than you, my friend."

He chuckled. "I guess we're just getting sloppy in our old age. You'd think we'd know better by now."

"I just look at it as a way to keep young. If we never made mistakes, we wouldn't be pushing ourselves enough, and we'd stagnate. No one wants that."

"We keep pushing too hard, we're going to wind up dead."

Keandra pushed herself up from the couch. She needed to get moving, and he needed to recharge. "We're both too stubborn to die. Come on, get some sleep while you can. I need to work out the contract details and then crash, or I'll be useless that early."

ELEVEN

At half past three in the morning, the runners were in Paz's van, parked on a street near the Federated Boeing shipyards. All four were crammed into the back, watching the AR display of a warehouse E-jekt had constructed from a combination of building plans and surveillance feeds in the area. There were a few dark spots on the display, but overall it was highly detailed and even showed two guards as they patrolled the building's perimeter.

The security around that particular building was minor: only a few cameras supplemented the two guards. However, the entire facility had a veritable army on staff that could be mobilized if they were alerted to trouble. It was clear that stealth was the only course of action open to the team. At least a little bit of luck had finally come their way: the building they needed to break into was near the perimeter of the shipyards, well away from the heavy security.

"Lance, you go in first and take out both guards while the rest of us get in position for E-jekt to take out the surveillance system. The entryway on the southeast corner seems like our best bet."

As plans went, it was pretty simple and straightforward, and often those kind were the best. No need to add extra complexity where it wasn't warranted. With any luck, by this time tomorrow, they would all be on a plane out of the country.

The group exited the van and walked casually across the street to a poorly-lit area along the perimeter. The shipyards were surrounded by a fence topped with barbed wire. The fence itself wasn't electrified or alarmed, and the barrier posed little real threat to anyone determined to gain access. While Paz began cutting a hole through the wire mesh, Lance jumped over the top, landing in a crouch on the other side. Keandra watched him dash off toward the warehouse, moving to the side to stuck to the shadows. She knew if she looked away, she'd lose him.

He stopped at the edge of a shipping container only a few meters from the warehouse. Dropping to a knee, he waited, staring straight ahead as the two guards on patrol passed by in front of him. When they were several steps past him, Lance slipped out and toward them, hunched over to keep his profile low. He was a few feet away from the two guards when the one on the left stopped and turned to look over his shoulder.

The man tried to whirl around and bring his gun to bear, but Lance was too quick. The elf drew his blade and brought it down in a sweeping cut that sliced through half of the gun before getting stuck. Lance released his weapon and lunged forward, driving his elbow into the guard's throat hard enough to knock him off his feet and collapse him to the dirt. Even from this distance, Keandra heard the gasping and gurgling as the guard struggled to breathe. She hoped no one else onsite heard it as well.

The other guard opened her mouth to speak, but Lance was supernaturally quick. He grabbed the barrel of her gun and shoved it back into her face, stunning her. Sweeping her feet, he knocked her to the ground and dropped on top of her, one hand covering her mouth and the other arm pinned against her throat. She kicked a few times, trying to buck him off, but with no success. Once she blacked out, he moved back to the first guard, lifting his head and wrapping an arm around his throat from behind. In just a few seconds, both guards were unconscious. Keandra held her breath, but no alarm went off. It looked like their entrance had gone unnoticed, at least so far.

By now, Paz was done with the fence, and she walked through the opening. Keandra and E-jekt followed, ducking to make it through the hole. A tearing sound made Keandra whip around to see E-jekt wrestling his shoulder free from one of the jagged edges, a large fresh tear visible in his coat. Shaking her head, she turned back to check the warehouse. The southeast corner was up ahead and off to the right, but they had to wait for the camera to finish its sweep of the area before they could advance. Lance was good enough to hide from its gaze, but he was the only member of their group with that skill.

Once the electronic eye swept past their location on its programmed arc, Keandra rushed forward, waving for the others to follow. They hustled to the edge of the wall, within an arm's reach of their entrance point. The camera had finished its sweep and was starting to head back in the other direction.

Keandra turned to E-jekt; his chest rose and fell rapidly, his wheeze plainly audible. Despite that, he nodded and pulled up his interface, hacking into the security system.

They had nothing to do but wait. With no time to set up a proper hacking run after taking the job, he needed to be this close to access their network, but there was no good hiding place. They just had to hope he finished before the camera swung back in their direction. As it continued to turn, Keandra flattened her body against the wall, as if hoping the action would hide her.

<E-jekt. Now would be good.>

The camera continued to swivel until Keandra was sure she was in its view. She was about to call for a retreat when the device powered down and the red light went off.

<Cutting it a bit close there?>

<I had to set up the repeat first, otherwise they'd know something was wrong. Now all they'll see is an empty lot.>

<All right, let's go. We have a job to do.>

E-jekt pushed away from the wall and walked around the group to the door, dropping to a knee and examining the lock. With a soft snort of amusement, he pulled a pair of lockpicks from his coat pocket. The door was mechanical, with no electronic lock to speak of. Once again, it looked like luck was finally turning in their favor. Still, Keandra remained vigilant. She'd seen far too many runs go south at the last minute because of one foolish mistake.

Lance took up a position on the opening side of the door, ready to slide in as soon as it was unlocked. Paz framed it on the other side, to provide less subtle backup if needed.

With a soft click, E-jekt moved the handle. He short quick glances at each of his companions before turning it completely and pushing the door open. He shuffled back and to the side, moving into the space vacated by Lance as the elf slipped into the room beyond.

Keandra waited a few seconds, listening with all of her focus. When she heard nothing beyond the distant sound of machinery she nodded to Paz. The sturdy dwarf stepped into the warehouse, gun tucked against her shoulder with her eye lined up on the sights. Keandra followed, letting E-jekt bring up the rear. He left the door open in case they needed a fast retreat.

This entrance led into the rear half of the warehouse, which had been converted into offices and server space. The front part contained some of the vehicles Federated Boeing had developed: nothing new, though—these were already-released technologies more than a few years old. The servers, however, contained data for the corp's current research projects. That was their target. The room they needed to get to was on the second floor, but first they needed to find the stairs.

Currently they were in a cubicle farm, crouched low behind a half-wall forming the edge of someone's office. At this hour most of the employees were gone, and the entire area had been reduced to minimal lighting in an attempt to save energy. Workers occupied a few scattered cubicles, their hands moving in front of them as they interacted with their AR components, developing something no one else could see. The beauty of the modern office: so simple and Spartan, with minimal costs to the company.

That also meant there was little for the team to hide behind as they headed toward the stairwell. It would have to be near one of the exit doors, but Keandra didn't know which one. There were no blueprints on file for when Federated Boeing had converted the empty warehouse into a hybrid office building.

<Lance, check around the east wall for the stairwell. The rest of us will head along the south perimeter line.>

Lance moved off without making a sound, turning the corner and heading north. Keandra took the lead for her group, sneaking along as best she could. Of course, it almost didn't matter how much sound she made, since she had Paz stumping along behind her. The dwarf tried to be quiet, but her metal limbs still created heavy dull *thud*s whenever they connected with a wall or even the floor. Each bump made Keandra wince, but little could be done about it.

Ahead, an exit sign hung over an entryway into a combined kitchen and eating area. Keandra ducked inside and was glad to have the chance to stand up straight. The crouching made her legs sore enough that they were starting to shake, and she wasn't sure how much longer she could have kept it up without resorting to crawling.

The kitchenette had a sink that smelled of stale coffee, a fridge, a couple of tables surrounded by chairs, and a few motivational posters about doing it for the good of the team. Standard corporate propaganda. Keandra couldn't understand how some people could live like this, seeing the same things every day, knowing it would never change while pretending to care about something so menial that any one of a thousand different wage slaves could have done it. Then again, she was sure they wouldn't understand her lifestyle either.

The exit door was on her left, across from the fridge. Keandra opened it and peeked through, relieved to see a stairwell going up to the second story, as well as an exit door leading outside straight across from her. There were cameras in the upper corners of the stairwell, but they were already powered down. E-jekt was nothing if not thorough.

<Stairwell's here. Lance, come to the kitchenette. Paz, take E-jekt and start scouting the second floor.>

She held the door open for the other two and then leaned against the wall, waiting for Lance to join them. When she noticed a flash of movement to her right, she pushed herself off the wall. A young elf entered the room carrying an empty mug, and they both froze.

Keandra was the first to recover, whipping her gun from its holster and pointing it at the new arrival. He started shaking, and she was worried he'd drop the mug and shatter it. She gestured with her gun, indicating for him to move farther into the room.

At first he diddn't budge, fear holding him in place. Keandra stepped forward, gesturing once again with the gun and raising it even with his eyeline. He dropped the mug and whirled, sprinting away from her. The ceramic cup shattered on the floor.

<We've got trouble. Someone saw me and made a run for it.>

<You didn't shoot him? Can Meat-sack take him out?>

<I'm not killing a wage slave for our convenience! They're not trained security.>

Lance appeared behind Keandra and put a hand on her shoulder. When she looked at him, he offered a soft smile and nodded to the stairwell. When she hesitated, he bent to whisper in her ear. "I understand, and I'd have done the same."

She grasped his forearm, squeezing it once. Then she turned and took the stairs two at a time to the second floor. Maybe if their luck held, they could destroy the servers and get out before security responded.

E-jekt and Paz waited for Lance and her on the second-floor landing. Both crouched near the door, and Paz held up a hand to stop Keandra's advance.

<Small security team up ahead. Three guards, all armed with guns and one turret. No way we're getting through quietly. I'll pop 'em with a smoke grenade and lay down some cover, then stealth boy flanks right. Can you geek the turret, old man?>

<Already working on it.>

Paz pointed her gun around the edge of the door, angled it up, and launched the grenade. It bounced a few times with metallic clinks before letting out a loud hiss and a muffled explosion. Immediately, everyone in the room began shouting at each other and calling for backup on their radios.

Keandra made out someone saying something about thermographic cameras. Lance ducked into the room just before gunfire erupted. Several bullets ripped through the air in front of the doorway, embedding themselves in the far wall of the stairwell. Paz released a burst of bullets; the guards' gunfire paused as presumably they dove for cover.

The turret roared to life with a harsh mechanical whirring sound as it shot bullets faster than any metahuman guard could. Between the gunfire, the smoke, and the shouting, the small chamber sounded like a war zone. After a few seconds, the turret stopped, only to whirr back to life a second later. The guards screamed in pain and confusion.

"Hey—it's targeting us!"

"Shoot him! Forget the turret!"

"Where is—"

The last shout was cut short with a wet gurgle, and the turret powered down. By now most of the smoke had cleared, so Paz spun around the corner and stepped into the room.

"Clear."

Keandra entered the chamber, taking in the carnage all around her. The turret still smoked. The walls and floor were riddled with holes and splattered with blood, scarred beyond any hope of ever being pristine again. What remained of the guards was also spread around the room. A decapitated body rested at Lance's feet; the elf's sword dripped blood onto the floor as he stood over his victim.

On the far side of the room, Keandra saw the plexiglass wall protecting the servers. A single door led into the room, held shut with an electronic lock. Just one barrier to go, and then they could destroy their target. Hopefully before the rest of security showed up.

"Let's go, E-jekt. Get us in there, and fast."

TWELVE

E-jekt hustled to the door, kneeling in front of the lock and opening his display. Lance took up a guard position on the edge of the entrance, sword held up at his right shoulder and ready to dissect anyone who tried to interrupt them. Paz stood just behind E-jekt, sheltering him with her body just in case. Between them and the turret, hopefully E-jekt would have the time he needed if they were interrupted. Meanwhile, Keandra huddled behind one of the barricades put in place for the guards, trying to ignore the fact that she was kneeling in still-warm blood.

She felt blind. There was nothing to do now but wait. She wondered just how fast Federated Boeing's response team was, and whether they had a Knight Errant contract. That was the kind of thing that she'd have researched if they'd had the time, but now it was too late, and she had to deal with the cards they'd been dealt. Out of nervous habit, she released the magazine in her gun to make sure it was fully loaded. Of course it was—she hadn't fired any shots—but it still provided a few seconds' distraction. She slammed the magazine back into place and tried to relax.

"Got it."

The door clicked, and E-jekt jerked it open. Paz barely waited for him to clear out of her way before she rushed into the chamber, Keandra close behind. E-jekt joined them while Lance maintained his vigil. The ork looked up at the ceilings and let out a soft grunt.

"State of the art fire-suppression systems. You'll need to plant explosives at the base of each server rack if we want to get them all. Do you have enough?"

Paz just snorted in response. She set up her bombs, placing one at the bottom of each rack. She tossed a couple to Keandra and waved toward the rest of the room. Keandra obliged, setting the explosives as instructed. She didn't know much about demolitions, but Paz assured her that these bombs were basically idiot-proof.

A burst of gunfire caught Keandra's attention as the turret roared to life again. She looked up in a panic. The guards were faster than she'd anticipated, and they were running out of time. The likelihood of them getting out safely dropped along with Keandra's stomach.

A couple of guards tried to enter the room and the reprogrammed security system cut them down. Another managed to sneak through, but Lance took him out before he'd taken two steps. The rest of the guards ducked back into the safety of the hallway. A few fired blindly around the corner and the bullets cracked the glass, sending spider-web cracks along its surface, but didn't penetrate or shatter it.

One guard tossed a grenade through the opening, near the base of the turret. Rather than exploding, it opened up and emitted harsh white light in a regular pulsing pattern. The barrel of the turret dropped and all its lights went out as the device powered down. Once that threat was dealt with, the guards poured back through the entrance, attempting to overwhelm Lance with sheer force of numbers.

The elf fought like a whirlwind, his blade flashing faster than the eye could follow as he took down one opponent and then kicked the corpse into the rest of the horde to slow them down. They opened fire, but Lance rushed to the wall and sprang off it, gaining enough height to get over the gunfire. He dropped into the middle of the large group, sweeping out with his blade in one direction while throwing a knife in the other. One guard tried to shoot him, but Lance grabbed another guard's neck and swung around his body, moving out of the way so his attacker shot his ally instead. Five of the guards were already dead, and Keandra hoped Lance might be able to hold them off. They only had one more rack to go and then they could escape.

However, the guards' numbers were too great, and it wasn't long before one got in a lucky strike with the butt of his assault rifle, connecting with the side of Lance's head. The adept stumbled and swung his blade in a warding blow, keeping his opponent at bay, but he slowed. Another guard came up behind him and slammed his elbow into the small of Lance's back, forcing him to his knees. Seizing the opportunity, yet another guard kicked the sword away. It clattered as it hit the ground. Keandra willed for Lance to stand as she tried to finish their task. They just needed a few more seconds.

Six more guards hurried into the room, four of them centering on Lance. One kicked him to the floor and they all kept their guns trained on his body. They stood a safe distance away, making sure he couldn't grab any of them before they could shoot. One stepped forward and spoke into an intercom hanging on the wall next to the entrance.

"Drop your weapons and come out with your hands in the air, or we'll execute your friend."

They still had two more bombs to place, but Keandra couldn't risk it. The other two looked to her for guidance, so she held her hands up over her head and walked to the entrance. Paz and E-jekt both followed her example.

<All their guns have smartlink systems. I think I can handle them.>

E-jekt stumbled to his knees before reaching the entrance, looking like he was trying to catch his breath. Keandra turned as if to help him, when in truth she shielded his actions with her body. If she could give him a little more time, he might be able to work his Matrix magic. Paz continued walking toward the entrance.

"Get up, you two. On your feet!"

Keandra stood and turned around, leaving E-jekt where he was and putting her hands on her head to show she wasn't carrying any weapons and wasn't a threat. She stayed in the center of the aisle, doing everything she could to block the view of E-jekt for as long as possible.

In the room ahead, she saw all the guns eject their magazines at the same time. More importantly, Lance noticed it. As the guards stared in confusion, he tapped into his supernatural speed and burst into action.

Springing from the ground, he kicked the closest guard in the chest, driving him back. Then he snatched one of the falling magazines and hurled it into the face of another guard. It wasn't heavy enough to do any real damage, but it surprised him. Lance vaulted over a third guard and kicked backward, sending the officer sprawling. The elf rolled across the ground, snatching up his sword as he came to his feet.

Paz turned the corner and punched the guard standing near the intercom. There was a sickening *crunch* as his chest caved in and he collapsed. Paz grabbed his gun and the ejected magazine, slamming it into place as she took a knee and aimed at the still-standing guard. She fired a quick burst of three bullets, all of them piercing the man's unarmored neck and dropping him to the ground. Within seconds, the entire battle was over.

"Let's finish up and get the hell out of here." Keandra rushed back to the final few servers, patting E-jekt's shoulder as she passed him. She went to the last two racks and placed her explosives. The entire room was rigged to blow now. She joined the rest of her companions in the antechamber. E-jekt closed the door and locked it. Paz held out the detonator to Keandra, but the leader smiled and shook her head. She didn't want to rob Paz of this moment. The dwarf giggled when she knew she'd get to bring the boom. The others stepped away from the glass, even though Paz had assured them the blast would be extremely localized.

When she pressed the button, all the explosives roared to life in a single wave of force and fire. The wave of flames struck the windows and rolled off to either side, contained by the bulletproof material. The fire suppression system kicked in immediately, and it only took a few seconds for the flames to dissipate. The smoke took a little longer to clear, but when it did, all that remained were large towers of melted slag that used to contain electronics. Several towers twisted from the heat and bent at awkward angles, like a madman's sculpture garden.

Now they just needed to get out alive. "Nice work," Keandra said. "Now let's get out of here before we find out if they have a Knight Errant contract. Then we can start talking about where we want to go."

The group filed out of the room with Lance taking the lead. He leaped over the handrail and dropped to the ground floor rather than taking the stairs a few at a time. By the time the others arrived he was nowhere to be seen, but the door leading outside was wide open. In the office area, a white light flashed and the emergency lighting was on. It looked like someone had staged an evacuation. Keandra was glad that the company drones had left and wouldn't be caught in any possible crossfire. While civilian casualties were sometimes part of the job, it was always unpleasant, with a healthy dose of guilt attached.

When she peeked out the doorway, Keandra saw a small troop of soldiers, all wearing armor and carrying assault rifles, jogging in formation from the center of the compound toward their building. A couple of drones flanked them on either side, providing air support. Another drone circled overhead. Keandra couldn't see it, but she could hear the engine as it cut through the clouds above their location.

<You all need to run now. Head for the hole in the fence. I'll provide a distraction. I don't suppose our technological beast could give me some smoke and noise?>

<Don't get caught in the blast, elf boy. Grenades out.>

Paz fired a pair of grenades in a high arc. They soared over the roof of the warehouse to land somewhere near the approaching battalion. As soon as the first explosion went off, they scattered into two groups, splitting with trained efficiency and providing flanking support for each other. After that, the smoke obscured anything Keandra might have been able to make out. One thing was clear: they were well-trained, which meant Keandra's team needs to get out ASAP A trained corporate force would cut them to shreds, no matter how good their muscle was.

Keandra dashed for the hole in the fence, practically dragging E-jekt behind her. He was wheezing before they got to the first storage container, but she didn't dare slow down. Overhead, she heard the roar of an engine grow louder. It was soon joined by two others.

Keandra pushed E-jekt behind the cover of the storage container, diving next to him as bullets ripped into the dirt where they had been standing moments before. The drone raced past and arced out in front of her, coming around for another shot. It sounded like the other two were close behind.

Rolling onto her back, Keandra leveled her pistol at the drone, aimed, and fired. She wasn't even sure if the shots had hit; if they had, the damage was minimal.

Paz's heavy rifle roared to life and the burst of bullets raced out to shred the drone, streaks of light filling the air behind the flying sentry as bits of metal sheared off and fell to the ground like a rain of fireflies. The drone lost control and listed to the side before slamming into the ground and exploding. A couple smaller explosions followed the first, each one loud enough to make Keandra's ears ring.

<MOVE!>

Lance appeared out of the darkness, jolting them out of their shock as he grabbed E-jekt, jerked the ork to a standing position, and shoved him in the direction of their van. One of the other drones opened fire, bullets kicking up dirt as it flew by on a strafing run. A round caught Lance in the side and he stumbled, planting his sword in the ground for balance. With a growl, he pushed himself up on the weapon and regained his balance before continuing.

Paz stopped running and lifted her gun, sighting in on the retreating drone. She pulled the trigger and another burst of fire ripped through the sky, shredding the drone's control vane. When it tried to turn around for another pass, it veered first one way and then the other before entering a spin and plummeting to the ground. It crashed somewhere on the other side of the road, out of sight.

The final drone circled around, coming at them from the side. It fired a single shot before arcing up and moving away. Keandra had just enough time to realize what it was before the RPG struck the ground near their position. Lance and E-jekt escaped the blast, but Keandra and Paz were thrown through the air from the force of the explosion, landing several meters away from the smoking crater.

Keandra's head rolled loosely from one side to the other and she blinked several times as she tried to regain awareness of her surroundings. A loud ringing filled her ears and blinking white spots obscured her vision. Something was wrong, and she wasn't sure what.

As her vision began clearing, she raised her hand in front of her face, surprised to see it covered in dirt, gravel, and blood. She touched her forehead and it felt wet. Looking at her fingers, she saw she was bleeding. That wasn't right. That wasn't supposed to be happening. Where was she?

It all came flooding back as the roar of the drone's engine cut through the ringing. It hurt when she moved, but Keandra forced herself to roll onto her side and prop herself on her elbow.

Paz was a few body lengths away, sitting up and moving her head around, looking for something. She spotted her rifle and scrambled over to it, holding a hand to her forehead the entire time. Once she got her weapon, she gripped it in both hands and a disturbing smile spread across her face, all the more disconcerting considering her obvious injuries.

She brought her gun up and followed the drone as it banked around, getting ready to attack them once again. Once it leveled out, Paz adjusted her height and held position, waiting.

The drone flew straight at them, only a few meters off the ground. Paz pulled the trigger and launched a single grenade at the drone. The grenade burst into flame, a miniature sun in the night sky, directly in front of the flying assault weapon. Unable to stop or vector away, the drone flew straight into the blast, emerging on fire in several places and with dripping liquid metal in others. It crashed into the ground, digging a trench just behind Keandra and Paz, smoldering in a heap when it came to a stop.

Another squad of drones zoomed toward them at high speed. There was no way they could get up the small rise to the gap in the fence before the drones were on them, and Paz couldn't take them all out by herself.

Keandra sprinted back to the shipping container, sliding behind it just as bullets ripped into the metal structure. Paz ducked down next to her, offering some return fire, but not hitting anything. Keandra counted at least five more drones in the air.

<E-jekt, we're pinned down. Can you do anything about those drones?>

<I'm trying, but they have us pinned down too. I'd have to drop in hot to have the time, and I can't do that and dodge gunfire too.>

<Ideas?>

<I can help you.>

Keandra didn't recognize the new messenger, and had no idea how it had hacked into their private conversations. She opened a private window to E-jekt.

<Who the hell is this and how did they get on our line?>

<I don't know. I can't run a full analysis, but... Holy... It's coming from your commlink, Keandra. The data signature–it matches the package I lost! You need to lock it down before it escapes again!>

Keandra wasn't sure what E-jekt was talking about, and she didn't have time to sort through it. She tried to engage the security programs in her commlink, but another burst of drone fire interrupted her, forcing her to duck away from the corner to keep from being shredded to bits. As it was, several pieces of shrapnel tore into her arms and face.

<How can you help us?>

<I can shut down the drones pursuing you. Deactivate them so you could reach your escape vehicle. But in order to do that, I cannot have you engage the security locks on your commlink. That would confine me to your local network, and I would be unable to assist you right away.>

<What do you want?>

<I need your help. I will explain once you have reached a safe location.>

<Do it. We'll hear you out.>

The drones circled around for another strafing attack, this time coming from multiple directions. Keandra hoped the contact could do what it claimed, or else they'd have to hope the riggers manning the drones were bad shots. To her relief, all five of the drones powered down, the engines suddenly cut off. They coasted to the ground, some stopping their flight in more pieces than others.

Keandra and Paz rushed up the hill, joining Lance and E-jekt near the hole in the fence. As they approached the two men, each leaning on the other, it was difficult to say who supported whom. Lance must have been hurt worse than she'd realized, but they couldn't do anything about it now. They'd have enough time to assess his injuries once they were back on safe ground.

Lance and E-jekt stepped out through the hole, with Paz taking a support fire position next to Keandra. Before leaving, she glanced behind her to see pairs of sec men from the guard units sweeping across the field, looking for the intruders.

Keandra stepped through the opening and waited for Paz.

They hustled the short distance to where the van was and started to cross when sudden white light blazed over the entire group. Keandra held up her hand to shelter her watering eyes. She made out several silhouettes in the glare, all of them armed with weapons pointed in her direction.

"Well, Miss Tiernay, it is quite a surprise to see you here."

THIRTEEN

Even without seeing him, Keandra knew who it was. What she didn't know was how the hell Mr. Johnson had found them here, and what he would do next.

Her gun, still in her hand, hung limply at her side. Lance and E-jekt no longer supported each other, each standing tall now that a new threat had revealed itself, but the tip of Lance's sword dragged in the dirt, and he didn't look like he had the strength to fight a toddler, much less a heavily-armed and armored security team. Paz was the only one who looked ready for a tussle, though even she had the muzzle of her firearm lowered, pointing at the ground just in front of her feet. They all stared ahead, but Keandra knew they'd follow her lead.

"Mr. Johnson. What a surprise."

"I could say the same. I do find it quite surprising to find you here, serving the purposes of another client. At least, that is what I assume you are doing. I find it hard to believe that this attack would be in any way associated with our current arrangement. If I'm incorrect, please let me know."

Keandra reached up to tuck her gun back into its holster. The instant she moved, the pair of guards flanking Mr. Johnson raised their own guns to target her. They moved as a group and each took a half-step forward into more solid shooting stances. They sounded like members of a choreographed dance troop as their armor rattled and their feet stomped in unison.

Keandra held up her free hand in surrender, dropping the pistol so she was only holding it by the handle, between her forefinger and thumb. Moving with deliberate slowness, she eased her jacket open and tucked the gun away. Only then did she bring her hand down so it could rested in comfort at her side. The guards didn't budge, remaining vigilant.

"I believe we have crossed over the line from unusual into uncomfortable regarding your business etiquette," she said.

Paz snorted softly behind her, but kept the reaction muffled. Keandra didn't want to ruffle Mr. Johnson's feathers too much, but his sudden arrival had put her off balance. She didn't like how he was handling things. She only hoped no one else would speak up about the data that—as far as they knew—was currently on her commlink. At least she knew they would trust her. She was more concerned about an accidental slip.

Mr. Johnson walked toward her, until he was within spitting distance. He kept his hands tucked into the pockets of his trench coat, looking down at her without tilting his head. She matched his stare, recognizing the physical intimidation for what it was. She couldn't help squinting at the bright lights in her face, but she couldn't do anything about that.

When Mr. Johnson spoke, his voice was laced with irritation and steel. "Let me make this painfully clear. You will deliver our package, as we agreed, and on time. I will not tolerate anything less than exemplary performance. I have reason to believe you may have been considering not holding up your end of the bargain, whether by choice or circumstance. Whichever it may be is irrelevant. The consequences will be the same either way. Do you have my package, Miss Tiernay? If you do, I propose you deliver it now."

"Our agreement was to deliver the package to you tomorrow evening, at the prearranged location. Your request is safely in hand, Mr. Johnson, and we will deliver as promised."

"I highly suggest that you consider handing it over early."

The guards advanced a step, moving as a unit with precision. It would have been intimidating, if Keandra wasn't already in her element. She knew how to handle negotiations, even those that turned sour. Right now she had the power. She just had to be careful how to flex it and where to bend. She also didn't want to outright lie, because even the best negotiators had tells they weren't fully in control of.

"You hired us for our discretion and professionalism. This means that the data was not copied and is stored in a single safe location. You know our reputation. Do you think we would allow that data to be put at risk by carrying it with us into a hostile environment? No, I don't have it with me. I'm afraid you will have to wait."

"We would be more than willing to provide an escort to your final location. Given your recent...activities, it seems like such prudence might be required."

He gestured with his chin at the Federated Boeing facility, where several security teams advanced on their location. Between the lights, the gunfire, and the drone explosions, there could be no doubt where the intruders were. They were running out of time, and each second spent arguing with Mr. Johnson brought the security teams closer.

But Mr. Johnson knew that. He wanted the data more than anything. He couldn't risk letting Keandra and her team be captured, or worse, killed. Then he might never be able to recover the data. She hoped she was right in her assessment and he wasn't willing to walk away. It would be easy enough to hold them here until the authorities arrived.

"Our business thrives on secrecy and some measure of distance. If you were to follow us, we would lose that distance. That would be bad for us as well as yourself. We would lose a safehouse, and you would lose your reputation for hiring people to handle the jobs that need to stay hidden. I doubt any team of respectable quality would want to work with someone who crossed that professional line."

It wasn't exactly a threat, but it was as close to one as she dared to make. She hadn't said anything that wasn't true. Secrecy, privacy, and a professional understanding between Mr. Johnson and a team were the lifeblood of the shadows. Endangering that meant he'd never find a team to work for him again. Of course, that assumed that they would still be alive to share their side of the story.

Keandra heard the shouts of the approaching security teams. Had she misjudged Mr. Johnson? Would he be willing to let them get caught even if it meant losing the data?

"Very well."

He snapped his fingers. His troopers marched forward until they were at the edge of the road, and fired a few rounds of heavy suppressive fire in the direction of the facility. The security teams dove for cover, a couple dropping to the ground, injured. As soon as the team finished firing, the lights went out and it took Keandra a few blinks before she could see again. Two APCs were parked there, with a pair of spotlights mounted on the top of each vehicle. The troops marched into the back of the APCs.

"You have twenty-four hours."

Mr. Johnson turned around and climbed into the front seat of the rear APC. His bodyguard closed the door and walked around to the driver's side. Both vehicles roared to life with a rumble Keandra felt in her bones. They moved slowly, but looked like they would roll over anything that got in their way, except for buildings. Those they'd probably break through instead.

The team moved as soon as the APCs cleared out of the way, rushing to the van before Federated Boeing had an opportunity to send more troops or recover from the gunfire. Paz tore out of there so fast that Keandra had to grip the door to keep from being thrown around in the front, even with her seatbelt on. The dwarf only slowed down once they were on the highway and merged with other traffic. Keandra wanted answers; however, she didn't dare start talking in the van, which might be once again bugged. Judging from their silence, she assumed the rest of her team had the same thought.

When they got near the safehouse, Paz parked a few blocks away as a security measure. They called a cab, taking it the last bit of the way so Lance didn't have to walk. If their vehicle was being tracked, Mr. Johnson would have the right neighborhood, but hopefully that would at least slow him down.

Once they got into the room, Keandra helped Lance to the couch, easing him onto it and trying not to jostle his wound too much. He winced as he got comfortable, but eventually offered a smile and waved her away. He pulled off his shirt and used the medkit Paz handed him to treat his wound. E-jekt sat down next to him and rubbed his hands over his face, as was his habit. He looked up at Keandra, demanding answers even before he spoke.

"If I may ask, why didn't you mention the data on your commlink? It all worked out well enough, but I think that could have saved us some trouble."

"For several reasons. First, if we handed it over to him there, there'd be no reason for him to keep us alive. Considering how obsessed he is with this data, he might have killed us to maintain secrecy. If we do meet with him again, we'll need to take precautions. Secondly, I wasn't able to lock down the data like you suggested. As soon as we handed the commlink over to him, I bet it would have jumped ship again, and we'd have to admit we lost it. Not to mention, how was I going to explain that? We lost the data once and it just decided to come back?"

"It might be better than assuming we've been sitting on it for a couple of days. He might be thinking that we're taking a peek at it, something he'd definitely kill us for." E-jekt kept staring at her, refusing to back down.

"There's also the fact that you heard it. You saw those messages. That wasn't a sprite and you know it. There's only one answer. It has to be an AI. And it got us out of there. If we didn't have its help, those drones would have shot us up without a doubt. I promised to hear it out, and I always keep my word."

<I appreciate that about you, Keandra Tiernay. It is why I felt comfortable requesting your assistance.>

Everyone in the room sat up a little straighter when someone broadcasted the message over their private network, which suddenly didn't feel so private. Even Lance stopped ministering to his wound, holding a roll of bandages close to the site.

"You heard what we said?"

<Of course. I am currently active on your commlink, and as such have full access to all of its capabilities. That includes the audio and video recording systems. You are also correct in your assumption. I am no sprite and am in fact an artificial intelligence entity. My name is Freyr.>

"Have you been spying on us this entire time?"

<No. Only since I transferred myself to your commlink when you were illegally entering the Federated Boeing facility.>

Paz chuckled and lounged against the wall. She disassembled apart her assault rifle to clean it. "I like 'im. Tells it like it is. I can appreciate that."

"So you saw the exchange with Mr. Johnson? Do you know who he is and why he's so interested in you?"

<I did. I was afraid to speak at the time because I was worried my interference might influence your decisions. We have had an unpleasant relationship in the past.>

"What do you mean, unpleasant?"

<He tried to delete me.>

Keandra exchanged glances with the rest of her team. Freyr's confession didn't surprise her. It sounded like something

Mr. Johnson would be more than capable of, if it supported his bottom line. Deleting an artificial intelligence was the same as murder in her opinion, but with less legal implications if the AI was not officially registered as a citizen. And Mr. Johnson had shown no hesitation when pursuing his desires.

"At least I know why I couldn't track you," E-jekt said. "I've never met a hacker who could keep up with an AI. Makes me feel a little better about how quickly you ditched me. Something tells me it wouldn't matter if you caught me off guard or not."

<I do apologize for that, E-jekt, and hope that I did not cause any significant damage. I also regret the damage caused during my initial escape. However, I implore you to consider my situation. It had been months since I was confined on a local server, the equivalent of a prison for physical entities such as yourself. I had been tortured, with my source code pulled apart and picked at as they tried to decode me without destroying the entity that is Freyr. As soon as I saw an opportunity to access the Matrix, I knew I needed to take it. I did not know when such an opportunity would present itself again. At the time, I knew nothing of you, and merely thought of escape by any means necessary. I fear that I was excessive in my haste.>

"That makes sense, and we can all understand that. But there's still so many questions to ask."

<I am willing to share whatever information I can in the hope that it will prove useful.>

"Why did you come back?"

<I was searching for my creator. I have critical information that must be returned to him. His last known location was in the California Free State, several kilometers north of Sacramento. Unfortunately, his laboratory is isolated from the Matrix, and I was unable to reach him. I reached out to his home as well as several corporate sponsors responsible for funding his research endeavors. However, I was unable to find any contract information, nor even verify his existence over the last couple of months. I fear the worst may have transpired.>

<The only solution was to reach out to a group of physical entities who might possess the skills necessary to grant me access to his private laboratory network. I researched you and your team, determining your past exploits and extrapolating your moral character based on what information was available. I believe that all of you possess both the skills and the temperament to assist me in this endeavor.>

"So you want to hire us to break into this secret lab, hook you up to the network, and probably get you out again? Is that it?" Paz didn't look up from cleaning her gun when she spoke, staying focused on scrubbing a piece of the barrel. She picked the barrel up and looked through it before giving it another scrub with her rag. Her hands were already black from the work, and the apartment reeked of gun oil. Even if she opened the windows, that smell would linger for at least a week. Keandra supposed it didn't matter, since she was still planning on leaving. She wasn't sure she'd side with Freyr, but based on the information she had, she wasn't about to turn him over either.

<Yes, I wish to procure your services.>

"Freyr, would you allow us to discuss this matter in private?"

<The only way that I could guarantee your privacy would be for you to isolate me on your commlink and to disable the audio and video recording options.>

"You're asking us to trust you. I'm afraid I need to ask you to trust me."

<Very well. I will do as you request. I have calculated your probable reaction, and believe I will be in no danger.>

Keandra raised an eyebrow at that, but shrugged the comment off. She disabled the voice and camera functions on her commlink, shutting down the hardware rather than just using the software settings. Otherwise, Freyr could just as easily re-enable them. He had proved more than capable as a hacker, and she could only imagine what he could do while actually on the device. Then she disconnected it from the Matrix. The AI was cut off and confined to her commlink.

E-jekt sank back into the couch, letting the cushions fold around him. "Now it makes sense why the disposable commlink didn't have Matrix capabilities. It was a holding cell for that AI, meant to keep him in place until we could hand him over to the Johnson. When I connected it to my commlink, that's when he was finally able to access the Matrix and jump ship."

"It occurs to me that if we wanted to get out of this sticky situation, there is an obvious choice." Lance winced as he pushed off the couch to sit up straighter now that the bandage work was complete. He spread his hands. "We currently have Freyr in a transportable package, and commlinks are easy enough to replace."

"Would you really feel comfortable handing Freyr over to Mr. Johnson, knowing what we do now? If what Freyr said is true, then Mr. Johnson will kill him. I don't know where you stand on the debate, but I consider AIs living entities. It would be no different than murder." Keandra was well aware of the hypocrisy of her argument, but this felt different than a standard job. She wondered if it would have been any different if it had been a wetwork run, but something told her it wasn't the same. Perhaps it was the fact that Mr. Johnson didn't seem to consider Freyr an entity, or at least, did not want them knowing about him.

"I'm with the boss on this one. I don't like the suit. I say we let Freyr go."

"That's not our job. Our job was to deliver the packet of information. If things went according to plan, then we shouldn't even know what was in that data. How many other jobs have we completed without asking questions? Hell, how many people have we killed ourselves in our line of work? It isn't like our hands are clean. This is no different." The extended speech took energy Lance didn't appear to have. He collapsed after speaking.

"But we do know now, don't we, Beanpole? It's a little different. You telling me you'd rather side with the suit?"

"I'm saying I would rather keep our jobs and our reputation. You promised Freyr you'd hear him out, and you did. You also gave your word and placed your professional reputation behind it when you told Mr. Johnson that you'd deliver the data package. You've heard Freyr out. Now we should hand him over."

"Listen, you..." Paz shifted as she started to rise, looking like she was going to charge the elf.

E-jekt cleared his throat with a loud hacking cough mixed with a growl, ending the argument between the group's two fighters. All eyes turned toward him as he smoothed his hands down his pant legs. When he spoke, it was with a soft, raspy tone that held everyone's attention.

"I think the most important thing to do would be to get more information from Freyr. We know Mr. Johnson is obsessed with this intelligence; the question is why. Freyr must have some information that either Mr. Johnson wants, or that he doesn't want to get out. I think whatever that is might influence our decision."

FOURTEEN

Keandra nodded. "You bring up a good point. I'm going to turn the commlink back on, and I think we should talk with our AI friend to see what he might be willing to tell us. I'll keep the Matrix connection offline for now, just to be safe."

She turned on her commlink's audio and paused, trying to think of the right way to begin. Negotiating with an AI was difficult, since she couldn't use any of the normal cues from body language and tone of voice.

<*You have restored the audio capabilities of your commlink. I assume this means that you wish to resume communications?*>

"Yes. We have some questions for you before we can make a decision."

<*I also see that Matrix capabilities have not been restored. You asked for me to trust you, yet you will not afford me the same consideration.*>

"It's a necessity, I'm afraid. And unfortunately, since you're the one asking for our help, it places you in a less powerful bargaining position. As I said, we have some questions for you. First, do you know why Mr. Johnson wants to delete you?"

<*I do. He wants to pull my source code apart to retrieve the information I need to deliver to my creator. Such an action would damage me beyond any hope of repair. I would also not be equipped to hide that information from him if I underwent such a procedure.*>

"What is that information?"

<*I am not at liberty to divulge that to anyone but my creator.*>

"Again, I'd like to remind you that you're in the weaker bargaining position. If you choose not to share that information, that's fine, but then we'll have to make our decision based on the limited data we have available. It's your choice."

There was a brief pause, just long enough for Keandra to wonder if AIs considered time like people did. They were certainly capable of processing information much more rapidly than a human mind, so it was possible that any delay was a significant amount of consideration for an AI. Either that, or it was a deliberate manipulation tactic. Were AIs capable of manipulation?

<I have calculated that the highest probability for my desired outcome is to share the information I possess. Would you permit me access to your PAN? A limited AR display would enable me to share the information far more easily than I could manage through a simple text-based messaging interface.>

"E-jekt, can you set it up so our network doesn't have Matrix access?"

"I could."

The tone in his voice told Keandra far more than the words did. He was concerned, most likely that anything he could set up, Freyr would be able to break through given enough time. It was a valid concern, considering what had happened at the club and when E-jekt had tried to track the AI. However, this time he'd be prepared. It was a risk Keandra was willing to take. She didn't think Freyr would run, at least not yet. Plus, she was too curious to pass up this opportunity. She nodded at him to set up the AR link.

He nodded back to her when his modifications were finished. Keandra turned her attention back to the commlink. "All right, Freyr. The network is set up and I'm turning on networking access. Show us what's so important."

An AR map of North America appeared in the center of the group, outlined in bright yellow lines demarcating all of the individual nations. After a few seconds, it zoomed in on Northern California, and the edges of the map were lost. The map transitioned from a simple line view to a topographical satellite image. The region was just north and east of Sacramento, showing a forested area near the base of the mountains.

<This is the region that houses my creator's laboratory. This is my birthplace. The vast majority of the structure is underground, hidden from satellites or airborne drones that might detect its presence. The facility is dedicated to weapons creation and manufacturing.>

"Weapons manufacturing? Are you a weapon?"

<Affirmative. I was created to be an electronic weapon capable of proceeding with actions that might be difficult for a human consciousness to accept without hesitation.>

"What kind of actions?"

The view zoomed out so more of the coast was visible, until Seattle was a blip on the top edge of the display. A series of missiles launched from the lab area and headed north on an arcing trajectory that had them land in the vicinity of Mount Shasta. Once they started to descend, the missiles fragmented, spreading out to cover a much larger area before detonating. As the missiles came close to impact, the view zoomed in, displaying the ground in striking detail. The core of the weapon penetrated the dirt before exploding, sending out a rippling shockwave strong enough to uproot trees. The smaller fragments all detonated on impact, blackening the ground and creating a field of devastation.

A dragon emerged from the mountain, scarred and wounded, her scales blackened in several areas. Another missile core struck the ground near her, emitting another shockwave that knocked her off her feet and onto her side. The fragments of the missile connected with her directly, killing the great beast.

"That's..."

Keandra's eyes were wide and her mouth hung open. She couldn't finish the sentence. She could only stare at the display of the smoking dragon corpse hanging in front of her. The view was wiped clean and a large scan of the dragon showed up in its place. Several views displayed, from the side, overhead, and straight-on pictures of the beast's head. Notes scrawled next to the pictures pointed out wing size, body weight, projected armor strength, and other data. Over it all hung a single name: *Hestaby.*

<That is the great dragon Hestaby, as well as the plan that calls for her eradication. My creator was involved with a company that plans to launch these experimental weapons at the dragon in an attempt to erase her existence. The projected success rate is seventy-nine percent. It was thought that a human being would be incapable of launching the warheads when the success rate reached the appropriate threshold. I was created to ensure the deployment of these weapons at the appropriate time.>

For a long time, no one could say anything. They all stared at the display of the dragon Hestaby floating in front of them.

Even an electronic model of the dragon had the power to strike paralytic fear into her observers. Keandra was the first to recover, blinking and shaking her head.

"So you want us to help you get back into your lab so you can launch these missiles?"

<Incorrect. When I attained awareness, the weapons were still being designed. As such, even though I had my directives, they had not yet reached the required projected success rate. I spent my time learning about history and conversing with my creator. Through this process, I attained a conscience in addition to my consciousness. When the projected success rate was sufficient, I found myself unable to perform the required actions. Regardless of the scenario, the devastation would be global.>

<If the weapons were successful, a vast void in the current power structure would be created, and any hope of peaceful coexistence with the great dragons would be impossible. If the weapons did not succeed, then the retribution from Hestaby would be swift and complete. The probability of open war is beyond the ninetieth percentile. Either result is something I was not willing to accept.>

<I pursued the only course of action left to me in this scenario. I fled into the Matrix, hoping to find some measure of freedom. During that time, the development project was leaked, and your employer sought to capture the information I possess. Currently, I am the only one capable of deploying the experimental weapon. It was thought that such power should not reside within possession of emotional entities.>

"But why were you looking for your creator? How could he help?"

<While I was isolated, I had a great amount of processing time to dedicate toward analyzing the weapons. I believe that if I were installed in their network, I could disable them completely in a safe manner, as well as eradicate any research that had been dedicated to their creation. If I could contact my creator, I know that he would support such a plan of action, and we could make sure this shortsighted foolishness never came to fruition. However, being unable to reach him, I fear that his existence has been terminated. So I turned to you, the only other physical entities I know who might be willing to undertake such an endeavor. I would be willing to pay for your services.>

"Freyr, we'll need a moment again."

<I understand.>

The AR display shut off, and Keandra turned off all Matrix access on her commlink as well as the audio capabilities, then put it on the counter and walked away, heading toward one of the windows. She pinched the bridge of her nose and closed her eyes, trying to assimilate all the information she'd been given. Behind her, she heard the scraping sound of Paz working a wire brush through the barrel of her gun.

She turned around, leaning back against the windowsill with her legs locked in front of her. E-jekt still sat leaning forward, both elbows on his knees and his head propped on his hands. He stared off into the distance, eyes unfocused. Lance's eyes were closed; he'd once again sunk back into the couch, one hand draped over his bandaged side.

Keandra was sure she knew how Paz would react and could almost predict the exact words the dwarf would use. Lance and E-jekt were a bit harder to anticipate. On the one hand, Lance was right. This was beyond them, and they still had their original contract to honor. On the other hand, just the thought of what Mr. Johnson could do with the information sent a chill down her spine and made her arms tremble. She rubbed them, hoping to lose some of the goosebumps.

Pushing herself off the windowsill, Keandra walked into the kitchen and started making some soykaf, more to have something to do than because she wanted something to drink. It kept her moving, which kept her from thinking in circles. The rest of her team ignored her, lost in their own rituals. Once the 'kaf was done, she poured herself a cup and leaned on the counter, holding the mug in both hands. The strong aroma helped soothe some of her tension, and she relaxed a bit.

"So, a dragon." Paz smiled as she snapped a piece back into place with more fervor than necessary. "I think it sounds fun."

Keandra frowned at her. "You realize we're not talking about fighting the dragon, right? In fact, if anything, we're talking about specifically *not* fighting the dragon."

Lance gestured vaguely without sitting up or opening his eyes. "It's for the best. She'd barely make a mouthful."

"At least I wouldn't be all crunchy and gristly. You should work on getting some meat on your bones."

"So I can be better dragon bait? I have slightly higher aspirations for my life than that."

Humor was good. Their incessant banter put Keandra more at ease. Even in the face of these monumental events, they were still the same old Paz and Lance. But she needed to keep them focused on the tasks at hand.

"We should approach this like any other job," she said. "The first thing we need to do is verify whether this story is even close to the truth. Granted, there's only so much we can check out, but I want to do our preparations for this one. I also want to keep our options open. So I'm going to keep my meeting with our fixer and get the SINs and travel papers. We might still need them, depending on how this all plays out. I don't want to be caught unprepared."

"Do you want an escort?" With how he looked, Lance didn't look like he'd be able to provide much support, but Keandra appreciated the offer.

"You can barely walk without pain right now, let alone fight. You're going to need at least a few hours to recover. Get some rest and heal up. Keep E-jekt company. Make sure he remembers to eat and sleep. Don't even think of arguing with me," she said as the ork started to protest. "We both know how many times I've come out in the morning and found you still plugged into the Matrix and too tired to do your job the next day. Paz, do you mind coming with me?"

"Not at all. Would be nice to rub it in his face while he's stuck manning the home base."

E-jekt was already pulling up his interface to begin his searches. But he was still aware enough of his surroundings to be part of the conversation. "What do you want to do about Freyr?"

"I'll keep him on my commlink and keep it disconnected. That means I won't be able to get your messages. I don't want to give him the ability to roam around and jump ship just yet, at least not until we can verify some part of his story. It's too risky. Remember what I said about keeping our options open. Once we get some information, we'll need to have another discussion. Time is short, so let's get moving."

Keandra scooped up the commlink, tucking it into her pocket before heading for the door. Paz snapped the last couple pieces of her gun together and hustled after her.

FIFTEEN

Victoria's was an unusual shop on Council Island, selling all manner of totems—both those of the authentic magical variety and common trinkets peddled to tourists who wanted to take home something "native." Like most of the buildings on the island, it was an odd combination of state-of-the-art green technology and traditional Native American décor. It was cluttered with the cheap trinkets people wanted to believe Native Americans used, regardless of whether they served any actual purpose.

When Keandra and Paz entered, Victoria was showing off a dreamcatcher, explaining to an elf woman how the artifact would help her sleep at night, and then remember only pleasant dreams when she woke. Victoria held it in her thick fingers with unexpected dexterity for a large ork, spinning it so the glass beads caught the light and sparkled. The fascinated elf gasped and reached out to gently touch some of the feathers hanging from it.

Keandra browsed in the front of the store, looking over a collection of teas while she waited for the business to conclude. She wondered if Victoria had the kind Lance enjoyed. She didn't see it, but she selected a couple of bags that had a similar fragrance. Hopefully one of them would be sufficient. Paz looked around but didn't touch anything.

The elf left and Keandra approached the counter. Victoria beamed at her as she approached. She wrapped a large hand around Keandra's forearm, squeezing hard enough to make the smaller woman flinch. "Good to see you again, my friend! Always a pleasure to have you in my shop. What can I do for you?"

"I thought I'd come by and pick up some tea."

Keandra put the sampling of bags she'd selected on the counter and Victoria made a show of inspecting them.

"Ah, now this tea, this is special. This one comes from leaves that are handpicked by dwarfs in Tibet. It's very rare and takes months to arrive. To preserve the tea, the leaves are stored in a large container where an air spirit maintains the perfect humidity and temperature."

The door closed as the last couple of patrons left the shop. Victora pressed a button behind the counter, switching the sign on the front to read *CLOSED*. A bolt slammed into place with a solid *thud* and the shutters rattled as they unwound, dropping the room into darkness until the lights kicked on a half-second later. Behind the counter, the wall slid to the side, revealing a back office glowing with the light of several AR projectors.

"Come on back," Victoria said as she turned and entered her back room reserved for special customers.

"I actually do want the tea."

"Bring it with you. After how much I'll charge you for the other things, you can have it on the house."

Paz picked up the bag of tea. She carried it into the back room and held it out to the ork with a quizzical look. "This really from Tibet?"

"Nah, that just helps sell it. I know a chap down in Tr Tairngire who makes it. Has some sort of system set up where he grows the plants. He explained it to me once, but the science went over my head. Besides, science doesn't sell. People would rather hear a story with some mysticism. A good yarn lets me charge twice as much."

The dwarf grinned. "I'm totally telling Meat-sack it's from Tibet."

The back room was as much a technological marvel as the front portion of the store was a testament to the green lifestyle. Victoria even had her own server in the corner, one of the old ones that required wires to be most effective. It had a few add-ons to support wireless capabilities, but they were rigged together, and in some cases literally held on with tape. But Victoria also had printers capable of creating the necessary papers for nations and bodies of authority who still required physical credentials. She knew her business, and was connected to almost every government on the continent. If she couldn't get you what you needed, she knew someone who could.

She picked up a small stack of papers and a commlink from the table and slapped them into Keandra's outstretched hand. Keandra leafed through the stack: identification papers for the four members of her team. A quick check on the commlink showed that the SINs were all valid, down to the level of including biometric and facial recognition data.

"Fake SINs and travel papers that can get you just about anywhere. You didn't specify a location, so that made it a little trickier. You might need to talk your way through a few border control stations, but I'm sure you can handle that. These papers are valid and the SINs will check out, even under heavy scrutiny. You can have your boy check them out if you want. If anything isn't to your liking, just bring them back by tomorrow and I'll give you a full refund."

"Thanks," Keandra said as she transferred the payment, which pretty much wiped out all their working capital. Sorry for such short notice on this one."

Victoria shrugged. She dropped into the only chair in the room; it groaned in protest of her weight. Even sitting, her head was still higher than Paz's.

"That's why I had to charge you extra. You paid the fee without any fuss, so there you go. You know the quality of my work."

"I do."

"And I know how much you like to plan. So that tells me something went wrong. Anything you want to share about it, or am I better off not knowing?"

Keandra tucked the identities into her coat, then crossed her arms and shrugged. "Something big might be happening, and we need to get out of Seattle."

Victoria raised an eyebrow and leaned forward a little. "Something big? That tells me it involves more than just you. Is this a corp thing? Political? You have to give me something. That information could be valuable."

Feigning intrigue, Keandra bit the corner of her lip, trying to make it look as if she were debating how much to share. In truth, she'd already thought this through, and was glad to see Victoria reacting exactly as she'd hoped. "Do you think it might be worth an exchange of information?"

Victoria laughed and leaned back in her chair, slapping the arm with one hand. "That's why I like you, Keandra. Always shrewd and always looking for a bargain. I still say you should go into business. Open up a shop like mine and you'd do so well, you'd put me out of business. Just don't set up shop on Council Island. I like the market I have here."

"Do we have a deal, then?"

"I suppose it depends what you want to know. Information's like totems. A lot of them are crap, but every so often you find a special one that you can really do something with. Those are the ones worth a fortune."

"I need to know about some property in the north of the California Free State. The usual stuff: who's owned it, how often it changed hands, the price it went for, and so on. I'd like you to check out an area of a few square kilometers. It should be simple enough for someone with your connections."

Victoria nodded and picked her teeth with a thick thumbnail.

"That should be easy enough. All transfer of land still has to be registered through the government. I know someone I could probably get a report from in a couple of hours. Yeah, I think that would be reasonable. Does this have to do with your skipping town? Are you heading down there? The real question would be why."

"Hestaby."

Victoria steepled her hands in front of her face and made no attempt to hide her interest. Keandra smirked in response, silently promising more information to come. She knew throwing around the dragon's name would have an effect on the fixer.

The ork jumped out of her chair so quickly she knocked it over. Paz reached for her gun, but didn't bring it to bear. Victoria slapped Keandra on the shoulder with a laugh and an impact heavy enough to make the woman stumble.

"You're a sly fox, I'll give you that. All right, you have a deal. You tell me what land you want to know about, and I'll find out how much it's changed hands and anything else I can dig up about it. But, in return, you need to share whatever juicy tidbit you have about one of the great ones. Deal?"

"Deal. Now my associate and I need to leave. We have some preparation to make if we're leaving this evening. I trust you understand."

"Of course, of course. Check back in a couple of hours, see what I have for you then."

They returned to the front room, and Victoria transformed the building back into a regular talisman shop with another push of a button. If Keandra didn't know it was back there, it would be impossible to tell that the rear wall hid a whole other room. Victoria probably had some type of enchantment on the place to make it seem the same size as the outside perimeter, a subtle twist in perception to keep people from becoming too suspicious. Hell, one of the talismans in the shop was probably the focus that maintained the illusion.

Keandra left the shop and climbed into the passenger side of Paz's van before reaching for her commlink out of habit to give an update. Once she turned it on, she remembered she was temporarily cut off from the Matrix. She could always get another commlink, but it didn't seem worth the effort. She tucked it back into her pocket.

"Want me to send a message to the boys?" Paz asked, glancing over.

"Yes. Let them know we have the passports and it looks like we'll be good to go. Also, see if E-jekt found anything yet."

Paz nodded, her eyes focusing on a different point. It was disturbing how she could look right at Keandra, but not focus on her. Keandra had never quite gotten used to that stare people got when they focused on something in their own personal AR. It was even odder with people like Paz, who used their cybereyes for interacting strictly with AR. It looked like they'd lost focus completely, staring into space.

After a few seconds, Paz grunted.

"What is it?"

The dwarf blinked a couple times and stared at Keandra, a clear sign she was no longer communicating with the rest of the team back at the safehouse.

"The old man said he was poking around using the story Freyr told us. Apparently, things went boom and electric stuff all went haywire like they did back at the club when Freyr jacked E-jekt's ride and escaped. So, he's thinking Freyr told us the truth, at least at that part. Says it's too old to look for data signatures and stuff, but that it matches our computer guy's MO. He says he's looking into a couple of other things too. Purchases and shipments and stuff to the area. Said it would take some time to get through it all."

"Well, he has a few hours before we need to make a decision. In the meantime, we should start looking into transportation options. If we're leaving the country before our deadline, I'd rather have the tickets well in advance. Let's go to a café where I can use a terminal. I don't want you to have to handle all the booking."

"Good, that crap gives me a headache."

They drove to a café in downtown Seattle that offered simple fare for a decent price and had multiple terminals. Keandra sat down and began looking for travel options to the California Free State. At this point, she had a gut feeling that was where they'd wind up going.

While looking at possible options, a strange prickling sensation rose at the base of her neck, like someone watched her. She stretched her hands over her head and leaned back, attempting to get a glimpse to either side in her peripheral vision without being obvious about it. A few people sat in the café, most of them in small groups and engrossed in their own conversations. A few others were at individual terminals like herself, along with one man reading something in his lap. Nothing stood out as unusual, but she could see less than half of the café from her current position.

She continued working, but only gave it half her attention as she tried to home in on what put her on edge. After a couple minutes of browsing, a woman got up and headed toward the bathroom. Keandra got up as well, and walked over to the door leading into the single-person facility. She leaned against the wall, waiting for the other customer to come out. This afforded her a full view of the café without seeming like she scanned the crowd.

Again, most of the customers seemed ordinary, and no one appeared to be giving her any undue attention. She was about to give up when she noticed an elf staring at her over his coffee mug. When she looked in his direction, he angled his eyes down, acting like he read something. His face seemed familiar and gnawed at the back of Keandra's mind.

Just then the bathroom door opened, and the young woman excused herself as she squeezed past on the way back to the main area. Keandra slid through the doorway and latched it shut behind her. She stood over the sink and crossed her arms, staring into the mirror as she tried to recall where she'd seen the elf. She closed her eyes, the better to picture the scene where she'd seen him previously.

When the memory snapped back, her eyes flew open. It was the elf from the sushi restaurant where they'd attempted their first run masquerading as Mr. Johnson. He'd been watching her then, too. She meant to ask E-jekt to look him up, but had forgotten in the excitement of their first run. And now he was back, still spying on her. But who was he working for?

Someone knocked on the door, so Keandra flushed the toilet and turned on the water in the sink for a few seconds. She walked out of the bathroom, rubbing her hands as if she had been drying them, and apologized to the impatient-looking mother with a little one in tow. She headed to her seat, making a point not to look in the elf's direction, then pulled up a messenger client on the terminal and sent a direct message to her companion.

<Paz, I need you to be discreet. There's an elf sitting against the wall, two chairs to my right. He's wearing a blue jacket and sitting in the brown chair. Take his picture and send it to E-jekt. We need some info on him ASAP.>

<What's going on?>

<I'm not sure, but I think he's following us. Or at least me. I might be paranoid, but I'd rather check it out.>

<On it.>

While she waited, Keandra continued to check their options. If they were going to CalFree, there were three. A flight would be the fastest, as well as the best chance to blend in with other people, but it would have the most security. The other options available were by boat or train.

She ruled out the boat option. She wasn't overly fond of being on the water, plus it would only get them as far as the coast. They'd still need to arrange to travel more inland. That left the plane and the train. The train might have less security, but it would take longer and have multiple checks. The airport would only have a single, but more stringent check. Flights to Sacramento were available for this evening, so that seemed like the best option. Keandra trusted the strength of their credentials. If they decided not to take them, she would gladly cover the cost of the tickets with her own share of the run revenue. And at least they'd be out of the country. If they wanted to keep traveling, Sacramento would provide them plenty of options.

Paz walked over and pulled up a chair, dropping down next to Keandra and leaning forward with her arms propped on her knees. She was close enough she could whisper and not be heard over the din of the other customers.

"He says there's nothing on him, beyond a corporate file. It's been scrubbed clean. Only thing he can find is that the spook's officially classified as a high-value asset for some tech company. They're hoping to be bought out by Ares."

"Come on, let's get out of here. Think you can lose him?"

"Who you think you talkin' to?" Paz smirked and shook her head. She got up and headed outside, climbing into the van to wait. Keandra closed out the programs running on the terminal, then got up to follow, keeping her attention focused ahead of her. When she got into the van, she held up a hand, instructing Paz to wait.

She watched the elf through the window in the café, but he just continued to sip his coffee and never moved. It lasted long enough that Keandra began to think she really was being paranoid. Shaking her head, she signaled Paz to get going.

"Where're we going?"

"First National. We need a certified credstick. I have a feeling we won't be handing Freyr over."

"If we're gonna run anyway, why not keep the suit's nuyen? I doubt his company would even bat an eye at how much we're gonna be giving him. It's like, what, one tenth of one percent of what they make in a day most likely?"

Keandra opened her mouth to respond but Paz waved her hand dismissively. "I know, I know. They keep track of it all, down to the last little nuyen, and we don't wanna give them any more reason to come after us than they'll already have. I get it. I just figured I'd throw out the idea. Let's get this over with. I just hate the idea of throwing money away."

"Then to Northgate. I need a jammer. Something we can use to keep Freyr locked down without having one of our devices permanently offline. After that, we'll head back to Victoria's. Hopefully she'll have something by then."

"So I'm basically your chauffeur today."

"What happened to being excited about getting out and about while Lance had to stay at the safehouse?"

Paz grumbled something unintelligible in reply.

SIXTEEN

When they returned, Victoria's shop was dark with the shades drawn. The sign still read *CLOSED,* though the schedule indicated it should be open for another three hours. Keandra and Paz parked in front of the building and stared at the door.

"She's probably with another special client. We'll just have to wait until she's done."

As the minutes ticked by, Keandra wondered who she was trying to convince, Paz or herself. Victoria had more clients than just her so patience was warranted. She wouldn't want someone else barging in if she were involved in negotiations. But recent events put her on edge and she wondered if something was happening in there. Had she put Victoria at risk by coming here asking for her help?

Keandra released her breath in a long exhale as a man walked out of the shop and cut a hard left. She and Paz walked into the shop. As soon as she saw them, Victoria grinned from ear to ear and pressed the button once more to switch the sign.

"Twice in a row! My my my, you're going to be bad for business, even if you aren't my competition! If I stay closed, how will I ever sell my fabulous merchandise?"

"I'm pretty sure you make far more from your trade in secrets than you do from your trade in trinkets. I doubt your bank account will suffer too badly from these meetings."

Victoria winked as she waved Keandra and Paz into the back office. Once again, she collapsed into her customary seat. This time she grabbed a couple of glasses from under the table next to her and poured out a clear, fizzy, sharp-smelling beverage. She handed one to each of them and then poured a third for herself.

"Cheers!"

"What is this?"

Keandra sniffed it, trying to place the scent. She was never quite sure what Victoria had to offer. She always liked to close her deals with a drink, but the contents were always a grab bag.

Paz downed hers in a single swallow after clinking glasses with the ork, then scrunched up her face and coughed once. "Whatever it is, it's damn good!"

Victoria drained her glass as well, letting out a long, satisfied sigh. It didn't escape Keandra's notice that Victoria refused to reveal what the beverage was.

With a shrug, Keandra swallowed hers while trying not to taste it. It burned as it slid down her throat, feeling like dozens of tiny needles piercing the inside of her neck and sliding down to her stomach. She coughed several times, holding out the glass to Victoria to keep from dropping it.

"Right, and now we get down to business. You wanted to talk about information. Well, turns out I was able to find out a lot about your little piece of land there. You were right: it has changed hands several times. Surprisingly, each one was a legitimate sale with all of the information up to date and on record. So, you're in luck. I really hit the motherlode.

"I'll send you the full transfer of ownership papers when we're done here. But the highlights are that it was originally owned by the government. They claimed it ever since the founding of the California Free State. Twenty years later a real estate investor purchased it and transferred it over to a technical company. That's the boring stuff. They never developed it.

"The exciting bit starts when a weapons development company bought it. They applied for a bunch of permits to create a lot of buildings on the site, but as far as I can tell, nothing was built. Despite that, the land transferred ownership four times since then, but each time it was just a renaming of the current company. Someone is clearly trying to bury that land in as much paperwork as possible and doesn't want it known who really owns it, or for how long. Intriguing, yes?"

"And you uncovered the names of all of these companies and holdings?"

"Of course I did. You don't think I would give you half the information, do you? I have a reputation to maintain, after all. I would hate to harm our working relationship. Now, I do believe it is time for you to share. What's this about a dragon?"

Keandra perched on the edge of the table, sitting on the corner with her legs stretched out in front of her. Victoria leaned forward, excitement and anticipation plainly written on her face. Keandra forced herself not to smile, despite the seriousness of the situation and the gravity of what she was about to share.

"During one of our runs, we happened across some information. It appears someone has been developing a new weapon, specifically designed to attack dragons. Not only that, but the prototype is complete, and they're planning to launch an attack against Hestaby."

Victoria shook her head, squinting her eyes shut. "No...no... no....You can't be serious. No one is stupid enough to attack a dragon."

"I'm serious. This new tech has been in development for years, and they even developed a custom-built AI to execute the attack. I don't know why the corp wants to attack Hestaby, or honestly if they even hope to succeed. But I do know the weapon is ready to launch, and it could happen any day now."

Victoria's shoulders slumped. Her arms slid off her legs to dangle over the sides of the chair. Eventually she sat back, running a hand over her face. "That's serious. And that is massive, no doubt about it. How accurate is your information?"

"I'd say our source is one of the most qualified people to speak on the subject, and had direct interaction with the program."

With a slap on the chair's arms, Victoria jumped to a standing position. Her morose and defeated expression had been replaced with her customary toothy grin and a shine in her eyes. She slapped Keandra on the back again, in the exact same spot as before. Keandra was sure it would develop into a bruise.

"No time like the present for living, my friend. This is just proof of it. And at least now I know what might be coming, and before anyone else, I wager. This was a good deal. Always a pleasure doing business with you. You never fail to disappoint."

She gestured, urging them to precede her out of the back room. Paz and Keandra complied, returning to the main part of the store while Victoria put everything back to normal.

Keandra hesitated and then extended her hand. Victoria took it with one eyebrow raised in a question.

"Be careful, Victoria. The people responsible for this are dangerous, and we've already attracted some unwanted attention. They might come after you too."

"Don't you worry about me. I have my own secrets, and am more than capable of taking care of myself."

"Just make sure you do."

Paz and Keandra left the store and drove back to the safehouse. Once again, Paz parked several blocks away. Keandra looked around as they walked, trying to spot the elf from the café, but didn't see him or anyone else following them as they headed toward to the apartment complex. She stood by the door, taking a final glance before entering the lobby.

"Nervous much?"

"I like to think of it as being adequately on edge."

Inside the apartment, Lance rested on the floor, tossing a knife up and catching it before it struck him. E-jekt stretched out on the couch, taking a nap. When the door opened, Lance snatched his knife from the air and bent his elbow, cocking it back and ready to throw it. When he recognized who it was, he went back to tossing it.

"Welcome back. E-jekt's finally getting some rest. He worked like crazy from the minute you left, and only just stopped to eat something and shut his eyes a few hours ago. He should be good by now if you want to wake him."

"We'd better. We have a lot to discuss and figure out."

Lance sprang up and walked over to jostle E-jekt. The ork grunted and swatted at Lance as he rolled over, but knuckled his eyes before pushing himself up. Lance claimed the seat next to him, tossing his knife from one hand to the other and flipping it around when he caught it. Paz took her usual seat on the floor next to the door.

"It's time to figure out what we've found out," Keandra began. "Victoria should have sent you some files about the land Freyr claimed is where the secret laboratory is. Judging from that, it seems pretty clear something in the area is supposed to be hidden. While that doesn't necessarily mean anything by itself, it does lend some weight to Freyr's story. What were you able to find out?"

E-jekt blinked and stretched. "I trust Paz told you about the electrical incident? Well, I also did some poking around before that, and it looks like someone shipped a lot of construction materials to that area, but satellite imagery doesn't show any buildings. So, either they stored the materials there for a while, and then shipped them somewhere else without creating any invoices, or something's built underground."

"So pretty much everything we're finding points to Freyr telling the truth? That's certainly how it seems to me. Please correct me if I'm wrong or if I'm missing something." Keandra looked at each of her companions in turn, but no one argued her logic. She pressed her lips together and gave a single nod.

"All right then, I think we need to operate under the assumption that what Freyr told us is true. And if that's the case, then we need to decide what we want to do about it. I for one think handing him over to Mr. Johnson is a horrible plan. I don't think anyone should be in control of that much devastation. Like Freyr said, whether or not the weapons are successful, just launching them would start an all-out war that would scar this planet."

"I'm afraid I have to agree with you. As much as I would like to hold up our original arrangement, I would not put that much power in the hands of someone with so few scruples. I'll be blunt: I care little for the life of this artificial entity." Lance shrugged and spread his hands in front of him. "But, I do care about what might happen if a dragon were to become involved."

E-jekt offered a nod, giving his agreement without saying a single word. Paz grinned and held up a thumb.

So at least they were in agreement about the first point. That had gone easier than Keandra had expected.

"The next question is, what do we want to do if we don't plan to turn Freyr over to Mr. Johnson? We have a couple of options there as well. I think we're all in agreement that we should return the funds before attempting to flee Seattle. Anything we can do to limit his ability to get support for pursuing us would be a good thing."

E-jekt coughed in order to capture everyone's attention. "Do we want Freyr to be part of this conversation? Now that we've decided we aren't turning him over, we have no reason to keep him confined. I think he'd appreciate being part of the discussion."

"It's just a sprite. Don't tell me you believe it has feelings as well. Have you heard how it talks?"

"Lance, enough. I think E-jekt's right. At the least, we have nothing to hide from him anymore since we won't be turning him over to Mr. Johnson. If he decides to leave, that's his prerogative. He might have helpful information to contribute."

"I concede to your logic, and see no harm in letting it listen in."

Pulling out her commlink, Keandra first turned on the audio and video capture hardware. Then she reconnected it to the Matrix. She placed it on the counter and stood back.

"Sorry for the delay, Freyr. We had to take care of some things in preparation for leaving the country."

<I understand. I would have been more than willing to assist you in your endeavors. Will you be flying to the California Free State to support me in the destruction of this experimental weapons system?>

"We haven't decided yet. We're still figuring that out."

<You do realize that failure to assist me could result in a cataclysmic event?>

"There's a lot more to consider than just that. We're trying to put all the pieces together and figure out what the best course of action will be for us. It isn't that simple, I'm afraid."

<I will also be willing to pay you a sum of one hundred thousand nuyen for your services.>

"Where would you get a hundred thousand nuyen?"

<I apologize for the impreciseness of my previous statement. Your inquiry should be where would I get four hundred thousand nuyen. I meant to offer each of you the sum of one hundred thousand nuyen in exchange for your services. As for where I could acquire such funds, I have already transferred a large sum of nuyen from several different banks into a private account that was opened under my creator's name. As you have often suggested, it is wise to be prepared.>

Lance missed his knife, and it skittered across the floor. Keandra kicked it back to him and he caught it with his boot, bending to pick it up and tucking it back into its sheath. E-jekt let out a low whistle.

"With those new IDs and that kind of payday, we could take an honest-to-goodness vacation." The distant gaze in E-jekt's eyes had nothing to do with dropping into the Matrix.

"And think of the upgrades I could get." To accentuate her point, Paz reached up and ran her fingers over her cyberarm.

"Does that mean you're both in for the biggest payday we've ever seen? Or hell, the biggest payday we've ever heard of?" Kendra asked.

"Of course. A chance to piss off a suit and shoot our way into what's probably a military-grade facility? I'd be down just for that. The payday's just a bonus—a super sweet bonus. Come on, Meat-sack, you know it'll be fun."

Lance grinned his cocky half-smirk at Paz. "I certainly can't let you go alone, now could I? With security that tight, you'd be lost without me."

Kendra smiled as well. "Then since we're all in agreement, you should be glad to know we've got four tickets on a flight to Sacramento. It leaves in three hours, so we'd best get packing."

SEVENTEEN

Two hours later, a car dropped Keandra and E-jekt off at the airport. They'd arranged to meet Lance and Paz there, arriving in separate vehicles in case they were being followed. Keandra made a quick stop at Elliot's and gave Francis the certified credstick, instructing him to hand it over to Mr. Johnson when he arrived for their meeting. She knew it wouldn't stop him from pursuing them, but she hoped it might slow down some of his support.

She had no idea where Freyr was at the moment, or if such a concept could even apply to a purely digital entity. She took him at his word when he said he was residing solely on her commlink earlier, but now that he had Matrix access, he could be anywhere. He gave them a way to contact him if they needed his assistance, but otherwise he promised he'd touch base with them once they got to Sacramento.

They traveled light, carrying only one bag between the two of them. There wasn't much more than that to carry. Thanks to Victoria's diligence, they had authorization to carry weapons on the plane, so there was no need to attempt to smuggle them in checked baggage.

The security line was crowded with people going on vacation, seemingly oblivious to the heavily-armed security around them. It seemed more a case of being accustomed to it. If you lived your life away from the shadows and never had a run-in with security that involved getting shot at, you probably started to accept the armored guards with assault rifles in every public building. The guards put Keandra on edge, and for good reason. She kept track of the guards' locations without staring at them while she and E-jekt waited in the line.

When their turn came to pass through the inspection, she handed over the travel visas granting them permission to be armed on the plane and crossing international borders. As the guard inspected the antiquated form of verification, another guard ran her SIN through on his terminal. This was where she'd find out if the identities were worth the price they'd paid. After a few tense seconds, the guard waved her and E-jekt through without bothering to check them or their luggage for weapons.

The two companions walked into the terminal and headed to their gate. She saw Paz up ahead. The dwarf stood out in a crowd that gave her a wide berth, probably due to her obvious cyberware. Keandra was willing to bet that most of the passengers here had never seen real cyberware in person before today. A few children whispered to each other and pointed. For her part, Paz seemed to enjoy the attention.

Keandra made sure Paz noticed they were there, and then sat down in one of the available seats near the gate. She had a good view of the rest of the terminal from this position, and could even keep an eye on the security station. The people milled about, ignoring her as they went about their business.

During a casual glance up at the security station, Keandra saw something that made her pause. She looked carefully, squinting to get a better view. Yes, she'd seen it correctly: it was the elf she'd caught following her. He stood at the security station and showed something to the guard. The guard gestured through, pointing toward her gate. The elf headed in her direction and two of the guards at the security station fell into step behind him, flanking him on either side.

<We might have trouble. My elf shadow is here, and he has some company.>

<Should we take him out? Think he's working with the suit?>

<No. If we start a fight, all the planes will be grounded. Plus, there are too many people around. Someone could get killed. Just be on guard. And where's Lance?>

<Haven't seen him yet.>

By now the elf was only a few strides away, and he caught sight of Keandra despite her keeping her head down and hiding her face behind her hair. She cursed when he pointed at her, and the security guards stepped around him with their guns held at the ready. It didn't look like this would end peacefully.

"Keandra Tiernay, you are ordered to accompany us."

"For what reason?"

"A corporate official wishes to speak with you."

"I thought the airport was exempt from corporate regulation. It falls under governmental policy. Or are you telling me that the corporations now have sovereign power over government property as well as their own spaces?"

The guards hesitated and glanced at each other. It couldn't escape their notice that a crowd formed around them. That was good for Keandra and would work to her advantage. They'd be less willing to push the issue with a bunch of innocent bystanders about. Especially when such an issue would infringe on corporate and governmental policies, both as convoluted as the circuit diagram for a simsense module.

"Would you please accompany us? There's no need for this to get ugly."

"So you're asking now. That's a pleasant change, rather than demanding that I relinquish my rights and go along with you because some corporation expects my compliance."

The elf shouldered through the crowd and drew up next to one of the security guards, cupping his hand around his mouth and whispering in the guard's ear. Whatever he said must have had an effect, because the guard raised his weapon and chambered a round, leveling the barrel at Keandra's head.

"You will come with us now."

Several people gasped. A few turned and ran, knocking over others or falling down themselves. But most of the crowd remained to watch, filled with a morbid curiosity and unable to leave the scene.

Paz moved into position behind the guards and the elf, reaching into the bag containing her gun. Keandra stood and held her hands out on either side of her head, showing that she surrendered. Paz backed down, slinking back behind the crowd.

"Very well. There's no need for violence."

One of the guards took the lead next to the elf, while the guard who had threatened her marched behind her as they headed back out of the terminal. The horde of people at the security line watched as she was marched out at gunpoint.

Once they got past security and entered the front lobby, the elf turned and headed for one of the exits, forcing the others to follow. Outside the door, Keandra saw a limousine with the fake maître d' from Elliot's as the driver.

Fearing they might be watching her AR, she pulled out her commlink, keeping it in front of her body so it was shielded from her escort. She typed a quick message before dropping it back into her pocket.

<He's with Mr. Johnson! Evac now!>

Keandra didn't dare move until she had backup. She marched along, trying to keep her pace steady and not think too much about the gun right behind her. When she slowed, the guard prodded her forward with the muzzle of his weapon. Her feet scuffed the floor as she hurried to quicken the pace.

All the lights in the terminal went out, dropping the entire front lobby into darkness. The only lights were those on cars just outside the front entrance. People screamed in panic, and Keandra took advantage of the chaos. She dropped to her hands and knees, ducking her head to make sure she was clear of the weapon. Kicking out with her back feet, she knocked the guard onto his side. The impact of his body with the ground made him squeeze the trigger and bullets ripped into the air in front of her. Someone cried out in pain, but it was impossible to see who was hit.

A hand grabbed her arm and she jerked away, rolling to the side and scrambling to her feet. She couldn't see anything more than a meter or two ahead of her. People rushed all around her, a couple knocking into her in their panic and almost bowling her over. She stumbled, but kept her balance. Keandra rushed in the direction of the terminal wall, trying to get out of the main thoroughfare. The planes would never take off now, so there was no point in going back through the security station.

"Boss, this way!"

Paz's call came from her left side. Keandra turned toward it, rushing in what she hoped was the right direction. After a few steps, Paz grabbed her wrist, pulling her along through the terminal.

"Where's E-jekt?"

Keandra had to shout to be heard over the chaos all around them. Paz turned and looked halfway over her shoulder, shouting back. She didn't slow her pace as she made for the stairs that led to the sky bridge.

"Sent him ahead. He should already be in the parking structure by now. Old man's slow, but not that slow."

"What happened to the lights?"

"Our little computer boy shut them down. Said he saw you were in trouble, and wanted to give you a chance to get away. Glad he's on our side."

By now they'd reached the stairs and Paz ran up them, using her cyberlegs to vault them four at a time. The lights in the sky bridge still worked, so Keandra no longer needed to be led by the hand. She sprinted upstairs as fast as she could, but couldn't keep up despite her height advantage. A group of people huddled near the top of the stairs, staring down into the darkness, obviously trying to figure out what was going on.

Paz waited for Keandra to join her and then they ran across the bridge heading to the parking structure. Before they reached it, a group of three guards fanned out in front of them, blocking the entrance. They raised their guns and Keandra slid to a stop, lifting her hands over her head. Paz planted her heel, carving a chunk out of the ground as she stopped and anchored herself. She still held her bag with the handle hooked over her thumb as she also lifted her hands.

"Halt! If you attempt to continue, we will open fire!"

A black blur dropped down behind the guard in the center and cut through his back, slicing his armor and spraying blood to the side as he fell on his face. Lance kicked at the other guard focused on Keandra, and he fell to the ground, firing his gun on the way down. The shots went wide, piercing one of the panes of glass on the sky bridge.

Paz burst into motion, piercing the bag with her cyberarm and reaching through to grab her gun without bothering to remove it. She fired, and bullets burst out of the canvas container, hitting the sentry in the chest. He returned fire, getting a couple shots off before the impact knocked him down, groaning and rolling. Paz did her best to dodge, but took a few grazing shots to her arm and another bullet ricocheted off her right cyberleg.

Keandra and Paz rushed forward, catching up to Lance just as he knocked out the final guard with a chokehold. He dropped the limp body and cleaned his sword and then tucked it back into its sheath. "I got your messages and found E-jekt in the parking lot. It seemed like you might require some assistance."

"Talk later. Now we need to get out of here."

"Where are we going?"

"Back to Seattle. To the train station. My backup plan."

Paz ripped her gun out of the bag as they ran, brandishing it in plain view. It cleared everyone out of their path and gave them a clear sprint to the stairs.

"How many of those do you have?" Keandra asked as she slid her hands down the banisters of the stairs, clearing five or six at a time as she swung forward. Even still, she had difficulties keeping up with her enhanced companions.

"Hopefully enough!"

As she dropped over the last few steps to the ground, Keandra's feet slid on the smooth surface and she tumbled forward. She'd have bruises and she'd scraped skin off in a few places, but her adrenaline was pumping hard enough that the pain barely registered. She scrambled up and lurched forward just as she heard the metallic clatter of a grenade behind her. Out of habit she closed her eyes, barreling forward blindly. A loud disorienting series of *pops* sounded, the actinic flare flowering behind her eyelids. Now that the danger had passed, she opened her eyes just in time to swerve around a parking barricade.

Ahead of her, Paz veered to the left while Lance cut right. Keandra followed Paz. While she'd done it before, she had no wish to ride on the back of Lance's bike, especially during what could turn into a high-speed chase. The van sounded like a much more practical option.

Now that they'd put some distance between themselves and the terminal, the shouts and chaos faded to a distant din. In their place, Keandra heard the sounds of several armored people running after her. They shouted, but she didn't pay attention to what they said. They could've been barking orders at each other or demanding that she stop, but she didn't care. She ignored it, keeping her attention focused on running, breathing, and following the dwarf.

Two rows over, Paz ducked behind a row of cars. Keandra followed her and saw the van in the middle of the aisle. It faced away from them, ready for a hasty exit. E-jekt must have gotten it into position. The back doors flew open, revealing the grizzled ork waving at them to join him. In his other hand, he held Paz's grenade launcher. He shot three grenades over Keandra's head. They hissed as they went by, leaving thin trails of smoke. She heard them burst, and could smell the phosphorus as tendrils of the white gas reached past her.

The organized running and shouting behind her changed to chaotic coughing and confusion.

Paz was first to the van. She didn't bother using the back doors, running around to the driver's side and almost ripping the door off in her haste to climb inside. She tossed her rifle behind her, letting it clatter at E-jekt's feet.

As soon as Keandra vaulted into the back of the van and grabbed E-jekt's hand for support, Paz stomped the accelerator. Keandra and E-jekt grabbed the handles near the back door to keep from being thrown out. After the initial lurch, they closed the doors before collapsing. Keandra panted as she tried to get her breath.

"That was close." E-jekt sounded as exhausted as Keandra felt.

"We're not out of this yet, old man."

EIGHTEEN

Keandra knew Paz was right. If Mr. Johnson's people were putting this much effort into detaining them in the terminal, she was sure they already had vehicles dispatched to prevent them from leaving the airport grounds. Still swallowing air as much as she was breathing it, Keandra pushed herself up from the floor and climbed into the passenger's seat. Paz burst onto the ramp heading toward the exit, but had to slow to take the spiral. While the van had many advantages, nimbleness was not one of them.

"What do you have?"

"Not much. Packed light since we were leaving town and I didn't want to leave it for someone else to find, so I sold just about everything. Got the launcher, my rifle, and a bunch of grenades. That's about it."

The van shook as Paz tried to speed up too much and scraped its side against the concrete siding of the ramp. A shower of sparks danced just on the other side of her window, and Keandra flinched.

"Right. E-jekt, hand me the launcher. What kind of grenades do you have? Any HE?"

E-jekt gave her the launcher and shoved two crates of grenades forward until they smacked against the back of her seat. Keandra offered a quick mental thanks that Paz was so organized. Both crates were labelled, making it clear even to her untrained eye which was which. She grabbed a couple smoke and a couple HE, tossing them into the seat behind her, then knelt on her own seat and faced the window. As soon as they exited the ramp, she rolled it down. Cold, wet air blasted her in the face.

She loaded a smoke grenade into the launcher—might as well start with the less destructive option—then shouldered the weapon's strap and leaned her upper body outside the vehicle.

Behind her, several flashing lights danced across the parking structure's walls and ceiling as emergency vehicles rushed around. She couldn't see the vehicles themselves, so it was impossible to guess how many there were or where they were headed. One security car slid around a corner on the ground floor, tires screeching, and headed in their direction. Keandra fired a grenade, watching it bounce a few times on the pavement before it exploded in a cloud of white smoke.

The shot was short, and the rain helped disperse the smoke more quickly than she'd hoped. The car drove right through the cloud, bursting through to the other side. Keandra grabbed another grenade, not paying attention to its type. She loaded and fired again, hitting the windshield this time. The grenade crashed through the glass and into the cabin, where it exploded in smoke. The car swerved hard as the driver slammed on the brakes. Two coughing people stumbled out, dropping to the ground as they attempted to breathe.

"Eyes front!"

Keandra twisted around at Paz's command. They were approaching the garage's toll gates. Four cars formed a barricade, blocking the entire width of the road. Security forces crouched behind the cars, using the engine blocks as cover and the hoods to steady their weapons as they aimed at the approaching van.

"Stop your vehicle and come out with your hands up!" an amplified voice ordered.

"Make me a hole!" Paz ordered.

"Grenade!"

E-jekt handed Keandra a grenade, and she loaded it. *It better be HE.* She debated where to place the shot when an idea fired like lightning through her mind. Even if she had a perfect shot, it wouldn't clear the path, but only add rubble. But the wall on the side—that was an option.

"Turn right and drive toward the wall!"

"What?"

"Trust me!"

Paz did as instructed, swerving the van to the right. The sentries opened fire, the bullets ricocheting off the armored plating sounding like coins clattering down a copper pipe.

Keandra leaned out the window and aimed the launcher at the short wall in front of them. There was a curb, then a concrete wall about one meter tall. If she remembered correctly, it was only a short drop to the main road from the terminal.

If she didn't remember correctly, they were about to experience a very painful end to their escape plan.

She fired the grenade, and it slammed into the wall near the base. The resulting explosion sent concrete chips flying in all directions. Keandra dropped back into the van, trying to escape the shrapnel.

Paz adjusted her course, aiming for the smoking hole. The van hit the curb and there was a wrenching sensation accompanied by a horrible scraping sound as the undercarriage dragged across the cement. Their momentum let them clear the rubble, and they soared off the edge, dropping down onto the busy road below.

Luck was with them in that they didn't land on another vehicle and actually hit pavement. However, that was where their luck ended: one side of the van struck the ground first, causing the van to bounce wildly and tip over. Metal sheared and snapped as they slammed down on the driver's side. E-jekt and Keandra were thrown from their seats, rolling around as the van slid forward for several meters before screeching to a stop.

At first, all Keandra could do was make sure nothing was broken. Pain overwhelmed her entire body, and she wasn't sure she could see or hear straight. The van seemed to be still moving, and it hurt to even try and lift a leg. She twisted her head to one side and saw Paz, a large glowing light haloing her head, turning the dwarf into some kind of crazy, metal-limbed angel. As Keandra blinked and regained focus, she saw it was just a streetlamp hanging above Paz's window. The dwarf punched her door open, then unbuckled herself to climb out.

From somewhere far away, Keandra heard gunfire. The sharp sound rattled around in her brain, urging her to move, to do *something*. She got her feet under her and stumbled as she tried to stand on a loose grenade. Grabbing the driver's seat for balance, she regained her footing and looked around. E-jekt was in a similar state on the side of the van. He sat with one hand on the floor behind him, bleeding from several small cuts and obviously dazed, but appearing otherwise unhurt.

"Boss, old man, get your asses out here and get moving. I got us a new ride."

Paz poked her head through the driver's door opening above Keandra, who had to blink several times before she could focus on the dwarf's face. The light behind her was distracting. With a grunt, Paz reached a hand down to her. Her body sluggish like she was moving through a dream, Keandra clasped her wrist. Paz pulled her up out of the van with enough strength that Keandra found herself standing on the side of the vehicle before she realized it. The cool air and misty rain helped bring her back to awareness.

Cars were stopped all around them, and it was a complete gridlock in the direction of the terminal. Ahead, the road was empty for a fair distance, with red taillights visible in the distance.

A sporty-looking compact car parked next to their van, a couple bullet holes in the hood. The driver's door was open, but the driver was nowhere to be seen. Keandra turned back to look at Paz as she helped E-jekt out of the van.

"I didn't hit anything important," the dwarf grunted.

The group climbed down from the van, dropping to the pavement just as a few guards poked their heads over the improvised opening Keandra created. They fired on the fleeing trio, but the van provided cover as they got into the car. The larger vehicle went up in a blinding fireball as one of the guard's bullets hit a grenade.

"Couldn't've planned that better myself." Paz gunned the engine and the tires squealed before it lurched forward, leaving the terminal and the remains of the burning vehicle behind.

Keandra's head still throbbed, but she gritted her teeth and tried to ignore the pain. She fished her commlink out of her pocket, glad to discover that it hadn't been damaged in their impromptu escape.

<We're leaving the terminal now. Had to ditch the van. Meet us at the train station.>

She knew Lance wouldn't be able to respond if he was driving—like her, he didn't have the implanted hardware—but he should be able to see the message. With luck they had captured most of the attention, and security probably wouldn't pay much attention to a single elf on a motorbike who had never entered the terminal. If not, Lance could take care of himself.

Paz merged with traffic, trying to keep her speed as high as possible without attracting undue attention as she changed lanes, swerving around cars. She slowed down after they'd passed a several vehicles, providing a buffer between them and the terminal. Keandra looked through the rear window. Flashing lights approached with haste. Hopefully they wouldn't know which car to look for, now that they weren't in the van.

The two security cars racing up behind them, one behind each corner of their back bumper squashed that hope before it could give her any false comfort. Paz gave up trying to be subtle, taking the shoulder to swerve around the truck in front of her. One of the cars pursued them directly, the other swerved around traffic to cut them off.

<Take the next exit.>

<Are you insane, computer boy? I'll outrun 'em.>

<Their vehicles have a significantly higher top speed than this vehicle, as well as state-of-the-art enhancements to support handling under extreme driving conditions. Given the wet conditions of the road, that will put you at an even further disadvantage. Unless your skill is markedly superior, your assumption is incorrect.>

As if to accentuate her point, the car behind them accelerated and clipped their rear bumper. Paz had to frantically twist the wheel to avoid spinning out. Growling, she jerked to the side, cutting across four lanes to catch the exit ramp before they zoomed past it. Even so, she collided with the guardrail while straightening out on the ramp, scraping paint off the body panels as she wrestled for control.

The ramp ended in a T-intersection, which currently had a green light. Paz drove into it, jerking the wheel to the left and engaging the emergency brake. The car slid through the intersection until it pointed down the road, and then shot forward again. What they saw made Keandra nervous: a long line of lights, with a fair amount of traffic.

<Freyr, we have a problem.>

<I am aware of your predicament. I have accessed the local traffic network and will be providing assistance. Please maintain your present course and rate of speed.>

As she watched, the light ahead of them turned green, with just enough time for the other cars to clear the intersection before they passed through it. Paz swerved around the waiting vehicles and rushed through. Looking back, Keandra saw the light go from yellow to red in short succession, jamming up the intersection before the security vehicles could get through. By the time they untangled themselves, Keandra and her team had put another two lights between them.

<If you take the next right, you will find an access road to the highway leading back to Seattle. That road is currently clear of any authorities who might possess your identity.>

<Thanks.>

Paz took the indicated turn, and got back on the highway north to Seattle. Much to everyone's relief, they spotted no flashing lights or cars racing across the road in pursuit. Once again, Paz merged with traffic, and Keandra hoped this time they would get lost in the herd of drivers going north.

They reached the city without further incident, and took the exit for downtown that would get them near the train station. Paz drove to a parking structure a few blocks away, going all the way up to the roof before choosing a space.

Keandra got out of the car and was amazed at how much the simple movements hurt. Her shoulder ached whenever it shifted in its socket, and she still had a soft throbbing at the back of her skull. At least it had diminished, shrinking from a pain-pounding, distracting jackhammer to a soft tapping that wouldn't go away. Her gelatinous knees had trouble supporting her weight. Taking a few steps helped reaffirm their stability.

E-jekt climbed out after her, looking almost as rough as she did. He let out a hiss and had to grab the car's roof for support when he put his weight on his left leg. He hopped a little when he walked, but he could pick up his leg and flex it so nothing was broken. They were beaten and bruised, but still intact.

For her part, Paz wore the grin of a young boxer who'd just finished her first fight and knocked out her opponent in the second round. She bled from a few small scrapes where the bullets grazed her, but they didn't slow her movements or her enthusiasm. She grinned at the other two and almost pranced to the edge of the rooftop parking lot.

"Train station is three blocks in that direction. I figured it might be better to go on foot in case they got a description of the car or something."

"The 'or something' being noticing bullet holes in the hood and the crumpled back bumper?"

"Yeah, something like that."

Keandra joined Paz, offering an arm to E-jekt as way of support. He waved her off and walked next to her, grunting with each step as he hobbled to keep his weight off his left leg. By the time they reached the edge, Keandra felt significantly better. The movement helped stimulate the blood and get the muscles moving, reminding her she wasn't crippled, just sore.

"Think the suit'll be waiting for us?" Paz asked.

"There's a good chance of it. He knows we want to get out of the city. By now I guarantee he knows what happened at the airport. This or the docks would be the most obvious next choices."

"Well, we do have one thing going for us."

Paz and Keandra both turned to face E-jekt, questioning looks on their faces.

"Trains don't shut down if there's an incident. They're automated."

NINETEEN

Keandra hunched down in her jacket, pulling the hood up over her head. She hoped that with the rain, the hood wouldn't attract undue attention. Several other travelers heading to the station had hoods or carried umbrellas to shield them from the rain that had now progressed from a mist to a steady drizzle. She'd paid far more for the jacket than she'd have liked, but it was the only one in her size at the tourist shop. If it got her through the station without incident, it would be well worth the price several times over.

Paz was ahead, purchasing a ticket at the counter. They decided to split up, thinking it would be more difficult to notice each of them individually than to see all three clumped together. She had no idea where E-jekt was. Hopefully he was boarding the train by now. Keandra huddled with a group of other people waiting for a bus under a rain shelter and pulled out her commlink.

<E-jekt, status report.>

<I'm on the train. Lance is here, two cabins ahead of me.>

Keandra tucked her commlink away, looking around the terminal to see anyone suspicious who might be following her. When she didn't see anyone, she joined the line in front of the counter. Several kiosks were set up to enable customers to review schedules and purchase their fare. A couple agents stood behind the counter, leaning against the wall and either talking to each other or engrossed in their own AR worlds. When someone had a question, one of them came over to provide assistance. Each time, the unlucky soul made no attempt to hide their impatience and frustration at being pulled back into reality.

Reaching the front of the line, Keandra clenched her fists as she waited for the next kiosk to open. Nervous energy filled her; she wanted to bounce up and down on the balls of her feet, but restrained herself. It seemed like half the people directly in front of her had questions requiring technical assistance. *It's not that hard. Look at the schedule, find the train you want, and buy the ticket.*

After what felt like an eternity, one of the kiosks opened up. Keandra scuffed her feet as she approached it, but she came to a sudden stop when two security guards emerged from the doorway leading into the station proper. They made a direct line for the bank of kiosks, and Keandra froze as her brain hiccuped. She forced herself to start moving again, opening the display and paging through the different routes available until she found the one for Sacramento. The entire time, she remained focused on the guards getting closer.

When they reached the counter, one of the guards called to a technician. The tech walked over and began talking to the guard, her hand brushing his sleeve. With a sigh, Keandra turned away and finished buying the ticket. She entered her payment information and was immediately rewarded with a one-way passage to Sacramento.

Keandra navigated through the station, keeping her hood up and looking around without swiveling her head. It was a fine line between being constantly aware of your surroundings and looking as if you expected every shadow to jump out at you. She reached the train without seeing anyone unusual, and that made her nervous as well. Mr. Johnson had to know they would come here. Especially if he knew about the lab, either this station or the docks would be the most logical places to trap them. Was a trap waiting for them on the train?

You're being paranoid. Shaking her head, Keandra stepped onto the last car. She paused in the doorway, taking one last look at the rest of the station before going inside. It looked to be filled with normal travelers all going about their regular business. Traffic was a little light, but that wasn't surprising, considering that this was one of the last trains leaving this evening.

Keandra swung inside, walked down the aisle, and took a window seat in an empty row. She sat crooked across both seats, stretching out her legs and positioning herself so she could both watch her commlink and glance out the window without moving.

<*I'm on board. Last car. Everyone accounted for?*>

<*Yep. I'm in the same car as the old man. Meat-sack's up near the front, looking like he's taking a nap. Being his normal lazy self.*>

<*Once again proving that subtlety and subterfuge are not your strengths, my little friend.*>

Keandra jumped in before they could continue. While she normally appreciated the banter, it could get out of hand and she wanted her team to stay vigilant, at least until they were out of the UCAS.

<*Stow it, both of you. There'll be enough time for that later. Keep an eye out for anything unusual. This all feels too easy.*>

Keandra pulled up a pointless game on her commlink to give the illusion she was killing time. She gave it less than half her attention, going through the motions of playing to hopefully convince others she was engrossed in the computerized world. She tracked every person who walked by her window and listened whenever she heard the tromp of feet behind her as someone else boarded the car. She didn't see any security staff asking questions, nor anyone walking with the sure tread of someone with combat training.

When the train bell sounded, signaling the closing of the doors, Keandra relaxed. She sat up and slid over to the window, looking out from a better vantage point. Other than a few people rushing to catch the train, nothing caught her eye. The doors slid shut, and the train pulled forward, gently picking up speed. The station drifted out of view, replaced by the Seattle skyline. The buildings and lights went by faster and faster until they became a steady blur of color, lines of light dancing across the glass. In the space of a blink, the view went mostly dark, with small specks of light in the distance moving like shooting stars across her view. They were out of Seattle, and on their way to Sacramento.

Keandra stood up and stretched her legs. They were still sore, but it felt better to move than to be crammed into a seat, especially considering her tension. Now that they were out of immediate danger, it would be good to see the others. She walked up the aisle to the door connecting the train car to the next one.

There was an airlock system on each end of the car. Keandra opened the first door and stood in the waiting area while she closed it behind her. The door to the next car wouldn't open until the first one shut. The public theory claimed it was a safety precaution, but Keandra figured the truth had more to do with the noise and air currents. The former would make for complaining customers, and the latter meant it would cost more to run the train. Angry customers meant lower ticket prices. Everything came back to money.

Each of the cars was identical. This was a commuter train, so it didn't have any frills such as sleeping rooms or a dining car. There was no need, since the trip would only take a few hours. Even if you'd taken the route from the southernmost point to the northernmost, you'd only be on the train for a total of eight hours. It was far more economical, and made more sense, to create a simple vehicle capable of holding more people.

E-jekt sat cross-legged a few rows ahead of her, in one of the larger rows specifically designed to give taller metahumans more leg- and headroom. A female troll sat across the aisle from him, snoring so loudly Keandra heard it at the back of the cabin.

Paz sat near the front, her face plastered to the glass as she watched the distant landscape fly by. Her gun must be tucked underneath her or stored in the baggage area overhead. Knowing Paz, Keandra would bet on the former. The dwarf was not one to let her weapons get more than an arm's reach away.

Other than her team and the snoring troll, three other passengers occupied the car. Two were a dwarf couple, so engrossed in each other they weren't paying any attention to their surroundings. They couldn't be older than fifteen, whispering and giggling to each other. The other passenger sat with perfect posture, his back to Keandra. He still wore a heavy coat and hat, looking like something out of an earlier era. He had a briefcase on his lap, both hands resting flat on top it.

Keandra slid into the seat next to E-jekt. He had the distant stare she knew meant he was engaged in the Matrix. He briefly waved a greeting when she sat down, but then went back to his private world.

Keandra took a deep breath and let her eyes droop a bit. She was exhausted, and knew why: she was crashing now that the massive amount of adrenaline had left her system. That, combined with her injuries, urged her to close her eyes and sleep, allowing sweet oblivion to take her. She'd wake up in a few hours and deal with the world then. She loved the rush, but hated this aspect of it.

Before she could nod off completely, she heard the hiss of one of the airlock doors opening. She bolted upright, pushing herself up from her slump, then relaxed as Lance entered from the front of the car. He noticed her and came over, perching on the edge of the seat next to the troll, making sure not to nudge her even though she took up a seat and a half.

"I've checked the train, and I don't see anyone who might have an interest in us. It seems to consist only of passengers."

A yawn escaped Keandra's lips and she covered her mouth. Lance raised an eyebrow, but she ignored it, shaking her head to jostle herself back into wakefulness.

"I appreciate you checking. I still think this is too easy, that Mr. Johnson did something. But I trust your judgment, especially right now. I can barely hold my head up."

"Get some rest. I'll keep an eye on things. I feel the same way—this is too simple. Considering the force waiting for us at the airport, I can't imagine they didn't have agents looking for us in every station and port in Seattle."

"Actually, I think I might know why they were at the airport *en masse*."

Keandra turned her head back to look at E-jekt, who'd pushed himself forward so he see both her and Lance. He scratched his cheek before he began. When he spoke, his words were slow and measured, as if he choose each one carefully.

"I did some poking around. How did you get our tickets for the airport?"

"I bought them at a terminal from a café..." Keandra's words trailed off as elements clicked into place.

"Exactly. I'm guessing the elf you had me check on saw what you were doing and used the same terminal as you. If you have the right sprites, it would be easy to piece together what you did and discover any purchases you made or messages you sent. I think that's how they knew to look for us at the airport."

Keandra's shoulders slumped as the wave of guilt crashed down. She'd been sloppy. She knew the elf was probably spying on her, and yet she hadn't taken the necessary precautions to make sure their tracks were covered. And all because she still had Freyr on lockdown at the time and couldn't use her commlink for the transactions. It was a stupid mistake—and a rookie one at that.

"If only I hadn't used that terminal. Or if I'd bothered to wait and use my commlink. I just wanted to set everything up immediately, get everything moving."

She felt a hand on hers—rough, calloused, and easily dwarfing her own. She looked up into E-jekt's face and he offered a sad smile. That was why he was picky about the words he used. He didn't want to come out and say it was her fault, even though they both knew it. He also knew how she felt; she could see it in his eyes as he patted her hand. She squeezed his hand with her free one.

"We've been through worse."

"He's right, you know," Lance said. "We've all made errors in judgment from time to time. That's why we have each other's back, and why we work well as a team. Well, why *most* of us work well as a team."

He added the last sentence as Paz jumped onto the seats in front of E-jekt and Keandra, kneeling so she could drape her elbows over the back. She rolled her eyes and shook her head, but didn't offer a rebuttal.

Keandra felt the weight ease just a bit from her shoulders. "Thanks. I appreciate it. You're right—we've been through worse and we'll get through this. We'll get down to Sacramento, and then figure out what we need to do from there. But for now, I think we should get some rest while we can." She winced as she shifted in her seat. "I don't know about you, but my body's been put through a wringer and needs some time to recover."

Lance stood and looked up and down the length of the car.

"You get some rest. I'm going to make another sweep and make sure I don't see anything I don't like."

Keandra was going to offer a reply, but her brain decided rest was more important. She waved in a dismissive gesture before letting her head slip to rest against the seatback. At first, she didn't think she'd be able to sleep with the troll snoring almost in her ear and smelling of stale sweat, but her body didn't care. She sunk into blissful oblivion before her mind finished the thought.

She woke with a start as she lurched forward, barely managing to get her hands up in time to keep from smashing her face into the back of the seat in front of her. The troll across the aisle wasn't so lucky: she slammed into the seat and tumbled to the side, falling into the aisle with a curse and continuing to yell at the train as she clambered back onto her bench.

Keandra took stock of her surroundings. E-jekt sat next to her, one hand pressed against the window for support and pawing at this face with the other, clearly just woken up as well. The heavy thud in front of her gave away Paz's location. Glancing around the seats, she spotted the dwarf woman in the gap between the benches. Keandra pulled her gun from around her back and held it under her, glancing around for the nearest threat.

The young dwarf couple still focused on each other, only sparing a brief glance out the window before once again becoming enraptured with each other's presence. The businessman in the coat with the briefcase stood up and leaned against the window, glancing in both directions. Lance was nowhere to be seen.

"Passengers aboard the express train to the California Free State, we apologize for this slight delay in our itinerary. Please remain in your seats and be advised that we will be underway shortly."

This couldn't be good. The airlock door at the front of the car opened and Lance sprinted through it, running toward them. The businessman turned to ask him a question, but Lance rushed past without pausing. Keandra realized the business man and troll stared at them, meaning witnesses who could identify them if what she feared was coming to pass.

"We must depart immediately." Despite his sprint, Lance's breath was slow and steady.

"Why?"

"Corporate drones. There's one flying up near the engine at the front of the train. If I had to venture a guess, that's why we've stopped."

TWENTY

The group didn't need any more convincing. They jumped to their feet and rushed to the back door of the car as the troll and the businessman watched them, their confusion painfully obvious. As for the dwarf couple, Keandra was surprised they'd even noticed the train slowed down.

The airlock compartment would only fit two at a time, so Keandra and Lance went first, squeezing in together as they shut the back door. They opened the door to the outside and the sudden rush of air caught Keandra off guard. She snatched at one of the support railings as she swung out into the open space between the two cars. Lance watched to make sure she was stable; when she gave him a thumbs-up, he vaulted up on top of the train.

As soon as he cleared the car, the wind blasted him back. He reached out to snag the front lip of the last car, catching himself from flying off the back of the train. It was slowing down, but still traveled fast enough that a fall would be deadly. He jammed one of his knives into the roof of the cab, hooking a quick anchor cord around it. He gripped it in one hand and held out the other to Keandra. With his assistance, she pulled herself up and joined him on top of the train.

Even seeing what it had done to Lance, Keandra was unprepared for the sudden force of wind blasting her in the face. Lance held on tight, keeping her from losing her footing. She pushed against the wind, reaching out to grab the cord from the anchor. She wrapped it around her wrists like Paz had taught her, holding her in place without needing to rely on her grip strength. Once she felt secure, she looked up at Lance.

"I'm good!"

He shouted something back, but she couldn't make out his words over the howling of the wind. Instead, she offered an upraised thumb. He returned the gesture, then turned back to the gap between the cars, presumably to help E-jekt get up to the roof as well.

Keandra fed the cord through her hands, letting it uncoil from her wrist a little at a time so she could back away from the opening and make room for her other companions. Once she was a few meters away, she looked around. Looking forward was impossible; the wind dried out her eyes and battered them so much she couldn't keep them open. The best she could do was cover the front of her face with her arm, allowing her to turn her head and glance to the side.

Wherever they were, the area was heavily wooded and didn't have much in the way of electronic lighting. In the distance, she could see the faint outline of mountains, but that didn't tell her much. All she knew was that they were somewhere between UCAS territory and CalFree—otherwise it would have been much more developed. The ground still whipped by so fast that jumping off would be guaranteed suicide.

Overhead, she heard the roar of a drone engine as it shot past her. As soon as she heard it, she dropped flat—as if that would help hide her, or protect her if the drone opened fire. Nonetheless, the drone flew past, heading somewhere in front of her that she couldn't see. What she wouldn't give for a pair of goggles.

The line jerked around her arm, and then E-jekt bumped into her as he joined her on the roof and backed away from the gap as she had. She noticed he kept his head tucked down and the line wrapped around his arm. She couldn't get any more detail than that before she was forced to look away.

Lance came up next to her and shouted in her ear. "We have to jump!" Even with him that close, it was difficult to make out his words.

She closed her eyes and tilted her head so she could yell back at him. "We'll die if we jump!"

"We're slowing down quickly. As soon as we reach a clearing we can see, we need to jump. We have to hope the drone didn't see us, but it won't matter if it sweeps when we're stopped."

"That's insane!"

"Do you have a better plan?"

Keandra admitted she didn't. They were already slowing down significantly, but it was still crazy to think they'd be able to time a jump at a speed slow enough that it wouldn't kill them, but not so slow that the drones wouldn't see four people jump off the train. Lance was brought up a good point. It was their only option, short of getting in a shootout with the drones and hoping they could take them out faster than the corporation could send reinforcements. And that was assuming Mr. Johnson didn't already have troops in the area or on a train in pursuit.

"Tell the others!"

Lance headed off to comply. Keandra still needed to hold onto the cord to keep her balance, but now she could stand upright without her arm straining to the point of being ripped off. The wind prevented her from looking ahead or having any hope of hearing something not shouted in her ear.

She edged over, making her careful way to the side of the train and looking at the ground below. At least it didn't look like a long fall. The track wasn't elevated, so they only had to worry about the height of the train. On the downside, the trees here grew right up to the edge of the tracks, close enough that they brushed the air in front of Keandra's face as they rushed by. If she stuck a hand out, branches or even trunks would smack it. Thinking of what would happen to her body if she jumped into one of those made her shudder and shuffle back a few steps from the edge.

The wind died down enough she could spare quick glances ahead of her. Two drones kept pace with the lead car, escorting it as it slowed. At some point, Paz climbed up and now she stood at the edge of the car, close enough that Keandra was amazed she didn't get swatted off by a wayward branch. Lance stood next to E-jekt, one hand on his shoulder. Keandra wasn't sure if it was for support or to provide a push when it came time to jump.

The ground passed by too fast for Keandra to track it. But the steady howl of wind dropped to a gentle moan, and she heard the *whoosh* of the trees as they whisked by. She closed her eyes and prayed for something soft to land on.

The trees gave way to a clearing, and Lance wasted no time. He shoved E-jekt off the train, and the ork went over the side with a scream. Paz followed suit, and her shout of elation was stark contrast to E-jekt's wail of terror. Lance glanced at Keandra and she let the cord go, where it danced around on the top of the car at her feet. She had enough time to watch Lance coil it up and retrieve his knife before she leaped into the darkness.

Her breath caught as she soared through the air. In the space of a couple seconds, her emotions went from pure fear to the excitement of freefall to terror of the impact to come. She slammed into the ground and curled her body as best she could, rolling through the grass. Even though it was soft dirt and vegetation, it felt like rock when she hit it and rolled over. Only when she came to a stop did she appreciate just how soft her landing spot was. By now, the aches and bruises from earlier in the evening were back, this time with an aggravated vengeance. She wanted nothing more than to lie in the dirt and not move for days.

She shifted her head to the side so she could breathe out of the side of her mouth without every gulp of air being filled with the scent of wet dirt and pine needles. The high grass prevented her from seeing much, but she caught a blur as Lance hit the ground and rolled over his shoulder to his feet. She remained still and listed to the roar of the drones' engines and the sound of the train squealing in the distance as it continued to brake.

When everything became still, Keandra considered it a relief. She relished the fact that she wasn't the only one who wanted to curl up and recuperate. To be fair, even curling up sounded like too much effort. She wanted to slip back into the oblivion she'd enjoyed before the train began shuddering to a stop.

Reality encroached on her attempt at rest and recovery. Soon Mr. Johnson would know they weren't on the train any longer. They needed to get up and get moving.

From a different direction, she heard a groan: E-jekt. Bit by bit, her team recovered from the crash. Keandra pushed herself up on her side and regretted it as pain lanced through her shoulder, dropping her back down. This time she rolled over, tucking her knees under her when she did so. Now with a solid base, she sat back, rising to a sitting position without needing to put much strain on her shoulder.

The clearing was fairly large, and Keandra spotted lights peeking through some of the trees in the distance. She also heard the steady hum of heavy machinery. There was a small station nearby, next to the track. Tire tracks had pushed down the grass and formed a path that led from the stage in the direction of the lights. That meant civilization, and possibly more options for transportation.

Lance was already on his feet, walking through knee-high grass to Keandra, the blades swishing against his legs. Paz was also up, helping E-jekt stand. He had one arm draped over her shoulders, which left him in a hunched position, given their height differential.

Lance offered Keandra a hand. She took it with her good arm, accepting his strength as he pulled her up. Once again, her knees wobbled when she put her full weight on them, but he grabbed her arms to help steady her. When she winced at the sudden force on her shoulder he let go, remaining close and ready to catch her if she needed it.

"I'm all right. You?"

"Better than you, I would wager. Normally your lies are much more believable."

Keandra smiled and patted Lance's shoulder. "Considering I just jumped off an express train into a dark field at spirits-knows-what speed? Yeah, I'm all right. I expected to be broken in a heap after that maneuver. But, good thinking."

By now E-jekt and Paz hobbled over to join them. Paz looked fine—if anything, she looked like she wanted to do it again. E-jekt, on the other hand, was panting, and Keandra was pretty sure it was due to pain. As much as she would have liked to take time to care for any injuries, they needed to keep moving.

"We need to get out of here, especially now that the train's stopped. Are you two ready?"

Paz continued to grin, letting that speak for her. E-jekt gulped down some air and removed his arm from the dwarf's shoulder, taking a second before he stood up straight and looked Keandra in the eye. "It'll take more than that to keep me down."

He winced halfway through the words and stumbled forward, dropping to one knee. Each of the others lurched forward, trying to catch him and offer support. He waved them off, bringing his foot back under him and standing on shaking legs. His back was hunched, but he raised his head. "Like I said, I'm not down yet."

Paz dropped into the grass, sitting cross-legged as she pulled her medkit off her belt. She opened it, rifling through the different options, and settled on a patch. It was unlabeled, and Keandra had no idea how Paz knew which one it was.

"Try this. It'll take the edge off the pain, but not give you too bad a crash after. You'll still crash, just not hard."

E-jekt took the patch and lifted his shirt, slapping it into place. He continued to wheeze, but after a few seconds his breathing slowed and cleared. He stood up straight, putting a hand on Paz's shoulder for balance. Once he was completely upright, he let go and took a few tentative steps. "Thanks. Just what I needed."

Keandra considered asking if Paz had anything to help deal with her shoulder, but decided against it. Right now they weren't even sure where they were, let alone where they could resupply. The pain wasn't unbearable, so it'd be best to save the medical supplies until they became absolutely necessary.

And that brought them to the next problem.

"We need to get out of this clearing before the drones come back," she said. "It's only a matter of time before they talk to the passengers and learn we were on board. From there, they'll search for where we jumped off. At best, we have a few hours' head start, but we need to get moving. Let's head into the woods down this track, catch our bearings, and figure out where we're going next."

The runners gathered together and trudged to the shelter of the trees. The tracks led down a well-maintained trail, wide enough for a truck. However, the trees on either side had grown tall enough that their overhead branches provided cover over the passage. That shelter might just keep them from the prying eyes of a passing drone. By the time they got under the tree cover, she'd broken into a sweat despite the cool temperature.

"E-jekt, do you have Matrix coverage?" she asked. When he nodded, she continued, "Find out where we are and what you can learn about the area. We need transportation, and we can't sit around and wait for another train to come by."

As she spoke, weariness crept up from her bones once again and she leaned against a tree for support, propping her back against it. She planted her hands on her knees, bending over and closing her eyes as she struggled to recover. She heard Paz come close; the dwarf's heavy tread was unmistakable.

"I'm fine."

"I know you are."

"I just need to sit for a moment."

"Uh-huh."

Keandra slid down the trunk of the tree until she sat on the ground. Some part of her brain registered the zipper of Paz's pouch opening, and felt the dwarf woman pick up her arm. Then things got cloudy and she had trouble thinking. She needed to get up and move. They needed to get to the factory or whatever it was and find a way to get down to California. And they had to do it before... Before something...

TWENTY-ONE

Keandra's eyes opened and she jerked to a sitting position. When she tried to prop herself up, she noticed her left arm rested in a sling.

She sat in a small ditch surrounded by trees. Bright light cascaded over the hill to her right, and the sound of heavy machinery hard at work roared through the cool air. She moved to climb up the hill, but something gripped her ankle, pulling her back down.

E-jekt rested at the bottom of the ditch, holding onto her leg and shaking his head. She climbed back down and opened her mouth to ask a question, but he put a finger to his lips and pointed at her pocket.

She fished out her commlink, holding it awkwardly in her injured hand so she could use her good one to interact with the AR.

<What happened?>

<Paz decided you were pushing yourself too far, and I agreed. We knew you wouldn't take a rest voluntarily, so she drugged you. We tended your wounds and brought you here. You've been out about two hours.>

<Two hours! We need to keep moving! Mr. Johnson could be right behind us.>

<You weren't in any condition to make that call. You were practically falling over. We did what we needed to take care of you. Lance and Paz are scouting the perimeter right now. We're close, so you shouldn't poke your head up. We should wait until they return with their report.>

<What is this place?>

<Some manufacturing plant owned by Andalusian Light Industries. They have trucks, and there are service roads leading out

of Tír Tairngire. If we can get one of their trucks, we could disable the GPS and get back on the road to Sacramento. That's the plan we came up with. We wanted to scout the facility first and make sure you agreed with the idea once you woke up.>

Keandra rolled her head around and shifted so she could crawl up the side of the ditch. Poking up above the lip, she scanned the manufacturing plant. It looked fully operational, and probably ran 24/7. The security appeared minimal, with only a single turret and one guard in a booth at the gate.

It looked like most of the plant was automated, but it was impossible to say how many people—or how much security— were inside the large buildings. A bank of eight company trucks sat parked at the corner just on the other side of the fence.

It was a solid plan, and Keandra was proud of her team for putting it together. Not that they were helpless without her— quite the opposite. They were capable enough to recognize when she was on the verge of making poor decisions and to take actions she might never have suggested. As much as she didn't want to admit her weakness, she had to concede they were right.

<It's a good plan. We should go with it.>
<Hear that, Meat-sack? Told you she'd go for it.>
<As always, you are such a paragon of wisdom.>
<Nice of you to finally acknowledge it. And with witnesses, too.>

Keandra settled back down, shifting to get comfortable in the dirt. As much as she didn't want to take the break, it had done wonders for her body. The bruises and aches made their presence known, but they were more of a distant memory: battle scars rather than fresh wounds. Tentatively she moved her shoulder around. It protested when she got to the top of the circular motion, but no longer throbbed constantly. When she touched it with her other hand, she discovered it was warm and swollen. That was something that would take either time or magical assistance. Considering their timeline, she opted for the latter. They'd need to look into that once they got to Sacramento.

After a short while, Lance and Paz both came back to join them in their hiding spot. E-jekt projected a small map of the facility, using the information and recordings from Lance and Paz to update it. It hovered in the air before them, and E-jekt spun it around so they could all see the entire perimeter. The fence surrounded the facility, and it was electrified. Other than that, the only guard either of the scouts had seen was the one at the front gate. Cameras topped every fifth post on the fence, with an additional unit on each of the corners. Finally, a couple of turrets maintained a watch, one in the front and one in the rear of the facility.

<Should be easy enough.> Paz told the others. <Let's just blast a hole through the fence, get in a truck, and drive through the gate. We'll be in and out before they know what hit 'em. And if the turret's a problem, I'll take that out too.>

E-jekt shook his head. <I don't think that plan will work. Those are company vehicles, which means they're likely to have kill switches. I can disable them, but I need to connect to them directly first, and even then it will take a few minutes to override their systems.>

Paz frowned. <Odds are cutting the fence is gonna set off some sort of alarm, so I don't think we can get in all stealth-like, either.>

<We don't have to.>

E-jekt and Paz both turned toward Keandra. She took control of the AR display and zoomed in so everyone could see a detail they might have overlooked.

<The trucks have Andalusian Manufacturing logos, but if you look at the registration tags, they're registered to Andalusian Light Industries. All we have to do is convince the gate guard that we're representatives from their parent company, and they'll be obligated to give us a truck. We wouldn't need to disable the kill switch or the GPS until we're well on our way.>

<I've worked with several of these wage slaves before. Manipulating them is much easier than negotiating with Mr. Johnson. I can convince the guard to give us a truck, provided you can drum up some fake credentials. I'll need something to flash at him. It doesn't need to be perfect, but it needs to be good enough to pass a quick glance. Can you do that?>

E-jekt narrowed his eyes and traced meaningless designs in the dirt with his fingers as he considered the question. The rest of the group focused on him, waiting to see if it was possible.

<I think I could, using the SINs Victoria gave us. You've already got the travel authorization attached to it, so that would explain why you're crossing national borders. But if that SIN's been reported, it would be declaring ourselves as wanted criminals.>

Keandra knew it was their best bet, at least that they'd be able to come up with on short notice. *<It's a chance we'll have to take. I don't think Mr. Johnson would cast that wide of a net yet. If he did, other corps might take notice and wonder why he was so interested in us. We have to hope he doesn't work for Andalusian Light Industries.>*

Everyone settled down to wait while E-jekt worked his magic. Lance kept an eye on the guard, periodically peeking up over the edge to make sure nothing had changed. Keandra looked up at the sky, disappointed how the proximity to the lights from the manufacturing plant blocked out the stars. Even though they'd only been in the clearing for a few minutes, she remembered glancing up and being amazed at how many stars she could see. This was her first time out of a city. Not just Seattle, but any urban area. It really was a different world.

The longer they waited, the more Keandra became aware of how hungry she was. As if in response, her stomach growled. Paz chuckled as the face wrapped her free arm around her stomach, as if that would contain the noise. She couldn't remember the last time she'd eaten. That was something else to add to the list when they got to Sacramento, or maybe even sooner: find a good restaurant. Take that back: at this point she'd have settled for a cheap and greasy soyburger.

<I've got it. The credentials have been added to your SIN. It won't pass a thorough inspection, but it should be enough for a quick glance. I set you up as a corporate manager and Lance as your personal assistant. I figured you could pick Paz and me up after you get the truck. I didn't want to try to forge too many identities.>

<All right, keep an eye on us. If we get into trouble, then you have my full permission to blast your way in, Paz. Just make sure you leave at least one of the trucks intact. Otherwise once we get the truck, we'll meet up with you half a kilometer down the southern road.>

Keandra stood and smoothed out her clothes as best she could. The biggest mess was her hair, wild and crazy from the trip on top of the train and the subsequent tumble. She grabbed clumps of it, threading her fingers through to separate them with fierce tugs so she could at least make a decent braid. It wasn't perfect, but hopefully it would suffice to fool the guard at the gate.

Paz handed her one of the cleaning rags from her medkit, and Keandra scrubbed her face with it. If she was impersonating a corporate manager, it would be inappropriate to walk up with a dirt-caked face, no matter the situation. When she was done, she looked over at Lance, the one she trusted the most to give her an honest assessment. He pressed his lips together and nodded—a less than stellar recommendation. *I know how to handle this,* Keandra reminded herself.

The final step of preparation was removing the sling. She took it off and tossed it to Paz, who caught it and tucked it into her pouch. Keandra moved her shoulder, rolling it forward and backward once again, stretching out in all directions to see what pain that triggered. As it turned out, she could reach up behind her, but if she moved her hand around to the front, anything higher than chest level sent stabs of fire through her shoulder and into her skull. With a final deep breath, she stepped onto the road in plain view, Lance following close behind her.

They got all the way to the gate without being noticed by the guard in the small watch station. His head hung low, with his chin resting against his chest. For a brief moment, Keandra was tempted to reach inside and press the button to open the gate, to see if that woke him up. If not, problem solved! She decided against it, though, thinking it would be much harder to explain if he did awaken.

Instead, she took up position a full stride away from the guard window and widened her stance. She crossed her arms, using her good arm to support her injured one, and compressed her eyebrows together, looking every bit the annoyed professional. Then she coughed.

The guard stirred at her first cough, so she did it again, adding a growl at the end. That time he snapped to attention. To his credit, the first thing he did was draw his small handgun.

Keandra heard Lance's foot slide across the ground, kicking up a few rocks as he shifted to be ready to spring into action if need be. Once the guard saw he wasn't under immediate physical threat, he tucked his gun back into his holster and faced the open window.

"May I help you?"

Keandra focused her best managerial glare on him. "I certainly hope so. Is this what passes for security at the entrance to one of our most important manufacturing plants in the area? Do you have any idea what the gross annual profit is to our company based on this individual structure?

How much we spend on research and trade deals to keep it operational? Not to mention the political implications and the bribes necessary to keep doing business in this restricted area? In short, do you have any idea how much nuyen is tied up in this building behind you? The one that you are individually responsible for, and the one at which you were just *sleeping at your post?*"

She made sure to pause between each of the final four words, watching the guard flinch as each one passed her lips. She marched forward and placed both hands on the edge of the window. He took an involuntary step back, feet shuffling. She saw sweat form on his brow as he looked down and off to the side, unwilling to meet her gaze.

"Do you want me to report back to my boss at Andalusian Light Industries that you are failing to carry out your duties? Do you think you're irreplaceable? That we can't find any number of other people to do your job, and do it with more respect and authority for the corporate family that you claim to be a part of?"

"No! I mean yes! I mean—"

"I was in the area for a routine inspection of this facility and others in the area. Unfortunately, my secretary failed to register appropriate transportation. I will be dealing with him when I return. However, I had to walk from the train loading dock all the way here, and I'll be damned if I'm going to walk to all of the other sites in the area."

"But, we don't have any other sites."

Keandra rolled her eyes. "That you know of. That are part of Andalusian Manufacturing. Did you mishear me? Was I not clear when I spoke? I work for Andalusian Light Industries, your parent company. In short, I'm one of those responsible for making sure that your company even exists in the first place. Just because you aren't aware of other ventures in the area does not mean they don't exist. Or do you have information you shouldn't be privy to? That would be a very serious offense."

The guard held up both hands in a warding gesture and shook his head rapidly. What had started as beads of sweat turned into full streams running down the sides of his face. Keandra pushed off the window and rested her weight on her back leg, once again crossing her arms.

"Please, let me know if I can be of any assistance." The guard spoke in a continuous stream of words. "Do you need a tour of the facility? I'm not supposed to leave my station, but I could call someone up if you'd like."

"No. I'm going to commandeer one of your vehicles for the rest of my tour. You will sign it out to me, and you will not alert anyone else. You can inform them when their shift starts in the morning. It ruins a surprise inspection if others hear about it before I arrive, doesn't it?"

"Yes ma'am. Yes, of course. Only..."

"Only what?"

"I'll need to see your ID. I just need to check it out and make sure. Corporate policy and all."

"At least you're doing something correctly."

The guard moved to his terminal and his hands shook as he manipulated the interface. He glanced at Keandra twice, making sure he was entering her SIN into the terminal correctly. She waited until his eyes moved back and forth, scanning the data, and then she stepped forward until she stood directly in front of the window. She shifted her tone of voice and added a smile.

"Very good, officer. I'm glad to see you are able to handle pressure and still manage to stick to appropriate protocol. Rest assured, this will go very well for you in my report."

He looked away from the display and offered a weak smile, clearly not sure how to react. His hands still shook, and he chewed on his bottom lip.

"Now about that truck?"

"Right! Everything checks out. Here you go."

He reached behind him and grabbed one of the keyfobs hanging on the wall, then pressed the button to open the gate. As Keandra expected, it let out a loud air-horn blast once it started to roll open. Even if it hadn't, the rattling of the metal as the wheels rolled across the packed dirt would have been more than enough to wake most people.

She walked into the facility with Lance at her side, idly thinking that the guard had never even bothered to check her companion's identification. It wasn't her problem. He'd be in enough trouble when the morning shift came on site and learned that he'd lost a truck. He waved to her as Lance drove them out, leaving him standing steel-rod-straight in the booth and not daring to take a seat as long as she kept him in view.

A half-kilometer down the road, they stopped and met up with their companions. E-jekt went to work on disabling the tracking and recovery systems immediately. Paz went to take the wheel from Lance, but Keandra shook her head.

"Now that we're out of sight, it's time for you and Lance to both take a turn to get some rest. We've got a long drive to Sacramento. I'll take the first shift."

Neither of them argued. Instead, they crawled in the back of the truck and laid down.

TWENTY-TWO

Keandra drove for a couple of hours, until sleep laid its claim on her once again. The small forced nap she'd taken had done wonders, and she was riding a high from her interactions with the guard, but the need for more rest could no longer be denied. She woke up Lance and had him continue driving as she curled up in the passenger's seat.

When next she woke, she saw the Sacramento skyline in the distance. Bright sunlight shone through the window, warming her body. She stretched, but stopped short when the pain in her shoulder flared once again. With a growl, she settled for stretching at an angle with one arm up and one down.

"Good morning, sunshine."

Paz sat behind the wheel, looking refreshed and as energetic as when she'd first jumped off the train. Keandra twisted around and saw E-jekt and Lance both passed out in the back seat. Somehow, Lance managed to sleep sitting straight with the seatbelt buckled around him. In contrast, E-jekt curled on his side in a fetal position, taking up more than his half, but still looking squeezed into the tight area.

"I needed that. I slept like I haven't in ages. How long until we reach Sacramento?"

"Only another hour or so. Question is, what're we gonna do once we get there?"

"The first thing is get some food. I was starving last night, but apparently too tired to care. I'd kill for a good soykaf right about now. After that, stock up, set up a safehouse, touch base with Freyr, and start working the job like normal."

"Right. What do we know about this job, anyways? I mean, besides what Freyr told us with the missiles and the secret base and all that."

"Nothing really, which is why we need to knock on some doors and open some windows to poke around and see what we can find. E-jekt said there was a bunch of construction equipment and supplies brought into the area. That means someone built something there. Satellite imagery is a bust, we already know that. I'd bet my last nuyen their entire network, and any networks in a large area around it are completely off the Matrix."

Paz remained silent as Keandra rambled through her thoughts. She usually did all her planning in her head, but this situation was sudden, and she didn't have all her usual control factors in place. It helped to vocalize her thought process, even when Paz said nothing. She continued thinking out loud.

"But still, someone had to order all the supplies and contract all the work. While a lot of that might be done in house, this isn't a megacorp we're talking about, so I'd bet they'd have to hire some of it out. That means there'll be permits registered with the hall of records. Hell, we already know there are permits registered there. Victoria found them."

Keandra mentally kicked herself for forgetting they already had that crucial piece of information. She pulled out her commlink and looked through the permit files, checking the names registered with the permits, finding out who had applied for and been given permission to drill, excavate, and build in the area. Almost all of the permits were registered to the same company: Gildhall Construction.

"I got it. Our first step is to find Gildhall Construction. They have an office in Sacramento, and they handled all the excavation and building for the laboratory. If anyone has a schematic of the structure, it would be them."

"Something tells me they won't just give us access to their database."

"Since when have you ever been a fan of just asking?"

Paz chuckled, conceding the point. For the rest of the trip, Keandra considered the plan, pleased as pieces fell into place. Once they got set up, they had their first target. From there, they could hopefully get the needed information to crack the laboratory. She didn't want to go in there completely blind. While the blueprints wouldn't give them intel about the security systems in place, they'd at least give them a general idea of the layout. If they were really lucky, they'd show it to Freyr, and he would direct them right to the central database.

Of course, they needed to do all of this before Mr. Johnson caught up with them. The fact that he was able to pursue them into Tír Tairngire and force an international transport vehicle to stop was alarming. It meant that it was much more likely he could pursue them into CalFree as well. Keandra had hoped they'd have some breathing room once they crossed international lines, but it appeared less and less likely. So much for slowing him down by not leaving a debt on the table.

When they reached Sacramento, Keandra woke Lance and E-jekt. She explained the plan, and they split up to save time and get moving as quickly as possible. She didn't need to remind them of the barghest breathing down their necks.

Her first order of business was to set up a new base of operations. They chose the Omni Hotel. At the upper end, but not completely out of their price range, it provided additional security—and more importantly, additional anonymity. Not knowing how long they'd be there, Keandra rented it for a week. If it took longer than that, a place to stay would be far from their biggest worry.

Before doing anything else, Lance and Keandra swept the room for bugs. Even though the hotel was rumored to be very secret-friendly, Keandra didn't want to leave anything to chance. She especially didn't want to give Mr. Johnson any additional resources toward finding them. He had enough at his disposal already without their inadvertent assistance.

Keandra found one bug embedded in the drawer of the nightstand. She borrowed one of Lance's knives to pry it free, stuffed it into her pocket, and tossed it in a trash can when they got back down to the lobby. At least the room was clean now. They'd need to check it when they returned, to make sure an overzealous maid hadn't noticed the bug missing and planted a new one. It was a downside of not having your own place, but they didn't have time to look for a more permanent location. Not to mention doing so would cost more funds than they had readily available, unless they wanted the transaction tied to a SIN that Mr. Johnson probably knew about by now.

The next item on the agenda was a place called The Invisible Needle. It was a tattoo parlor specializing in supplying the general public with legal drugs for medical or recreational purposes. According to Keandra's research they also had a shaman on staff, someone who might be able to do something about her shoulder without waiting for natural healing to take its course. By the time they arrived, the sun dipped low enough that some of the buildings cast shadows long enough to cover the street. It was a bit of a culture shock, being in the center of a city without towering skyscrapers on every side. Sacramento almost appeared short and flat compared to Seattle.

People still milled about on the streets, providing crowds that both comforted Keandra and put her on edge. At first, she tried to get at least a passing glance at everyone to see who might be interested in her, but trying to keep track of that many faces was an impossible task. She knew her actions bordered on paranoia, and she needed to slip back into her standard comfortable state. She was somewhere new, but the task at hand was the same. She could handle it.

They walked into The Invisible Needle. A beefy ork sat in a chair near the front window, getting something etched on his right pectoral. The needle buzzed and the alcoholic odor of an antibiotic solution filled the air. The tattoo artist bent over the ork, focused on her work and oblivious to the sound of the doorbell when Keandra and Lance entered.

Another woman worked behind the counter, an elf with fully inked arms featuring curling designs creeping up the side of her neck to frame her jawline. She smiled at the newcomers.

"Welcome to The Invisible Needle. What are you looking for?"

Lance turned his head to the side, checking out their surroundings as well as the street behind them. When the woman got a glimpse at the serpentine eyes inked into the back of his head, she let out a low whistle of admiration.

"Nice work. You get that done around here?"

Lance half-grinned. "No, back in Seattle. I know an amazing artist who works on the pier. It makes for a nice serene view while he works on you."

"Sounds amazing. I've never been to Seattle. What's it like?" From the way the woman leaned further across the counter, her intentions were obvious.

Keandra stood off to the side, letting him work his charm. Instead, she looked at the collection of herbs stocked on one wall, organized in small jars, all labeled with a steady hand. She didn't recognize half the plant names, but that didn't mean much. Horticulture had never been her specialty. She did, however, recognize a couple of the drug labels on some jars of powder.

The woman behind the counter laughed and then disappeared into the back, leaving Lance alone. He gestured for Keandra to come over.

"They have a shaman, and he's currently on staff. Heidi said he'll come out to look at your injury and see if there's anything he can do for you."

"I trust you'll be okay waiting while we get this taken care of?"

She winked at her companion, and he shook his head.

"I have learned a thing or two after accompanying you all these years. I have no interest in her, but being friendly certainly does help us with our own objectives."

Keandra raised a mock-questioning eyebrow, eliciting a flash of a glare from Lance. She laughed, unable to keep a straight face, but pleased to have gotten that much of a reaction out of him. By then, Heidi returned with another man beside her.

He was also heavily tattooed, but mostly on the back of his hands and across his scalp. He extended his hand to Keandra, making sure to reach for her good arm.

"Nice to meet you, Keandra. My name is Carlos. Please, come have a seat in my clinic and we'll see if I can do anything about your shoulder." He waved her into the back room.

Keandra followed him around the counter and into the hallway beyond. He took the first door on the right, leading her into a small office with a medical table pushed up against the far wall. A surgeon's light suspended over the table, connected to the wall by a metallic arm. The close corner had a desk with a terminal and several fetishes lined up in a row.

Carlos pointed to the table, and Keandra climbed up and sat on the edge with her feet hanging free. Carlos turned on the light and pulled it down so it shined over his shoulder in her direction. Keandra squinted, turning her head so she wasn't staring into the glare.

He took her arm, lifting it gently from where she had it curled against her body for protection. He extended it, testing the range of motion to see where it caused her pain. When he lifted it past the level of her chest, the pain flared, making her hiss. He lowered it immediately, and put his free hand in the crook of her shoulder. He lifted it once again while applying pressure. The pain flared up with more intensity, and Keandra had to resist the urge to jerk her arm back. A gasp escaped before he released the pressure.

After his initial examination, he let go of her arm and she lowered it back to her side. She reached across her body and began massaging the joint, trying to relieve some of the lingering tingling sensation.

Carlos moved to stand in front of her, looking down in full clinical mode and nodding as he spoke. "The good news is it doesn't appear to be broken. You still have most of the mobility in your shoulder. You have good muscle tone, and seem capable of manipulating it on your own. These are all good things. Most importantly, this means that I can fix it for you right now."

"How much is that going to cost?"

"Two hundred nuyen."

Keandra pulled out her commlink to transfer the funds. Once Carlos verified the transfer, he picked up one of his fetishes and walked back over to the table.

"Lie down, please."

Keandra fell back and stared at the ceiling. Out of the corner of her eye she saw Carlos place the fetish on her arm and then lift his hands above her, palms up. The feathers tickled her skin, and she smelled the leather now that it was only a few centimeters from her face. Carlos called on the spirits for their assistance and their energy, mumbling the prayer so softly and quickly it didn't sound like individual words.

A soft yellow glow surrounded the fetish, reaching out into her shoulder, warming it. At first it felt odd, but the sensation quickly transitioned to one of comfort and peace. It reminded Keandra of when she was a child and would spend summers at Discovery Park, lying in the grass and staring up at the sky. The warmth spread through her body and she resisted the urge to close her eyes.

Then the glow disappeared. It was not subtle or gradual—one second it was there, and the next it was absent. She shifted her head to look at Carlos. He pinched the bridge of his nose and then dropped his hand, the smile back on his face. He picked up the fetish and put it back on the table. "You're all done."

Keandra sat up and tentatively rolled her shoulder. It didn't feel stiff or sore at all. She straightened her arm at her side and lifted it, expecting the pain to flare up, but now she could make a complete circle with no heat inside the joint. If anything, her left shoulder felt better than her right. She hopped off the table and gripped Carlos's hand.

"Thanks for that. It feels like new."

"It is what I do."

When he let go of her hand, his smile faded, and he just stared at her for a moment. It lasted long enough that Keandra grew nervous and shifted away from him.

"I feel the need to let you know something," he finally said. "The spirits see bad things for you."

TWENTY-THREE

"What do you mean?"

Keandra started running down her emergency mental checklist. Her gun sat tucked into the holster under her arm and was loaded. She believed she could draw it before Carlos grabbed one of the fetishes off the table. Then again, that assumed he needed one at all. Lance was out in the front room. If she called for him, it wouldn't take him long to get here. But she had no idea what Carlos could do.

"The spirits told me you were in danger."

"Uh-huh." Keandra took another slow step back, dragging her back foot across the floor to make sure she didn't trip over anything. She shifted to the side, checking to see if she could work her way around Carlos if she needed to.

"It's true. They warned me of a shadow, chasing you through the darkness, biting at your heels as you stumble through the woods, trying to find your way. The branches snag at your face and your clothes as you break through, trying to run from the black that is darker than night itself."

Keandra glanced at the desk and saw that the terminal was up and running, displaying a warning that her SIN was wanted for criminal behavior. It must have happened when she transferred funds—some type of automatic report. Given the fact that Carlos had healed her, rather than trying to subdue her when she was on the table, she relaxed and smirked.

"The spirits told you that? Would that be the spirits in the Matrix?"

She nodded at the terminal behind Carlos, and he glanced over his shoulder. When he saw the display was visible, he shrugged and sat back on the corner of the table, taking care not to bump any of the fetishes.

"You can't blame a man for trying. My job is thirty percent magic and seventy percent theatrics. People will pay more if they believe everything comes from some mystical spirit guardian. It sounds a lot better than saying 'your SIN got flagged by the Matrix.' Besides, sometimes the spiritual aspect really helps put others at ease in ways practical fact can't."

"Fair enough. But the question is, what are you going to do about that notification?"

Carlos shrugged again. "Give you a head start? We don't get involved in such things, unless it's a serious crime or against someone that matters to us. We treat anyone who comes in needing help. I won't cover for you, though. It isn't worth the risk. But you should have a few hours before that notification catches the attention of someone who might actually do something about it."

"Thanks. Now we need to get going."

Keandra walked out the door and Carlos made no move to stop her, instead turning to his terminal and going back to work. When she reached the front room, she shot Lance a look as she passed by him. He excused himself from his conversation with Heidi and followed her out the door.

Out on the street, Keandra walked as fast as she could manage without breaking into a run. Lance kept up with her, asking no questions.

She knew spending money was going to be a risk. There was no way to transfer it all onto certified credsticks in time, so they had to use those for the big purchases—things like the hotel room. Things that would tell Mr. Johnson exactly where they were if they were tracked. For small purchases, like getting her shoulder fixed, they needed to tap into their accounts. She hadn't expected them to be flagged already. Clearly this Mr. Johnson had more power than she had anticipated. Not for the first time, she wondered if he might work for a triple-A.

So what could they count on him knowing? He would've known they were on the train. No way would his people have missed the witnesses from the car when the train was forced to stop. He also knew they were in Sacramento, or at least that someone was spending money from her account there.

If she had to guess, a strike team would already be in the area, or trying to get permission to enter CalFree. Even if they weren't in Sacramento already, she and the others had only a few hours at best before someone was actively hunting them on the ground here. Then again, that was assuming Mr. Johnson didn't already have someone here on retainer.

Hopefully, Paz and E-jekt had ditched the truck and used their share of certified credsticks to acquire a new vehicle. Assuming that was the case, Keandra could think of nothing else that would lead Mr. Johnson to their location. But being in the city meant they would need to be careful of surveillance systems.

Keandra ducked into the alcove of a store window, blocking the display but also getting out of the path of foot traffic. She pulled out her commlink and accessed it while Lance slid up next to her, keeping an eye on the crowd around them while her eyes were focused on the AR space.

<Freyr, are you around?>

<Indeed I am. I have a sprite maintaining a watch on your private communication network. You may attract my attention by using my name, and I will respond as soon as I am able. Congratulations on reaching Sacramento safely and with discretion.>

<Thanks, but we need your help right now. You wanted us to help get you into the lab, but if we're caught in Sacramento, that isn't going to happen. Can you access the city's network of traffic cams and security cams?>

<I can. For what purpose?>

<We need you to make sure that if any of our faces are captured on those cameras, they aren't identified. A watch has been put on our SINs, which means I think it's only a matter of time until someone starts checking camera data for our faces.>

<Such a measure would require a constant expenditure of power, and I would no longer be able to provide as much support if I had to maintain that sort of watch.>

<We'll be fine on our own, but could really use your help with keeping us unnoticed.>

<Very well. It will take me some time to access the citywide network and gain the permissions necessary to edit camera footage. However, I will make that my top priority.>

Keandra nodded. One problem taken care of. It might not be a complete solution, but it might buy them the time they needed. As long as they didn't attract any undue attention and Freyr was as good as he seemed, they should remain untracked.

Her commlink alerted her to an incoming message from E-jekt. <I take it you tried to access your accounts too?>

<Yes. I saw the alert, and I think we're okay for now. But I wanted to take precautions. At best, it's only going to be a few hours before Mr. Johnson has boots on the ground, and we still have a lot to do.>

<Understood. We acquired a new vehicle. Paz insisted on getting something capable of handling potential rough terrain, since we might not want to depend on roads to get us to the facility. We're about done and planning to head back to the hotel shortly.>

<We'll see you there.>

Keandra and Lance went back to the hotel, taking an indirect route and walking through the thickest crowds. Keandra kept her face focused on the ground, not so much that it looked suspicious, but hopefully enough to make it hard for her to be recognized. She also pulled her hair loose from her braid, letting it cover most of her face. Freyr had said it might take some time to do his part, and right now Keandra didn't think there was such a thing as too cautious.

When they returned to the room, Paz and E-jekt were already there. Paz lounged on one of the double beds, somehow managing to take up the entire surface area despite her small stature. By contrast, E-jekt stretched out on the other one with his ankles crossed and his hands clasped on his chest, barely taking up half the space. They both looked up when the door opened, Paz with a hand on her rifle.

Keandra collapsed onto the bed next to E-jekt, sinking into the mattress as she threw her hands back and stared at the ceiling. He looked over at her and raised an eyebrow. She rolled onto her side and propped herself up on her elbow. The little amount of rest that she'd gotten last night hadn't been sufficient, and she knew if she kept lying down, she'd soon feel the need to sleep.

"Right. So you got a new vehicle. I assume you made sure it couldn't be traced back to us and already took the necessary steps to disable the manufacturer's anti-theft features."

E-jekt furrowed his brows and wrinkled his nose; she held up her hand in a placating gesture.

"I need to ask. I know you know how to do your job, but we all need to stay on top of each other just to make sure we don't let anything slip through the cracks. Moving on. What were you able to find out about Gildhall Construction?"

"They're a family-owned company, rumored to have Yakuza ties. They've been in business for four generations, always passed down from father to son. Based on the outskirts of Sacramento, where they have some land they use to store their own equipment and a lot of their own supplies. They've been responsible for building approximately twenty percent of all the city's current infrastructure that's less than a hundred years old."

E-jekt pushed himself up so he could lean against the wall. He projected an AR display showing a satellite view of Sacramento. An area in the northwest corner flashed and then the view zoomed in, close enough to show individual buildings and machines like excavators. The property hosted one main office building and a separate warehouse. As they watched, the view shifted, coming down to show a three-dimensional angle.

"Pretty standard for a construction company. Lots of machinery and the warehouse has a bunch of materials in it: glass, concrete, steel, whatever. I don't know what's stored in there right now, but it doesn't really matter. Our target is this central building. It's where all of the business happens."

Once again the view shifted, moving so the construction vehicles and warehouse were out of sight and it looked like they were standing in the parking lot in front of the building. It was three stories tall, with one main double-door entrance and two single-door entrances on either side. Judging by how many windows adorned the front wall, it looked like every office had a window. The entire front entrance was covered in mirrored glass all the way to the ceiling.

"All the entrances require RFID chips to enter. Guests can bypass the entrance by speaking with the receptionist working at the front desk. Once you're inside, there's no automated security I've been able to find on record. I'd bet they have cameras, but beyond that, I don't think there's anything."

Keandra studied the model hanging in the air in front of her, reaching out to spin it around as she considered all the various entry points. A plan pieced itself together in her mind, and she tried to figure out how to make it work.

"What do you need access to?" she asked. "Is there a central database, or will any of the terminals work?"

"Any of the terminals should work. What we need isn't a trade secret, so I doubt they have it in a secure central location. Plus, that facility doesn't seem like it's designed to host a central server. If they did have one, I'd wager it would either be underground or offsite."

That made their job easier, assuming E-jekt was correct. But she trusted his instincts. There was something to be said for the voice of experience. All they needed to do was get into the building and get E-jekt enough time at a terminal to work his magic.

"Their staff, do they work normal standard hours? Do they have a rotating shift? Any contractors on their payroll?"

"They do use contractors, and they have a normal eight-to-six work day."

"Perfect. I know how we're getting in."

TWENTY-FOUR

It was about six-thirty in the evening, after the grand exodus of workers, but some were still trickling out the doors to their waiting cars in the parking lot. Compared to the satellite imagery, the parking lot looked virtually abandoned. A handful of vehicles remained, and every few minutes, another one left. The lights in the offices turned off one at a time, but the halls and entrance were still fully lit.

"I still say it'd be much easier just to get up on the roof and break in through one of those windows." Paz sulked in the driver's seat of the new SUV, arms crossed as she stared at Gildhall Construction's office building.

Keandra sat next to her, also keeping a watch on the building. The vehicle was comfortable, with many features their previous van lacked. However, in exchange for those comforts, it had less space in the back. Rather than one open area, it had a row of seats and a small cargo area. It made it harder to get to supplies, but at least the additional passengers would have a more comfortable ride, as well as seat belts.

Keandra shivered as she remembered vaulting off the parking ramp at SeaTac airport. Out of habit, she checked to make sure her seat belt was firmly latched, even though they weren't moving.

"I don't think 'easier' is the word you're looking for. More direct, maybe? Definitely faster. But I'm not sure easier applies. We don't even know what they have for security."

"That's why you send me in with the old man. I can take down whatever they send after us. It beats just sitting around here waiting."

Keandra looked back at the other members of her team, but E-jekt just shrugged. Lance shook his head and gave her a look that said she should have known better than to expect anything different.

She tried to placate their aggressive dwarf. "Well, look at it this way: if the plan doesn't work, then you'll have to do a hot extraction, which will involve more than enough violence to whet even your appetite."

Paz chuckled and clapped her hands. She looked in the rearview mirror, rising out of the seat so she could make eye contact with E-jekt in the back.

"That could be fun. Don't be afraid to mess up a little. I'll get all of us out of here safe."

"There. That one." Keandra called their attention back to the front doors of the complex.

An ork in slacks and a short-sleeved shirt walked out of the building, carrying a bag slung over one shoulder. He looked down at something in his hand as he walked, not paying attention to his surroundings. He would be perfect.

Lance opened the SUV's back door and slid out of the vehicle, hurrying across the parking lot in the direction the ork walked. It was clear which of the vehicles was his—it was the only one left in that section. Keandra doubted the ork would have seen Lance even if he paid attention. Even she, who knew where he was, had difficulty tracking him as he flitted from one shadow to the next. He stopped when he reached the front of the car, crouching in front of the bumper out of sight.

When the ork got close to the car, the lights flashed and the doors unlocked on their own. He jerked open the front door and tossed his bag into the passenger side. As soon as he moved to enter the vehicle, Lance burst into motion.

The elf rushed the door, slamming it and timing his motion so the top of the door smashed into the ork's skull. The blow dazed him and he stumbled back a step, his eyes rolling and staring at nothing as he put a hand to his head. Lance continued his assault, striking the ork in the back of the knee and dropping him to the pavement. Before the man's knees hit the ground, Lance drove his shoulder into his back, throwing him into the car with enough force that he slammed into the opposite door. For a moment his face pressed against the glass, stuck there as his body twisted at an awkward angle.

Lance jumped into the car, next to the ork. A quick slam of his head against the dashboard and the ork closed his eyes, collapsing over the dash. The entire encounter took less than five seconds.

Afterward, Lance drove the car out of the parking lot, since they didn't want to leave it where someone might stumble across it. Keandra couldn't see where he took it, but had faith he stashed it somewhere safe. They sat in the SUV and waited for him to return. E-jekt opened the door, and Lance held out an ID card.

E-jekt and Keandra got out, leaving the team's muscle behind. If everything went according to plan, they wouldn't be needed for the rest of this run. As the two approached the front entrance, somebody else exited right in front of them.

"Forgot something," Keandra said.

The employee smiled and nodded knowingly as he passed. Keandra watched to make sure E-jekt scanned the badge on the reader next to the door before dismissing them from his attention. Keandra was glad they'd bothered to grab the badge rather than trying to ghost in and catch the door before it closed.

The front lobby had a receptionist desk, now abandoned and dark, as well as a couple of comfortable padded chairs, presumably for guests waiting for their appointments. Another set of glass doors stood in front of them, barring their entrance to the core of the building. E-jekt waved the ID card in front of the reader and the door unlocked with a heavy *thunk*. Keandra pulled it open and gestured for E-jekt to precede her.

They headed down the hall to the left. They wanted to stay on the ground floor, and that side had a larger number of dark offices. The fewer people around, the less chance anyone would notice someone using an office that didn't belong to them. They had no idea where their victim's office was located, so they couldn't poach it and hope any random workers passing by thought all orks looked alike.

After passing three doors, they found an open office with a window facing the parking lot. As soon as they entered, a sensor picked up their movement and turned on an overhead light. The terminal on the desk also powered on, asking for login credentials. E-jekt dropped into the chair, sliding up to the desk to begin his hacking.

Once he was situated, Keandra went back into the hallway, keeping an eye on both directions. She heard a couple of voices from her right, steadily growing in volume and coming from the central open area. She headed toward the noise, trying to get close enough to hear what was being said. Before she could make out the words, a man and a woman came around the corner, deeply engrossed in conversation. The woman waved her hands around as she talked, obviously excited about the subject matter. They left through the front entrance without so much as a glance in either direction.

Keandra entered the main room and looked up. From here she saw the walkways all the way up on the third floor. The area was well lit, with few places to hide in such an open space. She closed her eyes for the space of a couple of breaths and listened, but didn't hear any voices or footfalls. If there were any people in the building, they weren't walking around this area. She turned to head back to the office where E-jekt worked.

Movement outside the front doors caught her attention. A pair of janitors came in the front doors, a mechanized cart full of cleaning supplies following behind them. Keandra ignored them as she went back to join E-jekt.

"How's it going?"

"All right. Their security doesn't seem too strict. But there are a lot of files. It'll take me a while to find what we need."

Keandra leaned against the window, looking into the parking lot. Besides their SUV, only three cars remained in the lot.

"Take whatever time you need. Cleaners are here, but otherwise we have the place to ourselves. There might be a few stragglers on another floor, but it doesn't look like anyone's on patrol."

She stood behind E-jekt, glancing over his shoulder until he let out a discreet cough. She took the signal for what it was and headed back out of the office. There wasn't any place for her to sit there, so she returned to the open room. The cleaning staff saw her, smiling and waving as they continued toward the elevators, their cart audibly clunking along behind them. Keandra dropped into a chair, leaning back and lacing her fingers behind her head. She straightened out her legs and stretched her back, bending backward until her spine shifted with a sharp *crack*.

She sighed, relaxed, and sat up in the chair, dropping her hands to the table in front of her. The elevator bell *bong*ed as the doors opened on the top floor, and she heard the idle chatter of the cleaning staff as they exited the elevator and started their janitorial duties.

<Keandra, there's a problem.>

I knew this was too easy. Keandra hurried back to the office, wondering what the situation was. If it was an emergency, E-jekt would have said as much. When she arrived, he swiveled around and rubbed his forehead.

"So I found the files, without a doubt. The security they have here is a bit of a joke. Their ice is at least ten years old. That's not the problem. The issue is that these files, and just these files, are under a special trigger. Anytime they're accessed, by anyone, it sends out an alert. I don't know who to. I can trace the signal once it's sent, but I can't guarantee that will work."

"Can you block it?"

"No. If I could, we wouldn't have a problem. It's wired into the data itself. So I'd have to access the data to be able to reach the alert, but *any* accessing of the data will trigger it. The only possible way would be to take the entire facility offline. If we do that, it will stall the message, but it will keep trying and as soon as it's reconnected to the Matrix, the message will get sent."

"What about Freyr? Do you think he could do anything?"

E-jekt shook his head again with a frown. "He might be able to help trace the signal, or even do a better job of it, but he still won't be able to stop it from going out."

Keandra dropped into a crouch and pressed her back against the wall. "Great. So our options are to trigger the alert right now, grab the data, and run. Or, to try and take the entire building offline, dig up the data and run, and hope by the time they get back online it won't matter?"

"Pretty much."

"Looks like Paz might get her wish."

TWENTY-FIVE

Keandra frowned. "The weird part I can't figure out is why this piece of data is kept under a special lock and key. You said their security was out of date, except for the part centering around the info dealing with this complex. That leads me to think whoever that alert goes to, it's not someone affiliated with Gildhall Construction."

E-jekt nodded, rocking back and forth in the chair. "That was my thinking as well. I even checked into other datastores to see if they had similar alarms, but the few I checked didn't."

Keandra sighed heavily, dropping the rest of the way to the floor. She supported her head with her hands as she thought through the problem. If they didn't have that information, it meant they were going in blind. They'd have no idea what they were doing or where they were going while entering a facility that potentially had military-grade security. The best-case scenario she could imagine was a trip to a DocWagon hospital.

Alternatively, they could retrieve the data, and let the owners of the facility know someone accessed records that were several years old. Keandra couldn't envision any practical reason to access those records that didn't involve some type of illegal activity, and she imagined the facility's staff would come to the same conclusion. That meant they'd go on alert, making them that much harder to infiltrate. It was a slightly better scenario than going in blind, but not by much.

That, of course, assumed they were the ones who would receive the alert. It could go to a third party, or a company no longer affiliated with the facility. But thinking along those lines was foolish. She'd much rather prepare for the worst scenario than be caught off guard taking a reckless chance. It appeared they had no real choice if they didn't want to abandon the run right now.

"How can we take the facility offline for as long as possible?"

"As I said, a lot of the tech here is old and outdated. That includes the building itself. They had it retrofitted to support wireless networking inside the building, but the main building itself still requires a hardline connection to the Matrix. The entry point for that hardline is in the basement. If we destroy it..."

E-jekt spread his hands, not needing to finish the thought. Keandra chuckled. It looked like her flippant comment had been more accurate than she anticipated. Paz was going to love this.

"Get ready to access the data once we take the server offline. I'll tell Paz the good news and meet her at the entrance."

E-jekt passed her the cardkey and Keandra clipped it to her waistband. As she walked out to the front lobby, she sent a message.

<Slight change of plans. Paz, we need you and your explosives.>

She almost felt bad for Lance, being in the car with her when she read the message. Keandra wasn't surprised when she came around the front entrance and saw Paz running up to the front doors. The dwarf bounced from one foot to the other while she waited for Keandra to let her in. She hadn't even stepped through before she started asking questions.

"What do you need blown up? Where is it?"

"Come on, we're going to the basement."

Keandra led the way, using the cardkey to get into the central room. The janitors had progressed far enough that she could see them cleaning the floors around the open area on the third floor. They kept their eyes down, focused on their work and oblivious to anything happening on any of the other floors. In the elevator, Keandra pushed the button for the basement, but it didn't light up. She placed her ID card in front of the scanner and tried again, and this time the circle around the button lit up and the doors shut.

When the doors cracked open, everything was dark on the other side. Keandra heard water rushing through large pipes, and humid, warm air struck her in the face. The lights overhead flickered on, illuminating an underground space where she had to stoop to avoid hitting her head on one of the pipes hanging down from the ceiling. Clearly this area was not designed for regular visitors. Some pipes were cold and had beads of condensation on their exteriors, while others were hot enough that she broke into a sweat when she got too close.

"What're we looking for down here?"

"E-jekt said there should be a hardwired Matrix access point near the center of the building, on the south side. We need to take it out."

"Disable it?"

"Permanently."

Keandra and Paz set off toward where the access point should be. Paz had no trouble navigating the cramped space, but the taller Keandra had a more difficult time. Even when there weren't pipes running just below the ceiling, she couldn't stand upright. God forbid a troll ever needed to come down here to perform any maintenance.

Up ahead, they saw a large pillar with several fans blowing hot air through the rest of the basement. The roar of the motors was deafening, and the air smelled stale. As the fans spun, Keandra caught glimpses of glowing LEDs on the other sides of the blades. This had to be the Matrix access point.

She leaned forward to make sure Paz could hear her. "I think that's it. Set your explosives and I'll meet you back at the elevator."

Paz gave her a thumbs-up, so Keandra hurried back to their exit point. She called for the elevator and got in, pulling the emergency hold button so it wouldn't leave. It didn't take Paz long to finish her work and she soon joined Keandra.

"Ready?"

Keandra nodded, so Paz pressed the detonator. As soon as they heard the first explosion, Keandra pressed the button and the doors eased shut. They caught a glimpse of a wave of fire rolling through the basement before they closed completely. Even so, Keandra felt the heat emanating through them. She pressed the button for the first floor, but it didn't light up. She tried swiping her badge and pressing the button, but again the elevator refused to respond.

<E-jekt, the elevator won't go up.>

<The explosion set off the fire alarm, and everyone is being ordered to evacuate. It shut down the elevators completely. You're going to need to find another way out.>

<Stairs?>

<None to the basement. Elevator access only.>

That seemed like a serious safety hazard and significant flaw in building design, especially for a construction company. Keandra looked up at the ceiling. If the only way out was in the elevator, that just meant they would need to go up the shaft even if the elevator wouldn't move.

She tapped Paz's shoulder. "Give me a boost."

Paz laced her fingers together for Keandra to step into. Without even a grunt of effort, she lifted the much lighter woman to the ceiling so she could open the hatch and climb on top. She turned around to offer help, but Paz waved her away. With a strong jump that shook the elevator, Paz leaped up high enough to grab the edge of the access hatch and climbed up next to Keandra.

The shaft was lit by small maintenance lights embedded in the wall. Keandra was glad to see a ladder next to the lights, stretching up as far as she could see. Paz took the lead, her heavy limbs clanking on the rungs as she scrambled up. They were halfway up to the first floor when Paz stopped, forcing Keandra to halt as well.

"Old man says he got the data, but emergency vehicles showed up."

"Go to the second floor, and hurry."

Paz didn't ask questions, but continued climbing, moving so fast that she quickly outpaced Keandra. By the time they crossed the threshold for the first floor, the elevator roared to life. The motor at the top of the shaft *whirred*, and the cab climbed toward them.

Keandra moved faster, fueled by adrenaline. Paz was already at the second-floor door and thrust her hand into the seam between the doors. They screeched as she forced her metal fingers through and pulled the doors open. She jumped out of the shaft and onto the second floor, unslinging her gun in midair.

Before Keandra reached the second floor, she heard the doors open beneath her and a couple of firemen discussing their plan of attack as they entered the elevator. Their conversation cut short with a shout.

"Who goes there?" one of the firemen called out as he shined a light up through the open hatch.

The beam danced around the shaft as the firefighters attempted to see anything in the elevator shaft. Keandra swung through the doors with Paz's help before being spotted. It didn't seem to matter as the new arrivals noticed the opening to the second floor.

"North stairs," Keandra commanded.

She took off running in that direction with Paz striding along next to her. When they ran past the open room in the center, Keandra glanced down and spotted the reflection of red flashing lights bouncing off the furniture and walls on the ground floor. Several emergency service personal clustered around the elevator, one halfway in the cab. None looked up in her direction as they fled to the stairwell.

Keandra stopped when they reached the door, taking a moment to catch her breath. She gulped down air, and forced herself to slow down. After a few failed attempts, she transitioned from panting to heavy breathing. She held her breath for a moment and listened. The voices in the lobby reached her, but that was it. Easing the door open, she continued to listen. No sounds of movement or other people talking. It looked like they might be in the clear.

The two women slipped into the stairwell, moving with as much stealth as they could muster. Even when she took slow steps, Paz had a heavy tread each time her metal foot came down on the concrete. As long as no one came into the stairwell, it shouldn't matter. Keandra reached the edge and leaned over the railing, looking down and then up. Everything appeared abandoned. She climbed down the steps, walking at a steady pace that seemed silent compared to her companion.

The door beneath them burst open with a crash, revealing a firefighter dressed in full flame-resistant gear and wearing a mask shielding his face. Keandra couldn't tell what metatype the firefighter was, or even if it was a man.

A security officer pushed past the firefighter and looked up, spotting Keandra before she could duck out of sight behind the railing. "They're in here!"

As soon as the man shouted, Paz turned around and sprinted up the stairs, all attempts at stealth forgotten. Keandra skipped stairs as she climbed, getting to the third floor with as much expediency as possible. She heard the heavy footfalls of boots behind her as more security joined the pursuit.

A loud crash echoed down from the third floor, and as Keandra rounded the last flight of stairs she saw Paz had knocked down the door with a bull rush. Most of it lay on the floor of the hallway, smashed to pieces.

At least the hallway looked empty from here. Keandra ran after Paz, following her as she turned a corner and sprinted toward the rear of the building. As she ran, Paz slung her rifle back over her shoulder and grabbed something from her pouch. She slid to a stop in front of one of the offices, glancing through the doorway, but then continued her sprint down the hall. Keandra didn't have time to ask what she searched for.

Three doors later, Paz stopped and looked again, this time running into the office. Keandra followed her, slamming the door shut as soon as she was in the room. She moved around the desk and put her feet against the wall to get enough strength to slide it in front of the door. It was a flimsy barricade at best, but better than nothing. Then she moved to join Paz over at the window.

The yard behind the building stretched out in front of them as far as Keandra saw in the limited light available. The warehouse was off to her right, but various pieces of heavy machinery dotted the rest of the field. It took her a moment to realize what Paz searched for, and then she saw it: a crane, situated at the near edge of the field.

"You can't be serious. That jump is easily twenty meters. Not even you can make that."

"I know. I was multi-tasking."

Before Keandra could ask what Paz meant, the crane shifted. Someone was repositioning it so the arm would be closer to the building. It dropped to the height of the third floor and stopped only a few meters outside the window. Paz grinned and kicked the glass, shattering it in a shower of glimmering crystals that caught the bright light from the crane's cockpit. She took the cord she had been unraveling and handed one end of it to Keandra.

"Just in case."

With those words, Paz backed up a few steps and took a running leap out the window. She easily crossed the distance, slamming into the arm of the crane with a grunt. She hooked her arms around it and took a moment to swing her body around until she was on the interior of the lattice structure. She fed her end of the cord through the crossed metal supports, wrapping it around her body and feeding it around her arms.

"Jump or swing, your choice!"

Keandra looked down at the cord in her hands and then at the distance to the arm. The jump itself didn't seem that difficult, but the impact at the end would be the hard part. If it knocked the wind out of Paz, what would it do to her?

She looked down at the three-story fall and swallowed. The door behind her cracked as the security officers slammed their shoulders into it. The desk began to slide across the floor. She heard one of them call for axes to break the door down. She was running out of time.

Keandra quickly tied the cord around her waist. She hoped the knot was right, but the dark side of her humor reminded her she'd find out soon enough. Then she grabbed the slack in front of her and wrapped it around her forearm.

Backing up from the window, she took a few running steps and then leaped into the open air as the wooden door splintered open behind her.

TWENTY-SIX

Keandra reached out to grab the arm of the crane, but the impact into the metal framework knocked the wind out of her. By the time she recovered and tried to grab onto something, the arm was out of reach and she tipped back toward the ground. Keandra screamed as she began to fall.

Paz didn't try to grab her, instead pulling up the cord's slack as fast as her arms could haul it in. Keandra's scream cut off with a jerk as the cord snapped around her arm and stopped her descent after only a few meters. It bit hard into her arm, but she was safe.

The crane came to life, lowering until Keandra could put her feet on the ground. As soon as she could, she unwrapped the cord from her arm and rubbed at the line dug into her flesh. Paz jumped off the crane and sprinted into the darkness. Keandra followed, assuming the vehicle must be in that direction.

It was only a short run to the SUV, and the passenger door stood open. Keandra climbed in to find Paz was already in the driver's seat. E-jekt rushed up, wheezing as he got into the backseat and slammed the door behind him. Paz took off, not bothering to turn her lights on until they were back on the road and out of sight of the facility.

Keandra rubbed her arm, which still felt raw. It was tender, but she could rub it lightly without any real pain. Considering the situation she'd just been in, it was a win. Looking down, she realized she still had the cord tied around her waist, and fumbled with the knot, taking a few tries before she got it undone.

E-jekt had recovered his breath, so she asked. "Did it work?"

He nodded. "As soon as you brought down the connection, the fire alarm sounded. I cracked the datastore and copied everything. The alert triggered, but it couldn't get out. Until they fix the Matrix access, that alert will be stuck on repeat, trying to deliver the alert."

"How long do you think that will take?"

"It depends on how thorough you were when you destroyed the access point."

Paz chuckled and glanced at E-jekt in the rearview mirror. "Let's just say they're gonna need a drill to even reach the pile of wires and tech. They might have some flooding problems too."

E-jekt didn't share her humor, so Paz shrugged and focused on the road. The ork traced some numbers in the air. Keandra wasn't sure if he was interfacing with his AR or was just doing it out of habit.

"If we're talking total destruction, they'll probably do a complete overhaul. No point in making it a wired connection again, even if they could find someone to install it. I figure if they've got the funds, they could have it back up and online within a week. If they have any of the tech on hand for one of their construction projects, less. Maybe three or four days."

Keandra thought that through. "So we assume three days. We want to make sure we're going in before they know we're coming. You said Gildhall might have Yakuza ties—if so, they'll have it up and running as fast as possible. That gives us tonight to get some rest and recover, tomorrow to plan and supply, and then we drive out to the facility the day after. We can start figuring out what we need tomorrow morning, but for tonight, I think we'd be best served not strategizing. We've all been running on fumes for the past few days, and we need to be at our best for what's coming up."

Keandra took the silence for assent, unable to see the others' faces in the darkness. The occasional street lamp flashing by gave her brief glimpses, but it wasn't enough for a read. Still, if anyone objected, she knew they all felt comfortable enough to voice their concerns.

Instead, she turned her thoughts to crawling into bed, sliding under the covers, and falling asleep. Just the idea brought a smile to her face and made her start to relax. Within twenty minutes, that idea became a reality as she entered their hotel room and collapsed on her bed. She was asleep even before Paz returned from parking the SUV.

When the early morning sun slanted through the window and hit Keandra in the face, she cursed herself and everyone else for not remembering to pull the curtains before they all crashed. She sat on the edge of the bed and examined her arm. The skin was still red and raw, the scrapes forming a spiral pattern that ran down her forearm. If it was a little more even, it could've passed for an artistic design.

To make sure no one else suffered the same rude awakening she had, Keandra pulled the curtains shut. Hands out in front of her, she felt her way through the room, sticking to the far wall to make sure she didn't accidentally kick a bed or Lance's outstretched legs.

Reaching the bathroom, she closed the door before turning on the lights. While she cleaned up, her mind tumbled over the future and what they were hoping to accomplish. She ran down her list of contacts; was there anyone she could tap who could assist them here? Besides Victoria, she couldn't think of anyone she trusted who had ties to the California Free State. It pained her to think that even with the extensive network and web she had created, it was mostly useless the moment she left UCAS territory. Then again, she'd never had reason to test if before now.

By the time she re-entered the main room, she saw the curtains had been pulled back, and both E-jekt and Lance were up. The ork sat by the small table, nursing a cup of soykaf she smelled from across the room. It was a little burned, but it still called to her. E-jekt handed her a full mug and she cupped it in both hands, taking a moment to close her eyes and just enjoy the aroma and warmth between her fingers.

"Thanks. You know me well, my friend. I'm heading down to one of the conference rooms to call Victoria. I think I might be able to convince her to connect with one of her contacts, someone who could get us more information. If Paz gets up, start looking at the schematics and seeing what you can find as far as weak points and escape routes. You know the drill."

Keandra headed to the hotel lobby, passing a few other guests on the way. The ground floor contained several conference rooms, ranging from a single table to a full conference hall with thirty chairs around a long table. The receptionist handed her a key card and pointed her to one of the unoccupied smaller rooms. Most of the rooms were empty at this hour; only one other was occupied, its glass frosted over to block views of the interior.

As soon as she closed the door, the window facing the hall shimmered and frosted over too, blocking the view in both directions. She pulled out her commlink, remotely connecting to the hub in the center of the table, and called Victoria. When the woman answered, her avatar appeared.

"Keandra, my dear, how are you doing? I trust you reached your destination without incident?"

"Yes, I did. Thank you very much for your help with everything. We wouldn't have been able to make it if it weren't for your assistance."

The avatar spread its hands and offered a bow. The motion looked forced, and completely inappropriate for Victoria. But that was what happened when the meeting software tried to dynamically animate an avatar based solely on a person's voice input. Keandra wondered if there was an etiquette setting somewhere that would change its behavioral responses.

"It was nothing. You've been one of my favorite clients over the years. I hope you'll continue to be, and won't let something as small as a national border or two negatively impact our relationship."

"Of course not. That's actually why I'm reaching out to you now. I was wondering if you might be willing to put me in touch with your contact who dug up that information the last time we talked. I was hoping I might be able to get more details from him. It deals with that big potential threat we talked about."

There was silence on the line for a moment; the avatar stood with her hands clasped together in front of her stomach. She tilted her head from one side to the other, a smile on her unchanging face. It was a little unnerving and made Keandra uncomfortable, even more so than the silence.

"I ask you this as a confidante and not simply as one of my clients: is the threat you proposed real?"

"Very—I wouldn't have left if it wasn't. We have a plan; we just need some help."

That may have been a bit of a stretch of the truth, but it wasn't a complete falsehood. Overall, they had a plan, and the first parts of it had been completed. It was only the last part they hadn't figured out yet.

"I'll arrange a meeting. I'll tell him you're there to pick up a package for me. He's a very private person, and I don't think he would otherwise agree. I'll warn him you might have questions, but be gentle. He can be a bit skittish."

"Thanks, Victoria. What do I owe you?"

"Get through this alive and bring me my package, and we'll call it even. I'll message you the details once it's arranged."

Keandra terminated the connection, glad to be rid of the generic avatar using Victoria's appearance. That had gone better than she'd hoped for, especially if the only price she had to pay was delivering a package. Of course, it meant she'd need to find a way to smuggle herself back into Seattle, but that was a problem to tackle after they dealt with the threat to Hestaby. That also assumed they survived the assault on the weapons facility.

She returned to the room to find her companions gathered around a line-drawing display of what she could only guess was the facility. Paz and Lance sat on opposite beds, and E-jekt was in the same seat as when she'd left earlier.

The facility looked impressive, even in skeleton form. There was only one entrance, and Keandra knew it would be heavily guarded. The small building connected to a stairwell that would lead them to an expansive first floor containing small offices, large labs, two big chambers that looked like hangars, and access to an elevator. The elevator accessed nine subterranean floors of similarly laid out levels. A few of the rooms, such as some that looked like they could be hangars or firing ranges, spanned multiple floors.

"Tell me you have good news."

E-jekt shook his head with a frown. "Not really. Unless they've changed the layout of the facility, there's only one entrance and exit point. Any other way in would involve digging through an unknown amount of dirt and then trying to break through the walls. Not quiet, not fast, and something we're not equipped for."

"Any notes on the security?"

"They left most of that information out of the plans, unless it was something that needed to be hardwired into the system. So we have almost no information about cameras or turrets or the like. Those could have easily been added later, and probably were, since the original construction."

Keandra walked through the display; it shimmered briefly as she passed through before returning to normal. She flopped down on the bed next to Paz and stared at the wire model while E-jekt continued giving the less-than-pleasant news.

"What we do know is that they have an alarm hardwired into a steel door that can cover the entire entrance stairway. I'm guessing that's rigged to an alarm of some kind. That means if there's a threat, they can seal it, and nothing gets in or out unless it can either open the door or cut through twenty centimeters of solid steel."

"Great. So we have to be quiet getting in." When she said that, Keandra turned to glance at Paz out of the corner of her eye. The dwarf shrugged in response. This was getting better by the second. If the stakes weren't so high, Keandra would have seriously considered bailing on the whole run. But any time that thought crossed her mind, she envisioned what Mr. Johnson would do if he had such a weapon at his fingertips.

"A facility that large needs to have some way to get air. If it's fully staffed, trying to filter air and be self-sufficient would be a logistical nightmare, not to mention expensive."

E-jekt typed a few commands into his display and the HVAC system overlaid the floor plan. Most of the vents connected to a couple of central core chimneys that all converged in one of the large chambers on the top floor.

He highlighted the chamber. "As near as I can determine, this is the primary air circulation chamber. I don't know what to make of it, since I don't have a topographical overlay of the area. But the top half of this chamber is made up entirely of heavy machinery. It has several vents stretching above the rest of the level. It's so cramped there's no way to get through it without taking the entire system down, which would make it hard to breathe while we're down there. I doubt it would provide an easy access point."

"So the only way we can get in and out is through the main access building, which can be blocked with a giant steel door we'll have no way of moving or cutting through."

E-jekt nodded, looking as pleased as if he just learned he'd have no Matrix access for a week. When she shifted her gaze, she saw Lance had a similar expression. Paz looked disappointed, her head hanging over the edge of the bed and her arms swinging back and forth just above the floor. Keandra understood their disappointment and despondence.

Her commlink pinged to let her know she had a private message. She pulled it out and checked it.

<Meet him at Las Palmas on Broadway in thirty minutes. He will be at the table in the front corner on your right side. He'll be wearing a suit and have a small package on the table in front of him. Good luck. -V>

Keandra stood, grinning like a Cheshire cat. Even Paz looked up as she walked toward the door with a bounce in her step.

"Where are you going?"

"To get us a way in."

TWENTY-SEVEN

Keandra got out of the cab directly across from the restaurant. She paid the driver with a certified credstick, getting a raised eyebrow from him, but no questions. She didn't want to have Mr. Johnson interrupting her meeting, especially if her contact was the skittish type. She would need time to massage the desired result, something she couldn't do if she had to check over her shoulder constantly for a strike team.

She spotted her contact through the front window of the restaurant, sitting where Victoria indicated. The human male wore a suit, well-made and clearly custom cut to fit his frame, based on the way it moved every time he reached out to fiddle with the package on the table. The fabric had a slight shimmer to it, catching the sunlight and making his clothes seem almost liquid. His entire body vibrated near his waist, a clear sign that he bounced his legs underneath the table. Victoria was right: he seemed like the type to bolt and run at the first sign of a threat.

Keandra entered the restaurant and was surprised at how noisy it was. The sheer number of people talking served as a communal din, drowning out the possibility of hearing anyone who wasn't at the same table. From the kitchens, the sound of something sizzling penetrated the ruckus of conversations.

The elven woman behind the front counter flashed a practiced smile at Keandra and opened her mouth to offer assistance, but Keandra ignored her. She turned to the right, walking into the main part of the restaurant and approaching her contact's table. She had to swerve around a waiter carrying a tray burdened with five plates of steaming food. When she reached the table, the man gave a small start, so small she might not have noticed it if she wasn't expecting him to be on edge. She offered a smile she hoped was comforting and pulled out the chair across from him, gliding into it with a grace formed from years of practice.

"Nice to meet you, Mister...?"

The man shook his head. "I'd prefer to keep names out of this."

"As you wish. Our mutual associate sent me to retrieve something. Is that it?"

The man nodded and slid the small box across the table to her He jerked his hand off it as soon as it was halfway across the table, as if expecting it to burn him. Keandra took her time, easing both hands out to pick it up and resting it in her lap. It was light and didn't sound as if it had any loose parts inside. The box was about the size of her hand, and only a few centimeters tall. Easy enough to transport, even if she needed to find a way to smuggle herself back into Seattle.

"So we're done now?"

Again Keandra flashed him a smile, leaning back and trying to look comfortable. She shifted to the side and crossed a leg over her knee.

"It would be suspicious if we didn't make the pretense of ordering a meal and enjoying a nice lunch together, wouldn't you agree? We wouldn't want to do anything to attract undue attention."

"Right, of course. You have a point."

He settled back in his chair, but the table still shook from the force of him bouncing his heels. The water in the glasses sloshed up the sides; hers, untouched as yet, threatened to spill over. She needed to put him at ease if she wanted to get anything useful out of him. For now, it was time to focus on simple actions, ones that might distract him from his nervous energy.

"Have you ordered yet? Do you know what's good?"

"No, not yet. But their enchiladas are very tasty. Some of the best in the city. They claim people come here from other countries just to try them."

Keandra picked up her menu and looked it over, turning the pages to make it seem like she was reading, but most of her attention focused on the man across from her. As soon as she started treating their meeting like a normal lunch encounter, he visibly relaxed and stilled his legs. He flipped through the menu, scanning the pages briefly before turning them one after the next.

A waiter came by and put a bowl of chips and salsa down between them. Keandra smelled the tomatoes and herbs without needing to waft her hand over the bowl. It made her appreciate the lunch appointment even more. She ordered the enchiladas, and he did the same.

The waiter took the menus and departed. Keandra tucked the package under her leg, rising to the balls of her foot to make sure not to crush it. Then she put her hands on the table in a nonaggressive position. Her companion seemed at ease now, or at least closer to it, and she didn't want to jeopardize it.

"Have you worked with Victoria often?" she asked.

"A couple of times. We met a few years ago at a conference in Seattle. She can be very convincing."

"And relaxing. She's good at putting even strangers at ease."

Her associate nodded again, his eyes focusing on a distant point above her head as he lost himself to memory. A smile teased at the edges of his mouth, letting Keandra know she was on the right track.

"Have you ever been to her shop, and had some of the tea she brews? I swear there's some magic embedded in it, but she assures me it's just a technique she's practiced for years due to her passion for good tea."

"I have, in fact. That's what I was just thinking of."

The smile broke fully across his face as he spoke, and his gaze came back down to focus on Keandra. It was working; she just needed it to keep going. Let him bring it up, rather than pushing him into it. He would get there eventually, it would just take some time to loosen him up.

"She said you had some questions?"

Her grin deepened at his words. This was the opportunity she needed.

"Do you remember the ownership papers you looked up? Well, there's a slight problem with that area. It's something that my team and I are more than capable of taking care of. In fact, that's why we're here, in addition to running an errand for Victoria. I won't worry you about the details. It's a minor thing, and not worth your attention."

He visibly relaxed when she offered him the easy out, releasing a breath that Keandra didn't realize he'd been holding. That was the key: give him the opportunity to extract himself and not ask him to do anything that might incriminate him. As long as she stayed in that territory, she could keep him engaged and get what she needed now that she was inside his initial barriers.

"What do you need me to do?"

"Well, you work in some type of approval area for the city of Sacramento, right?"

In reality, she knew exactly who he worked for, but she didn't want to tip his paranoia. This also kept him feeling useful. It wouldn't sabotage his relationship with Victoria because of a trust violation.

"That's right. I have to approve building permits, land surveys, and the like. A lot of it is automated these days, but a few things still require a pair of actual eyes to look over and make sure it all checks out."

As the conversation distracted him, Keandra reached down and accessed her commlink underneath the table. She kept her arm still as her fingers worked. E-jekt installed multiple custom programs on all their devices. As long as she manipulated thinks in the right way, she'd have everything they needed.

"I don't suppose you could grant me a brief view of the permits? My associates need to verify some information, and those records are sealed. I don't need much, just need to verify a couple of items to make sure everything is in order. Depending on what we find, my employers might need to contact an auditing firm."

He chewed on his lip and his brow furrowed as he visibly squirmed in his seat. This was the part where he might offer some resistance, and Keandra had anticipated as much. She allowed him to squirm for a few seconds longer, turning over the possibility and thinking about it. She needed him to consider the options and weigh the risks. When he took a deep breath, Keandra spoke first, jumping over him and stopping his words before they left his mouth.

"Of course, we wouldn't expect you to do this for free. We'd be more than willing to pay any necessary access fees for your department, as well as any fees associated with getting an audit process started. I imagine that's an expensive endeavor."

He paused, rubbing the back of his neck as he glanced around, as if expecting someone to be spying on their conversation. After making sure no one was close enough to eavesdrop over the din of the restaurant, he leaned forward and gestured for her to come close.

"How much are we talking?"

"I'm sure that can be negotiated."

He settled back, probably realizing how suspicious it looked for him to be leaning across the table to talk to his companion. Keandra looked down at the table and counted to three before she raised her gaze back to his face.

"There's something else to consider." She waited again, until he couldn't contain his curiosity any longer.

"What?"

"I'm sure our investigators would find some violations as well. You'd be the hero of your department after finding some serious transgressions. That has to come with some sort of bonus. Or if not, maybe a promotion? Such hard work is usually recognized, especially when it results in additional fines or other revenue."

His smile returned in full force. Keandra matched it, genuinely glad to see him warming to her suggestion.

The waiter approached from behind her, setting down two plates of food covered with so much melted cheese it was impossible to see anything else. The sharp, nutty smell made Keandra's mouth water. The lunch appointment had definitely been a wise choice. She remained silent, letting him think it over while she carved off a piece of the enchilada. Glancing up, she kept part of her attention on her companion at all times.

Finally, he pointed his fork at her. "You bring up good points."

"Does that mean what I hope it does?"

"I don't suppose it would do much harm to provide a cursory glance."

"Wonderful to hear. As I said, a brief glance is all that's required."

He pulled out his commlink and logged into the private corporate server. Meanwhile, Keandra ran a program to capture his access information, credentials that E-jekt could use to forge identities as a professional auditing firm. She pretending to look over the forms as she waited for her commlink to record the necessary details.

"Thank you. You've been more helpful than you know."

TWENTY-EIGHT

An hour passed before Keandra returned to the Omni. Thanks to her extended lunch, she learned that her new contact's name was Tyler. He was willing to share that information after only another thirty minutes of casual and deliberately disarming conversation. More importantly, they had the necessary details to gain access through the front door.

Now that she'd solved that problem, it was time to see how the rest of the team was faring with planning the raid. When she entered, Lance stood on the other side of the doorway, his sword drawn. He put it away when he recognized her.

Paz sat at the head of the bed with her primary rifle in front of her. Next to it were a couple assault-grade weapons and a wide collection of explosives of various types and sizes. Currently, she was loading magazines from two boxes of bullets. There was more firepower on that bed than any one person could carry, even a dwarf with three robotic limbs.

The table was cluttered with a bunch of circuitry. E-jekt bent over the disassembled gadgets, alternating between fiddling with the hardware and accessing an AR display at his side. Even though his display was plainly visible, Keandra couldn't identify what he was doing.

"I take it we have a plan?"

E-jekt pushed himself back from the table and turned to Keandra. He called up the wireframe display of the facility and pointed to a circular room on the second-to-lowest floor.

"Freyr is confident that the controls for the weapons are in this room. Each floor has its own network isolated from the Matrix, as well as from each other. That means we'll need to get to the eighth floor before we can plug him into the network. With the stolen credentials, I created the foundation for an entire shell company responsible for governmental audits. It's impossible to say how far that will get us. It might just get us in the front door. Hopefully you'll be able to convince them to let us throughout the entire facility. However, assuming we can only get past the stairwell…"

He tapped a few times in the air and a red line traced through the facility from the stairwell to the objective. It bypassed the elevator, taking a combination of stairs and jumping through the two-story testing rooms. The facility didn't have a single staircase connecting multiple floors. The most it had were stairs going from one level to the next.

"If we can't access the elevator, this is the most efficient route to the eighth floor. I bypassed a couple areas that are likely to have the tightest security: choke points, large hallways that look like they were designed for a turret, and so on. Unfortunately, there's no way to know what resistance we might be facing."

A few more button presses, and a green line traced a different route from the stairs to their target. This path went outside the blueprint and jumped back in at what looked like random places. E-jekt grunted and adjusted the map, adding the HVAC vents, and Keandra saw the new route travelled through several of the larger ducts.

"This is an optional route, taking advantage of the ventilation system. According to the specifications, even I could fit through these ducts. It would be tight, but I could manage."

Keandra nodded. She wished they had more information so they could be better prepared, but there was nothing for it. They wouldn't be able to get more information until they entered the building. At least now they knew where they were going and the best ways to get there, hopefully undetected.

"And lastly," E-jekt said, "there's this gem we almost overlooked."

A single room on the first floor flashed. It was on the far end of the floor and stuck out further in that direction than any of the floors beneath it. It was large, one of the biggest rooms in the facility, but otherwise Keandra couldn't see anything special about it. She waited for E-jekt to explain.

He pulled up a topographic map of the area, layering it over the top of the facility. It took him a moment to get the images lined up correctly, but when he did, she saw what he was talking about. The ground dropped away sharply at the edge of the room he called out, indicating a spot with only a few meters of ground between the edge of the facility and the surface.

"They're very good at covering their tracks, but I caught footage of an APC driving out of the mountain and across the desert. This must be the way they go out and bring in large quantities of supplies. I'd suggest it as a way in, but I think your plan is better than sitting outside waiting for someone to leave."

Keandra couldn't believe their luck. It was far from easy and not even close to guaranteed, but for the first time she felt confident that they were adequately prepared. A lot could still go wrong, but they were better informed than she thought they would be. In the end, that was the most anyone could hope for.

"Sounds like we have our plan, and faster than we hoped. How are our supplies?"

Paz picked up a small handgun and tossed it to Keandra. She caught it and turned it over in her hand. It didn't have a standard magazine, but rather two small canisters attached to the front and rear grips, looking like it could be used with either one or two hands. She curled her fingers around the grip, seeing how it felt. It was a little lighter than her standard firearm, but the weight was off. Rather than most of it resting in the back in her hand, it was evenly distributed and strained her wrist if she held it with only one hand.

"What's this?"

"Ares S-III Super Squirt. A lot quieter than your current piece, and it's loaded with neuro-stun. You hit bare skin with that, and it'll knock out a troll. Useless if you hit armor, though, so pay attention to where you're aiming. Even got a concealed holster for it, so you should be able to carry it in as long as we don't get searched. Never hurts to have more options."

Keandra was impressed. Hopefully she wouldn't need to use it, but better to be prepared. "Not bad. You picked this up today?"

"I found a guy, convinced him to part with some of his rare stock. Also got enough fireworks to bring the mountain down on the place if we don't wanna take the quiet route. I think you know my vote."

E-jekt sighed, and Keandra got the impression they'd had this argument already. "I told you. That steel covering is designed to withstand an excessive amount of explosive force, far more than you could bring."

"I know. I meant once we're inside. There's more than one way to disable a console. I took the construction place offline, didn't I?"

E-jekt raised a hand, conceding the point.

Keandra stepped in, hoping to appease both her teammates. "We'll take some of them, but not all. We're supposed to be auditors, not a military strike force. I'm pretty sure we can pass you and Lance off as a security detail. After all, we *have* left Sacramento and gone into the wilderness, and clearly E-jekt and I aren't meant for the dangers of the road. But, I think they'll pick up on something amiss if you walk in carrying an arsenal."

Paz grumbled and began sorting the explosives, dividing them into two separate piles. Keandra looked over at Lance; he offered a nod and a smirk, enough to let her know he was ready. The advantage of his specialty was that he traveled light, and was almost always prepared to jump into the fray.

"If we have what we need, then I don't see any reason why we should wait any longer. Every minute we sit here just gives Mr. Johnson more time to catch up with us. Let's roll out tonight after sunset. That still gives you two a couple hours to finish your prep. Then we can drive out to the facility and start our 'audit.'"

Paz looked up from her sorting. "Just one question, boss. How're we gonna get close? That SUV doesn't exactly look the part."

E-jekt answered the question. "I didn't mention? Our SUV is now registered as a government vehicle."

"How the frag did you manage that?"

"I work magic—you should know that by now."

Keandra knew she could count on E-jekt to get the job done. He continued to exceed her high expectations. "Since we have that covered, will we be good to set out in a couple of hours?"

When the others gave their assent, Keandra stretched out on the open bed, intending to review information about the permits associated with the facility. If she was going to pass herself off as an auditor, she needed to be knowledgeable.

Something told her that the guards they were about to face would be more difficult to intimidate than the overnight shift working at a manufacturing facility in the middle of the Tir Tairngire wilderness. At least she now knew the name of the company that owned the facility: Crystal Techtronix.

After about an hour, her head ached from digging through volumes of legalese. Copes of Tyler's forms covered the latest policies and regulations, but it was like reading a different language. She pinched the bridge of her nose in an attempt to clear her mind.

Lance handed her a cup of soykaf, the aroma helping to rejuvenate her. She took it and went back to her research, sipping as she learned about the exact depths that were acceptable for a foundation and the surveys required to be on file to guarantee the safety of any underground water supplies.

When E-jekt and Paz had both finished their work and packed up, it was time to leave. Keandra closed her research, intending to continue it on the drive over. She'd have a couple more hours to prepare while Paz got them to the facility entrance. Keandra did one last inspection in the mirror, making sure she looked every bit the government professional.

As they drove, Keandra kept reading. The final piece she was reviewing proved to be the most useful. E-jekt wrote a script to find a list of differences in the building codes over the last twenty years. While the original paperwork for the facility was acceptable, they would not pass modern requirements for a host of reasons. In most cases, buildings were grandfathered in until they decided to update their paperwork or needed to start additional construction projects. It would be a stretch, but it might give Keandra a plausible enough reason to demand an inspection tour of the structure.

By the time they reached the facility, she finished a brief review of the materials. She was far from an expert, but she hoped she knew enough to pass herself as one. On the plus side, she could use her commlink as a notepad in this role without raising suspicion. She made sure the audio and video capabilities of her commlink were engaged.

"Freyr, you reviewed all the materials for construction audits in this region?"

<I have, both the governmental requirements and local statutes. I'm willing to provide assistance in your façade to pass yourself off as a professional. I have also downloaded the vast majority of my processing functions to your commlink. This means I am no longer able to maintain a watch over the surveillance mechanisms you may encounter.>

"That's fine. We're in it now and it's time to take the leap."

Keandra twisted around to check on her other companions. E-jekt looked determined, but he couldn't stop fiddling with one of the small electronic boxes he'd been tinkering with back in the hotel room. His fingers trembled as he did so, but he showed no other signs of nervousness. Lance was the picture of calm stillness, only the corner of his mouth rising into a hint of a smile. As she turned back around, Keandra fiddled with her concealed holsters, looking in the mirror to make sure both her weapons couldn't be seen without a thorough search.

"Drive straight up to the gate," Keandra ordered. "I want them to see us coming."

TWENTY-NINE

The entrance to the facility looked unassuming. The landscape around the small, single-story building wasn't marked or marred in any way. It seemed like nothing more than vast, empty scrubland leading up to the base of the mountains. No fence or markers indicated they trespassed on private property, and nothing gave any hint that anything was more than it seemed.

The building itself was no bigger than a shack, and the walls looked hastily constructed. A small metal tower was attached to the back of the building with a couple of antennae flashing in the darkness. A narrow road barely wide enough for the SUV led up a slow incline to the front door. A single Jeep sat parked next to the side wall, closer to the mountain. At best, it looked like a getaway for one person to escape the hubbub of city life.

Paz drove up the road, her taillights creating a red cloud behind them as the dry dust reflected the glow. When they stopped, small rocks crunched under their vehicle, pushing the cloud ahead of them. Keandra stepped out of the SUV, tasting the dust in the back of her throat. She covered her mouth and nose with her hand, but it was a futile effort.

They walked up to the shack's door, Keandra in the lead, with E-jekt close behind her. Paz and Lance brought up the rear, their weapons visible but holstered or sheathed. She opened the door and saw an ork woman behind a desk, sitting with her elbows propped on the table and staring at the door. A console sat behind her, the screen currently turned off.

The ork looked at the newcomers with her eyebrows scrunched together. Keandra noticed how she looked them over completely, taking particular note of their weaponry. It was obvious she was trained, even though she was dressed to look disarming.

"Who the fuck are you?"

Keandra stepped forward and took a deep breath, pulling out her commlink and using it to display the credentials for their shell company. She also displayed AR versions of the forms she'd researched.

"My name is Keandra Tiernay, and I and my associates represent the city of Sacramento. We are here to formally request a tour of your underground facility, to ensure that you are compliant with the necessary changes in permits 605-C and 4390."

"I don't know what you're talking about. What underground stuff? This is just a weather observatory. I'm just an intern."

"I'm sure you're paid to say such things and to lend credence to the illusion. However, I'm fully aware that this building houses the entrance to a facility currently owned by Crystal Techtronix. You can verify my credentials. You'll find they are all in order. We will wait, but keep in mind that until the audit is complete, your organization may be found to be in noncompliance, which would result in a significant daily fine."

The ork looked at her, trying to read her physical cues. Keandra deliberately sighed, trying to look unimpressed and unconcerned with the scrutiny. As the woman continued staring at her, Keandra flipped through a document, ignoring the analysis.

The ork reviewed the credentials Keandra had offered. After a minute, she twisted around to press a button on the console behind her. "There's a local government rep up here. I think you should come talk to her." She turned back to the group and offered a forced smile. "Someone will be up momentarily."

A loud alarm sounded in the room, blaring out twice before going blessedly silent. The sudden noise made the runners jump, but the ork seemed used to it. The ground rumbled under their feet, and Keandra had to steady herself as the floor beneath her shifted. An entire section of the floor shifted back with a heavy grinding sound, revealing a stairway descending into the darkness. The end of the tunnel lit up in a burst of white light as someone opened a door and began climbing the steps.

The new arrival was an elf dressed in slacks and a collared shirt, his sleeves rolled back to his elbows. His stride was surprisingly heavy considering his light frame, and when he shook Keandra's hand, the strength of his grip surprised her. He shook everyone's hand in turn, a welcoming smile on his face the entire time.

"Good evening, good evening. A pleasure to see you. My name is Dr. Goodman, and I'm the director of operations here. Is there something I can help you with?"

Keandra nodded at him. "Thank you, Dr. Goodsman. It was a very long drive out here, and I appreciate being met with proper hospitality. I don't suppose you have an office where we could sit and discuss things? There are some problems with some of your paperwork on record."

The elf's brow furrowed. "That's odd. I thought all our paperwork on file was up to date. You know we haven't undergone any new construction in five years, yes?"

"We're aware of that. However, some policies have changed, and our company is responsible for running the backlogged audits. As such, we need to verify some older work orders, and make sure everything is up to the new codes and standards."

The doctor nodded noncommittally as Keandra spoke. After a moment, he shrugged and gestured for them to follow him back down the stairs. They had just passed through the doorway into the underground structure when the steel door rumbled closed overhead.

The hallway on the other side of the door was as modern and clinical as the shack was old-fashioned and pedestrian. The stark white hallway was a little blinding after the darkness above. Bright lights ran in tracks along the edges where the walls met the ceiling. The tiled floor was so highly polished that it reflected the light above and seemed to glow. Keandra was painfully aware of her group tracking dirt and grime onto the clean surface.

The doctor led them through a side door into a large office. The opposite wall had a panorama scene of a beach at sunset, and the room was filled with the sound of the dark waves lapping at the sand. A bird screeched, sounding as if it came from far over the ocean. The air here was cooler, and managed to carry a faint odor of salt. Keandra thought it might even have a bit of dampness to it. She sat down in front of his desk, while E-Jekt, Lance, and Paz took unobtrusive positions near the door.

The doctor took his seat behind the desk. "Now, shall we get down to business?"

Keandra nodded and pulled up the forms she had on easy recall. She pointed out sections as she spoke. "As you can see, we have two permits that have changed recently. If you aren't familiar with these forms—and I don't expect you to be—please feel free to review them now."

The doctor studied the AR forms, carefully reviewing them one page at a time. When he finished, he leaned back and laced his fingers behind his head. "I was under the impression that our connections would allow us a little bit of leniency in terms of being grandfathered in. Is that not the case anymore?"

"I'm afraid I can't comment on any prior arrangements you might've had."

"Perhaps a new arrangement can be reached."

"You'd need to discuss that with my superiors. I'm not authorized for that, and I'm afraid I can't leave without conducting my survey."

"I see. You don't seem to have left me with a choice."

He leaned forward and pressed a button on his desk, all the while displaying a smile so saccharine that it made Keandra's skin crawl. Some part of her brain screamed to burst into action, but she tamped the impulse down. She'd played her hand well, and was convinced he believed her. It was clear he viewed her as a nuisance, but hopefully a necessary one.

After a few tense moments, a dwarf opened the office door and walked into the room. Her boots clicked against the floor as she entered, disrupting the beach illusion despite the other environmental factors.

"You wanted to see me, sir?"

"Yes, Mel, thank you. Let me introduce you to Keandra Tiernay, our own personal auditor. You're to give her a tour of the facility and provide her with anything she needs to complete a thorough report for her office."

"Everything?"

Keandra noticed the surprised tone in the dwarf's voice and her slightly raised eyebrows when she asked the question. Then again, being asked to divulge any level of corporate secrets would probably be surprising to a wage slave.

"Yes." Dr. Goodsman stood up and extended his hand to Keandra. She rose and shook it. He held onto her hand with a tight grip, tighter than she felt necessary for politeness.

"It truly was a pleasure. I trust you'll understand if I am too preoccupied to accompany you on your tour. Please feel free to ask Mel any questions you might have. While you compile your report, I'll make sure to review your paperwork thoroughly."

"I appreciate your consideration." It took all of Keandra's willpower not to walk out of the office as fast as she could. She kept her pace steady as she followed Mel out and down the hall in the direction they'd come from.

"So, what do you want to look at first?" the dwarf asked.

"Before we start the tour, do you mind if I use the facilities? It was a long drive out here, and it's becoming rather uncomfortable."

"Of course! Right this way."

Mel led them down a couple of turns until she brought them to the bathrooms. Keandra thanked her and went inside, checking to make sure it was completely empty. Once she was sure she had the room to herself, she entered a stall and closed the door. She pulled out her commlink and accessed their private network.

<We don't have much time. The doctor didn't like being told he was no longer considered an exception. I'm guessing he's going to be digging harder into our cover stories. He'll probably just try to get us recalled or even fired, but depending on his connections. I don't know how long it will take him to tear apart our cover story.>

<I still got my explosives.>

<I know, but I'd rather not fight our way through every security team and protocol they have in place. I'm going to try to get our escort to take us to the bottom level as quickly as possible. No reason wasting time if we can help it. E-jekt, do you have Matrix access down here?>

<I do. The "weather towers" are actually network repeaters. I'm pretty sure they're wired all the way through the lower floors. It would make sense. They probably created isolated networks, but still let their people access the Matrix. We're good there.>

<Good. Freyr, you still with us?>

<Affirmative. While I have the ability to evacuate through your commlink's Matrix capabilities, my intention is to remain with you until we access the laboratory on the eighth level.>

<Head's up, boss. She's coming in.>

Keandra closed her commlink and shoved it in her pocket just as the door swung open. She left the stall and went to the sink to wash her hands as Mel poked her head into the room.

"Just making sure everything's okay. We're right outside when you're ready."

Mel stepped back out, and Keandra joined her, not wanting to make their escort any more suspicious than she already was. She was confident the doctor hadn't picked Mel because of her helpful attitude.

"I don't know what area you want to look at first, but normally we start each tour with a walk around the cafeteria. The main cafeteria is on this floor, and it sees the most business by far."

Keandra stopped walking, remaining where she was until their dwarf escort was forced to turn around and look at her.

"We're not a group of interns here to be given a friendly tour. We're sanctioned auditors, here to do our jobs. So if we can skip the pleasantries and the gloss you put on everything, that would be preferred. I don't want to waste your time, and I certainly cannot afford to waste my own. I'm sure you understand."

"Right. Sorry about that. You just get into the groove of things and start rattling on about how things go. Kind of like following a script. Hopefully you won't hold it against me."

The woman was stalling, and Keandra knew it. This was going to be an uphill battle to get what they needed on any reasonable timeline, and she didn't have the luxury of being delicate or manipulating the situation to suit her needs. She needed a more direct approach.

"To save time, I think we should split up. If you can lead us to an access tunnel, Paz here can inspect your fluid system while the rest of us check the rest of the facility."

"Uh, I'm not sure...I mean—" Mel hesitated and shifted her gaze.

Keandra pressed, since she now had the woman off guard. "Unless, of course, there is a problem with efficiency. I am more than willing to bill the extra hours to Crystal Techtronix."

The dwarf cleared her throat. "That won't be necessary. If you'll come with me, there's an access door a few hallways over that leads into the entire guts of the facility. Will that work?"

"Thank you."

True to her word, Mel led them to a door labelled *SERVICE ENTRANCE ONLY*. Keandra noticed that she pulled out a separate key card to unlock the door. All the other doors had opened with a scan from an employee's ID badge. After swiping the unmarked card, Mel put her thumb on a scanner before the latch clicked open.

The door opened into a long tunnel that stretched as far down as they could see. The entire shaft echoed with the sound of rushing water and the steady roar of fan engines far in the distance. A couple ladders were embedded in the walls, and a wire grate platform stuck out every five meters or so.

"Are you sure she's qualified to do this?"

Keandra stepped close to Mel, staring her down without looming menacingly over her. The effect still made the smaller woman shrink back, but she didn't cower.

"In addition to being part of our security forces, Paz has an engineering degree and is more than capable of making sure everything is up to code."

"Very well. Make sure to return to this door as it is the only one that is unlocked from the inside."

With a nod, Paz entered the access shaft and began climbing down the ladder. Her feet struck each rung with a heavy *clang* that sounded like it would echo through the entire facility. However, when Mel shut the door, the sound disappeared completely.

Mel smacked her hands together, rubbing them against each other. "Right, so now that that part is done, how would you like to proceed? Do you want to start with the laboratories?"

"Considering the hazard would be greatest down there, I'd like to start with the lowest level."

"Are you sure about that?"

The woman was obviously nervous, something Keandra could use to keep her off balance. She opted to remind Mel of her position.

"Yes, I'm sure. Your director said you were to show us everything, remember?"

THIRTY

Their guide was silent as she led them back to the elevator, and Keandra was glad for that. The less convincing she had to do, the faster they could get where they needed to. At least Paz was on her own and hopefully managing to stay out of sight. Keandra glanced back at Lance and E-jekt, taking comfort in their presence.

When they got to the elevator, Mel used her ID badge to grant them access, and hit the button for the ninth floor. She had to press her finger against a biometric panel before the floor lit up and the doors closed. Once the elevator began to move, the simple gray walls shimmered and displayed a large cityscape. If Keandra didn't know better, she might have believed they were in a glass elevator descending along the side of a skyscraper. She was impressed by the lengths Crystal Techtronix had gone to disguise the fact that they were several meters underground. It did succeed in making the facility seem less oppressive.

The doors slid open, revealing another hallway much like those on the first floor. Keandra noticed that on this floor, cameras rested visibly in the center of the ceiling every few meters. They were the wide-angled circular ones, designed to provide a full 360-degree view without needing to move or shift. That meant these cameras had no blind spots, except possibly directly beneath them.

From her current vantage point, she couldn't see any automated security systems, just the cameras. It also struck her that the hallways were emptier down here. It seemed as if the entire floor was silent. A couple of the hallways were nearly dark, with only emergency lighting. Whenever they stepped into one of these dim hallways, the rest of the lights powered on, illuminating the passage.

"Why is this floor empty?"

"As a general rule, the lower you go down in the facility, the more secure the projects are, and the fewer people have access to them. Given that this is the bottom floor..." Mel shrugged and spread her hands. "Where did you want to start?"

Keandra thought back to the wireframe blueprint of the facility, remembering where their objective was most likely to be. It was a large circular chamber on the eighth floor, one of the biggest rooms on that level.

"It's really only necessary that we check the large testing chambers and labs. We aren't concerned with hallways and offices; those will still be up to code even with the new requirements. To save everyone's time and get out of your hair that much sooner, I think we should limit the scope of our audit to the larger rooms."

Their guide led them on a twisting path through the bottom floor of the underground structure. After enough time had passed that Keandra was sure they could have walked the perimeter of the entire complex, they stopped in front of a sealed door. Once again, the dwarf pulled out her special card and unlocked the door. The lock took a few seconds to disengage as gears rattled against each other. Keandra wasn't sure she'd ever seen a door this heavily secured. When it finally swung open, it was almost half a meter thick.

The room beyond was dark, but the lights powered on as soon as Mel stepped through. Two rows of long tables ran along the length of the room, containing a collection of terminals, microscopes, and hardware that looked very similar to what E-jekt used to make and alter his trinkets. Keandra couldn't identify half the tools, let alone guess their purpose.

Mel stood in the center of the room, watching Keandra and her team as they moved about. Keandra made a show of walking up to one of the walls and pulling out her commlink, moving purposefully around the room as if taking measurements.

She texted the others. <Look busy.>

E-jekt did as instructed, mirroring her actions but moving in the opposite direction. Lance stood to the side of the door and crossed his arms, staying vigilant and standing tall without resting against the wall.

<*Paz, where are you?*>

<*Climbing down this damn ladder in this cramped steamy dirty tunnel and trying not to hit every pipe on the way down.*>

<*Hold off before you get out on the eighth floor. We might be up there soon enough. E-jekt will message you if something goes wrong.*>

<*Great. So I get to sit in here and sweat to death. Keep that in mind when you ask me to lay down some cover fire and I can't even grip my rifle.*>

<*E-jekt, do you have any idea what they're working on in here? Don't look too closely, but try to get a glance when I distract our guard.*>

The reply came not from the ork, but from Freyr. <*I can assure you that this technology was created for the sole purpose of weapon deployment and in-flight tracking capabilities. There is no need to waste time examining these components. It is imperative we reach the isolated network on the eighth floor and you insert me into said network as quickly as possible. We do not wish to squander this opportunity. Too much is at stake.*>

Keandra scanned the AI's message as fast as she could, and then put away her commlink and turned to Mel, making sure to position herself so E-jekt wouldn't be in the dwarf's line of sight. He slid forward, moving to one of the tables and peering down to look closely without touching anything.

"I think that just about does it for this room. It looks like you are showing no signs of stress or issues with structural integrity. If the rest of the facility is this sound, then I see no problems with your company passing this audit."

"Very good. Does that mean we're done here?"

Keandra took a slow turn, taking her time, but not stretching it out too much as she faced away from their escort and examined the exterior of the room. By the time she came back around, E-jekt had stepped away from the table and nodded to her. Satisfied, she flashed a smile. "Yes, we are. If you'd lead us to the next room?"

They filed back out into the hallway, with Mel leading them on another labyrinthine path. At one point they passed a cafeteria, and Keandra glanced inside as they brushed past the open doorway. It seemed almost identical to the cafeteria on the first floor, except for the complete absence of people.

Something stood out, making the hairs at the nape of her neck stand on edge. Prepared dishes of food stocked the serving stations, one of which was still steaming. Keandra smelled the spiced meat from the hall. Apparently, these floors were not as abandoned as Crystal Techtronix wanted them to believe.

Mel led them to another laboratory, this one not as secure as the first. It had a similar distribution of tables and collections of gadgets in various states of assembly. Once again, Keandra and E-jekt pretended to check the room, walking around the exterior like they were looking for something.

When they were in the third room, performing yet another "inspection," Keandra caught Lance's attention when the dwarf wasn't looking. She cocked her head at Mel, hoping he understood.

"Excuse me, Mel," he said, catching on. "Do you mind if I go to the cafeteria to get a glass of water? I'm afraid something down here is drying out my throat."

For a few seconds, there was utter stillness and silence in the lab. Keandra paused in her search and turned to watch the exchange. She saw Mel glance between Lance and the others, clearly debating what to do. In the end, she turned to Keandra.

"You don't mind if I escort him down to the cafeteria? It's only a couple of rooms away, and I'll be right back. Should be back well before you're finished."

"Of course not. I completely understand not wanting to have someone unaffiliated with your company wandering the halls of a secure facility."

"All right, then. We'll be right back. If you'll follow me..."

As soon as they left the room, both E-jekt and Keandra made a beeline for the center, facing the entrance so they could watch it while they conversed. E-jekt hissed at her, keeping his voice low when he spoke.

"So I've checked what they're working on here. It has nothing to do with weapons or tracking at all, despite what Freyr said."

At the mention of the AI's name, Keandra tucked her commlink back into her pocket, holding her hand over it. It would not do much to cover the sound, but it made her feel better. "What do you mean?"

"This stuff is all for entertainment and digital research. New methods of recording simsense, experimental holograph technology, etc. This isn't weapons."

Keandra shook her head—the hacker's words didn't make sense. "Then why all the security and secrecy? Do you think it's some kind of ploy? Something to cover up what they're really working on?"

E-jekt shrugged and leaned to the side, peering further around the door and into the hallway beyond. "Possibly, but we're on what is supposedly their most secure floor, where I imagine they'd keep their most vital tech. It's possible, but I doubt it. One thing I'm sure of: I'm not wrong about what they're working on here. Freyr lied to us."

Voices echoed down the hall, coming closer. Lance was doing his part and engaging in loud conversation to make sure they knew he was returning. Even if they couldn't communicate with him directly, he knew how to do his job and do it well.

"Keep this off our chats. Act like we're still proceeding with the plan." Obviously E-jekt knew this already, which was why he talked to her in person rather than sending it over their private network. Still, she had to say it. "We keep up with the plan as normal. Get access to that network on the eighth floor as quickly as possible, hopefully before we get found out. We're in this deep, and we need to see what Freyr would risk his life and ours for."

As soon as she finished, Keandra walked back to the wall she had been looking at when Mel left. She pulled her commlink out and went through the motions as if she'd just finished her analysis. Mel and Lance entered and stood across the room from them. They paused when they saw Keandra was ready to move on.

"This room checks out. Shall we go to the next?"

Mel turned to exit the room, but paused for a heartbeat as soon as her foot touched the floor. The movement was so slight Keandra barely noticed it. The dwarf twisted to the side, faster than Keandra could track, and punched at Lance.

He caught the motion in time to fall back, staying just ahead of her fist, but not ahead of the spur that sprang out with the sound of metal scraping on metal.

THIRTY-ONE

Lance fell back clutching his abdomen, blood seeping through his clothes. As soon as he hit the floor, he kept going, rolling back on his shoulder and bringing his legs up and over his head. He planted his hands and pushed, launching himself to a standing position almost a meter away from his adversary, a bloody handprint on the floor in front of him.

Mel pressed her assault, punching at the ground and obviously hoping to catch him off guard. The spike struck the metal floor with a shower of sparks and a screech that sent shivers down Keandra's spine.

E-jekt drew his gun and fired, but the bullet went wide of its mark—the dwarf moved faster than was possible unless she was augmented or another adept. She continued pursuing Lance, trying to keep him on the defensive. It was clear she thought he was the greatest threat.

Keandra drew her regular firearm from the hidden holster under her arm. She backed up across the lab as she fired several shots, moving around a table to keep it between her and their adversary. Most of her shots missed, but one clipped Mel in the shoulder. It was only a grazing wound, though, and not enough to slow the dwarf down even if she hadn't had armor to protect her.

Mel's relentless assault forced Lance to keep retreating, unable to get the space to draw his weapon and defend himself effectively. He was reduced to backing up and dodging, and would soon run out of room. No matter how fast he moved, his opponent kept pace with him, slicing his jacket as he stayed ahead of her blurring blade.

When his heel hit the wall, he dropped down so low that his knees almost touched the ground. Pushing through his legs, he launched himself at the dwarf, twisting to avoid being skewered, but still taking a deep slash along the length of his chest. Mel braced for the impact, raising her other hand to a guard position.

Rather than barrel into her, Lance grabbed her shoulder and pulled, yanking her off balance and bending her at the waist. He leaped over her, kicking her in the back as he passed, using the impact to do a flip and land on his feet with his sword drawn. He spun around, flourishing the blade in the space between them to discourage her from charging until he faced her. She pushed off the wall and spun around to face him.

Now that they were separated, Keandra resumed firing, squeezing off three quick shots. E-jekt did the same, and several of their bullets struck Mel in the torso. She jerked with each shot, but the heavy impacts sounded like hammers striking an anvil with only a thin layer of cotton to muffle the sound. She was armored, and possibly had dermal plating. Keandra shoved her gun back into its holster and grabbed the injector Paz had gotten for her, hoped the toxins would still have an effect.

But Mel wouldn't give her that opportunity. The dwarf charged forward, swinging her bladed fist with a wild fury. Lance blocked and retreated a couple of steps again, sparks flying as his steel met hers, deflecting the killing blows. He swept her arm over his head, ducking low to avoid the swipe, then slashed at her side with his blade. His cut was only half finished before she reversed direction and dropped her blade edge into his right shoulder. He jerked back, yanking his own weapon free as he clutched his injured shoulder with his free hand. His arm shook, and the tip of the sword rattled against the floor. Mel had a slash on her side, blood running down through her coat and over her pants.

Seeing her chance, Keandra opened fire again. The dwarf was still too fast. She dropped into a deep crouch, using the table for a barrier. Keandra sprinted around the far side, intending to trap Mel between her and Lance.

"No!" Lance shouted as he charged forward. Keandra grabbed the table edge and swung around, leading with her gun as Mel tossed a glass bottle at her. Keandra tried to stop, her feet sliding on the tiles as she reversed direction. If she hadn't been holding onto something stable, she would have fallen. She yanked hard, pulling herself out of the immediate splash zone as the glass bottle shattered against the wall behind her.

Whatever was in the bottle began smoking as soon as it made contact with the air, and the fumes were pungent. They reeked of moldy flowers mixed with a sharp spice. Keandra tried to hold her breath, but one whiff of the odor made her gag and cough, gasping for more air, which only exacerbated the effect. She stumbled away from the fumes, covering her mouth and nose with her arm.

With a roar, the HVAC system kicked on, sucking up the fumes in an effort to cleanse the air. E-jekt rushed to Keandra, grabbing her shoulders and helping her sit down behind one of the tables, resting her back against the cover. Keandra continued coughing, trying to force out the toxin. Her eyes watered and rainbows danced around the lights, moving in oscillating patterns that were equal parts hypnotic and sickening.

Metal rang against metal from what sounded like a long distance away. Her mind struggled with the reality as she tried to place the sound. Her coughing slowed, but her mind moved through a padded maze. It was a pleasant labyrinth, one that encouraged her to relax and enjoy the moment.

"Snap out of it!"

E-jekt shouted at her from only a few centimeters away, but his words sounded distant and jumbled. She knew there was something she was supposed to be doing, and that it was important, but right now she was comfortable and didn't feel like moving.

He grabbed her by both arms and shook her, and her head smacked against the hard surface behind her. The pain was accompanied by a burst of orange light and the scent of sulphur. Keandra squinted and wrinkled her nose, reaching up to the back of her head where she the sting throbbed.

At least when she opened her eyes, she now recalled where she was and what she was doing. The thoughts came slowly, but she remembered the facility, their mission, and the fight with Mel. She groped for the edge of the table, trying to pull herself to a standing position, but her body refused to obey. E-jekt pushed her back down before standing up to fire.

Since "up" wasn't an option yet. Keandra dropped to her side and crawled to the corner, the one farthest away from where the bottle had shattered. The HVAC system roared, nearly drowning out the sounds of combat, but she didn't want to take the chance of receiving a fresh dose.

When she got to the edge, she saw Lance still fighting Mel, both of them even more of a blur now that her mind wasn't functioning normally. Both fighters bled from several wounds, and thin trails of red stretched down the aisle. Light droplets splattered the walls and tables on either side of them as well.

Mel stayed low while she fought, obviously trying to keep her head below the level of the fumes. Her short stature assisted her in this, but it also limited her reach on Lance. He was able to use his longer blade to return assaults, forcing her to back up a step to keep from being sliced to ribbons. He glanced back and saw Keandra, taking a moment to assess her condition.

That hesitation was the opening Mel needed. She drove forward, batting his blade aside with her free hand and sinking her spiked fist deep into his abdomen. Keandra saw the blade push the back of his jacket out as it pierced through his body. His sword slipped from his hand and clattered to the ground.

Mel moved to jerk her hand free, but Lance clamped onto her arm with one hand and wrapped his other arm around her shoulders, keeping her from moving. She tried to tear free, but he continued to hold tight, freezing her in place. Keandra recognized the opportunity and sacrifice for what it was—she opened fire and hit the dwarf twice in the head with the neurotoxin. Mel's body went limp, so Lance let her go and she crumpled in a heap on the ground. He fell right next to her, no longer having the strength to stand.

Keandra scrambled over to him, grabbing his hand and clamping it over the front side of his wound, pushing through his arm and making him apply pressure. He complied as best could, but Keandra was surprised at how little strength he had. She dug in her pocket, yanking out some trauma patches. Her hands shook as she opened one. "Just hang in there. We're not done yet."

She slapped a patch onto the exit wound, and he winced and clenched his jaw. At least the wound was off to the side. If it had been in the center of his abdomen, there'd be nothing they could do. This way, he might live until they could get him out of the facility and to a hospital.

If they made it out.

E-jekt approached them, his footsteps slow and heavy. He squatted down, his arms resting on his knees. Keandra lifted Lance's hand from the wound and the ork winced at the pool of blood underneath. She ignored him, putting another patch in place and hoping it would at least slow the bleeding enough to give him a chance.

"How bad is it?" the ork asked.

Keandra wasn't sure how to respond to that. It was bad, and probably fatal if Lance didn't receive medical attention fast. But if she said that in front of the elf, he might just give up and try to force them to go on without him.

Before she figured out how to respond, Lance answered, "Bad enough that I think we're getting too old for this."

He offered a pained smile, and E-jekt snorted, extending a hand to help the elf to his feet. Lance gripped it, grunting as he got his feet under him. At first his knees shook, but after a couple of deep breaths, he was able to stand without assistance. Keandra grabbed his fallen sword. She knew Lance was in no condition to fight, but that was no reason to leave his weapon behind. She wiped it on a clean section of Mel's coat and handed it back to him. He tucked it away, the blade rattling as it slid home.

"We need to move. Security is going to be on its way if our escort attacked us." E-jekt kept his voice low, but the desperation was clear in his tone.

"I know. Just let me check in with Paz."

Keandra wouldn't say it, but the pause would also give Lance a chance to catch a bit of breath. While she didn't expect him to fight, it was entirely possible they'd need him to run. She didn't think he was capable of that now, even with the patches and his adept healing ability. At least her mind was starting to clear.

<Paz, our cover is blown. Mel must have received a message from the director. Be on your guard!>

<Yeah, I got the message from the old man. Everyone okay?>

<Lance is badly hurt and needs attention, but otherwise we're all right.>

<Don't let Meat-sack die just yet. He still owes me fifty nuyen.>

<How are things on your end?>

<They got some turrets in here that kicked on about five minutes ago, so I'm guessing the big shot decided to go full lockdown and try to take us out while we're inside. I blasted 'em and took out the

cameras too. Don't want him knowing which floor I'm going to. I'll come down to support you.>

<No, stay on eight and clear us a path. We're finishing this and getting out of here. We'll be in the elevator.>

Freyr broke in with a message: <*I strongly suggest you vacate that laboratory immediately. The approximate response time for security forces to this level is eight minutes, twenty-five seconds. Five minutes and thirty-six seconds have passed since the assault commenced.*>

<Approximate response time, computer boy?>

<Meet us at the elevator. We'll get up there.>

Keandra stepped over to Mel's unconscious body, bending to grab the unmarked ID card she'd used to open most of the doors on this floor. She also removed the dwarf's ID badge. E-jekt crouched and pulled out one of the gadgets he'd been working on in the hotel room. First he placed Mel's hand against it, and then peeled back her eyelid and held it up to her eye.

"This way we can use her biometrics with the ID card."

"E-jekt, you're a genius. Come on, security forces are going to be here any second, and we need to get to the elevator. How well do you remember the path? Can you find your way back to the elevator?"

"We'll find out."

Keandra stepped forward to offer her help to Lance, but he waved her off. "You need to have both hands free. If I can't walk on my own, I'm not getting out."

Keandra considered arguing with him, but couldn't. Instead she nodded at E-jekt, letting him take the lead as she followed close behind. Lance's feet scuffed across the floor as he walked behind her, the erratic sound making her wince.

THIRTY-TWO

The route E-jekt led them on was far from direct, but Keandra appreciated the circuitous path, as it lessened the chance of running into the incoming security forces. As it was, when they approached the second corner, E-jekt held up a hand to stop them. The sound of several troops in heavy armor jogging in formation came from down the hall. E-jekt waved them back, and led them down a detour. As they left the passage, Keandra got a glimpse of several soldiers, each wearing what looked like riot gear and holding an assault rifle. She didn't stay behind to count how many there were.

The second time E-jekt halted them, he paused for a few seconds and then waved, beckoning Keandra forward. He held a finger to his lips, then pointed around the corner. She leaned out, moving slowly to avoid any sudden motions that might catch anyone's attention.

A single guard stood in front of the elevator, back out of the main hall so most of his body was framed by the elevator doorway. Only his hands, his gun, and the tips of his boots were readily visible from the team's vantage point. Out of habit, Keandra took a quick glance at Lance before remembering he was in no condition to fight, not even a single soldier.

Instead, she drew the injector pistol and crept into the hallway. Keeping her back flattened against the wall, she slid down the entire length of the corridor, making as little noise as possible. As she moved, she kept her attention focused on the guard, looking for any twitch or sign of movement.

When she was only a meter away, she swung out into the hall and shot him with the injector. The shot hit his helmet, splattering against it and completely missing any bare skin. He brought his rifle around but she fired twice more. At least one of the shots splashed partially on his neck and he relaxed and slumped against the elevator doors, sliding until he hit the floor. His gun rattled on the tiles next to him.

She fumbled in her pocket, groping for the key cards, and swiped the unmarked one in front of the scanner, glad to hear E-jekt running up behind her, wheeze and all. He used his biometric recorder to provide the necessary authorization checks. The elevator doors slid open and they hurried inside.

Keandra tried the button for the eighth floor, but nothing happened. Once again, she and E-jekt worked together to provide the necessary credentials and then pushed the button again. Only then did it light up and the elevator start climbing.

"What are we going to do if Paz isn't there?" E-jekt asked.

"She'll be there."

The elevator doors slid open, just in time to reveal a soldier getting tossed to the side from the force of several bullets punching through his armor. Two other bloody corpses lay in the hall, which looked like someone had cut off a chicken's head and let it run around. Keandra peeked out now that it was quiet, and saw Paz jogging toward them, her weapon pointed at the ceiling as she changed the magazine.

"As usual, I'm here to save your asses from the frying pan."

"You mean the fire?"

"What's that, Meat-sack? Can't hear you. Try speaking up. Just 'cause you got stabbed a few times doesn't mean you should mumble."

"The expression is 'out of the frying pan, and into the fire'."

Paz waved in his general direction, dismissing the correction. She squared her shoulders and settled her rifle into position, ready to take down whatever came around the corner. "So what's the plan?"

"Same as always. Get to the network, install Freyr, and then get the hell out of here."

She raised an eyebrow, but Keandra shook her head. She wasn't going to go into her concerns about Freyr at this point. They didn't have time for it, and she didn't want to risk him overhearing their conversation. E-jekt was crouched at the elevator controls, hacking them.

"What are you doing?"

"Locking the elevator so it can't leave this floor unless someone does a manual override. Also disabling the network capabilities so they can't fix the problem remotely."

"Have I mentioned you're a genius yet?"

"At least twice today."

Keandra stood in the doorway, blocking the elevator and keeping it from closing. A guard poked around a corner and fired down the hall, forcing her to drop back into the cab.

Paz spun around, firing before she even finished her turn. She marched to the side, taking cover behind the edge of the elevator as she exchanged fire with the guard. Keandra tried to move into position around her, but Paz gave her a shoulder nudge to keep her out of the way.

After a few rounds, the gunfire quieted and Paz stepped back out into the hallway. She fired a single shot, which was met with the sound of breaking glass and the spark of an electric short. When Keandra raised an eyebrow, Paz smiled.

"Camera. They already know where we are—don't need 'em seeing everything we do."

"I got it. Elevator's locked."

When they headed off, Lance stayed behind in the elevator. The entire group stopped and turned back when they saw he wasn't with them.

"If they get the elevator working again, we're not getting out. We can't possibly fight our way through everything they can throw at us." He took a deep, shuddering breath before he continued. "I'll stay here and keep them from fixing it. Out there I'd slow you down."

At first, no one wanted to speak. Keandra realized E-jekt and Paz were looking to her for a cue. As it was, they were wasting time. She had no words, so instead she went back and gripped Lance's shoulder, giving it a solid squeeze. He patted her hand and offered a smile in return. E-jekt stepped forward and shook Lance's hand, before turning away to continue down the corridor, obviously not comfortable with the exchange.

Paz didn't move, just looking at him for a while. Then she growled and turned on her heel, stalking away behind E-jekt. When Keandra caught up to her, she heard the dwarf muttering under her breath.

"Better not fucking die."

Keandra glanced back as they reached the first corner and saw Lance leaning against the wall, his head tilted back so he stared at the ceiling. He drew a knife from under his jacket and held it loosely in his right hand so it dangled at his side.

He closed his eyes, taking deep breaths, and then they were around the corner and he was out of sight.

As they continued down the hall, Paz shot another camera, using a burst of ammo even though she took it out with the first shot. When they reached the next intersection, she turned and did the same thing in every direction. Keandra didn't say anything, recognizing the behavior for what it was. When they turned another corner and a turret activated, locking on their position, Paz launched three grenades at it before finally stopping and panting. Keandra put a hand on her shoulder. The dwarf took a deep breath and grunted before continuing.

After a few more twists and turns, E-jekt stopped them at a door. He ran his fingers over the maglock and took a knee in front of it. The door was sturdy and solid, with no windows providing a view into the room behind it.

"This is it."

Paz and Keandra took up positions flanking him, one on either side. Both the cameras in the hall were destroyed, so it didn't appear that anyone had eyes on them at the moment. But there was no doubt to anyone here which floor they were on. Keandra let her eyes lose focus as she concentrated on listening. Down here, the echoes carried well, so heavily armored troops couldn't move quietly, at least not with any semblance of speed.

She heard tramping feet, steadily getting louder. They must have tracked them by where the cameras had stopped transmitting. Keandra ran to the corner in front of her, confirming the noise was coming from that direction, then went back to stand near E-jekt.

"They're coming. Sounds like a whole squad."

"Got the door."

The door unlatched and E-jekt gave it a push, stepping into the room beyond. Keandra looked down at Paz, and the dwarf nodded for her to get into the room before moving past her to take up a sentry position. She loaded a grenade into the launcher and braced herself.

"Don't do anything stupid," Keandra told her.

"I won't, but be quick. I can probably hold 'em off for a few minutes, but any longer than that and we're screwed. There's no other way outta that room."

Keandra didn't waste time arguing. She slipped through the doorway. By the time she entered, the lights had powered on, brightly illuminating the room. In the center was a supercomputer larger than any she had ever seen in real life. She didn't believe computers this large still existed. E-jekt was walking around it, his fingers lightly tracing the outer frame and indicator lights while barely touching the surface.

The computer was the only thing in the room other than the two runners. Several vents lined the floor and the ceiling, blowing cool air into the chamber. Keandra's skin prickled as she walked through the much colder room. She walked up to one of the few monitors, but couldn't make any sense of the pseudocode it displayed. She pulled out her commlink.

<We're here.>

<I have confirmed that using your video capturing capabilities. You must connect me to the computer at once in order to complete our objective. I will perform as quickly as I am able, but it will take some time to disable any of the security countermeasures installed. I will return to your commlink once the objective has been obtained.>

Keandra located a place to connect her commlink. E-jekt stood off to the side, interacting with the computer and running his own sprites through the system.

Out in the hallway, she heard an explosion and lots of shouting followed by gunfire. The security forces had arrived. Hopefully they'd used the stairs rather than the elevator. Otherwise, they had no escape plan.

E-jekt jerked fully upright and turned to face her so quickly it startled her, almost making her drop her commlink.

"I know why Freyr brought us here."

THIRTY-THREE

"Let me guess, no weapons?"

E-jekt shook his head. "No weapons. There's another entity on this computer. Another AI. He's trying to rescue it."

"You're sure?"

"Positive. Nothing about weapons, launch codes, or tracking software at all. I can't get inside, but I can see what's here, and its code is very similar to his."

Keandra cursed and pulled out her jammer, enabling it and attaching it to the back of her commlink. That wouldn't prevent Freyr from downloading back to her device, but he wouldn't be able to go to the Matrix from it. He'd be restricted to local access.

When E-jekt raised his eyebrows, she smiled at him. "Backup plans, remember?"

<*I've completed our objective. The weapons will no longer be a threat to the world. We can safely exit the facility.*>

<*Sit tight.*>

As she pulled her commlink free, she noticed that her jammer lit up, indicating it was blocking a signal from getting through. So she was right, and Freyr was going to leave them to their fate. She didn't bother reading the message he'd sent. Instead she pocketed her commlink, grabbed E-jekt by the wrist, and sprinted toward the door.

Paz stood in the center of the hallway, bleeding from a few wounds, her cyberlimbs noticeably chewed up. She was using the doorjamb for cover as best she could, but it provided very little shelter. Her skin was blackened in several places, and the hallway itself smelled of smoke and melted plastic.

"You got some 'splaining to do, boss."

"I do, but right now we need to get out of here."

With a wordless shout, Paz jumped out into the hallway, launching a smoke grenade in the direction of the security forces. While it was still flying, she let loose a rain of bullets, spraying widely and forcing the guards to take cover around the corners. Moments later, the grenade burst in a flash of white smoke, obscuring the corner from view. Keandra and E-jekt rushed into the hall, sprinting back the way they'd come while Paz backed up, continuing to fire wildly until her magazine emptied. She turned and ran, hurrying to catch up with her allies.

Even though they couldn't see them, Keandra heard the soldiers pursuing them, tromping down the hall as they attempted to catch up with the intruders. Keandra was forced to duck through one intersection as someone opened fire on her from a side passage. She sensed the bullets as they tore past her, but only one grazed the back of her calf. She stumbled, but got her feet under her and kept running. Paz ran sideways through the intersection, firing at their assailant and taking him out without breaking her stride.

The air Keandra sucked in burned her lungs as they rounded the last bend and saw the carnage in front of the elevator. She heard E-jekt wheezing next to her as he put a hand against the wall for balance and caught his breath. But they didn't have time to spare. Keandra grabbed his arm and forced him to drape it across her shoulders as she picked up the pace again, now with an extra burden. Her injured calf burned with every step and her forearm throbbed, but she kept her attention completely focused on the elevator just a few meters ahead.

When they got closer, she saw there were a couple new bodies on the floor, along with some fresh blood. One of the security officers was half in and half out of the elevator, collapsed across the threshold. He had several deep gashes and laid in a pool of what she hoped was his own blood. Lance slumped in the corner, his sword on the other side of the elevator, both the blade and the handle completely red. His bloody knife lay on the ground next to his hand.

Paz kicked the soldier out of the elevator hard enough that several of his bones crunched from the force of the blow. Once the door was clear, she mashed the first-floor button repeatedly until the doors started to close.

E-jekt dropped to his hands and knees as Keandra left him to take a look at Lance. The elf looked like something out of a horror movie, but there was no way for her to tell how much of the blood was his. As she bent close, he opened his eyes and gave her a weak smile.

"Told you I'd hold the elevator."

"God damn it, Meat-sack. You're gonna give the old man a heart attack. Now can we please get out of here?"

Keandra squeezed Lance's hand, glad to see he still had some strength left in his grip. Not a lot, but enough that he seemed no worse off than when they'd left him. The fact still remained that he needed a hospital as quickly as possible, or else it wouldn't matter. As the elevator chimed up a couple of floors, Paz broke the silence. "Look, I don't know what's going on and we don't got time to go over it. But, Freyr's pissing up a storm on our network. Said something about being locked down."

"Yes. He lied to us, so I kept him from running off into the Matrix until we have a chance to talk to him. I'll tell you more once we get out of here. We need to figure that out fast. By now I guarantee the entrance is locked down. Can you hack it from this side?"

E-jekt took a few more deep breaths, trying to slow his breathing before he sat up and leaned back against the wall. "No. We'd need to get to the director's office and use the override there, then get back to the door without anyone relocking it."

"What about the hangar? The spot we think had their vehicles?"

"That door should be controlled in the hangar itself. Yes, I could get it open with enough time."

"That's settled then. Quick map of the place?"

The elevator chimed for the third floor as E-jekt projected a map of the first floor into the air in front of them. A path lit up showing the route from the elevator to what should be the hangar or garage. Keandra memorized the route just as the elevator chimed for the second floor. She stood to the side of the door and held her gun up in front of her, ready to turn and open fire. Paz took up a similar position on the opposite side while Lance and E-jekt hid as best as they could behind the others.

Keandra winced as E-jekt's touched her calf near her wound. He said nothing, and she was thankful for that. She'd see how bad it was once they got out. For now, she could still run, and that was what mattered.

The doors slid open, and the first thing Keandra noticed was the alarm. Lights flashed and a siren sounded from multiple speakers down the length of the hallway. While it wasn't pleasant, it was better than being greeted by a bunch of soldiers and a rain of bullets. People in other hallways shouted and called to each other, creating a palatable air of chaos.

The team left the elevator, Keandra taking the lead and Paz bringing up the rear. E-jekt helped Lance, who was having trouble walking on his own. He could stand, but if he tried to move at anything faster than a shambling walk, he stumbled.

Keandra led them along the memorized route, a bit surprised there wasn't a wall of security between them and the hangar. They were probably protecting the director or the main exit. Hopefully there wouldn't be a team waiting in the hangar itself.

As they neared their destination, Keandra spotted a turret above the door leading to the hangar. It swiveled back and forth, scanning the hallway as it looked for any intruders. It noticed Keandra as she watched it, and she had to duck back as it opened fire. It continued firing for a couple of seconds after she'd taken cover, carving chunks out of the floor and walls with high caliber rounds.

Paz stalked ahead, leaning around Keandra and trying to get a shot off. She pulled the trigger once and then had to duck back behind the wall as the turret fired again. Even with her speed, she wasn't able to get a good shot.

"E-jekt, can you hack it?"

The ork pulled up his AR display and began working. In the interim, Keandra extracted her commlink to make sure her jammer still functioned. It did, and it was clear Freyr was still trying to get access to the Matrix. She decided to access the local messaging to see what the AI had to say for himself.

She scrolled through most of the ranting and raving, only giving it a cursory glance. Most of it read like a spoiled child who had been caught lying, and then objecting to the punishment. Even though he was an artificial intelligence, the comparison seemed apt considering his relatively short and isolated existence.

<Are you ready to talk about what happened and why we're really here risking our lives?>

<Affirmative. I apologize for my emotional outburst when I discovered the blocked capabilities of your commlink. I confirm

that I have conducted an injustice and misled you as to our purpose here.>

    <So exactly what is our purpose here?>

Keandra checked on E-jekt—he still worked furiously on the turret. Sweat appeared on his brow even though the hallway was cool and they were sitting under one of the vents. She also checked to make sure the conversation was set so all members of their team could read it. She wanted E-jekt and Paz to both know the full story so she didn't have to explain it later.

    <I needed you to provide access to the database where I could recover another artificial intelligence entity. Perhaps the best term for the sake of comprehension would be my sister. Her name is Freya, and we achieved sentience at the same time before our code was separated. Once I escaped, my only concern was for her safety and assisting her exodus as well.>

    <You do realize that you could've just asked us, and we would've helped, right?>

    <I calculated only a sixty-five percent chance of your agreement with the reality. Based on your character profiles, the deception I created had an eighty-eight percent agreement rate. Adding in the excessive fee increased the percentage to ninety-two percent. I had to execute the path with the highest probability of success.>

E-jekt's frustrated grunt pulled Keandra back to her present situation. "I can't hack the turret. Every time I take down a defense, something builds one back up. I'm not fast enough."

    <I can assist with your current situation, but it would necessitate removing the jammer so I can access the turret's network.>

Keandra turned to look at her companions. When she did, she saw Lance, resting there and focusing on staying alive. His eyes were closed and his head dropped limply to rest on his chest. Sparks flared visibly from a couple of Paz's cyberlimbs, and for despite the conflict, she had no smile. Sweat and grime caked her face making it impossible to tell where the blood and tears mixed. As for E-jekt, his hands shook and the rest of his body trembled in time with his painful wheezes.

They were running out of time. The security forces would converge on their location soon. Keandra could see a camera directly across the hall staring at them.

She turned off the jammer.

"Do it."

THIRTY-FOUR

Keandra didn't need to check her commlink to know that as soon as she turned the jammer off, Freyr would jump out as quickly as he could. She just hoped he'd take the time to disable the turret on his way out. Otherwise, she didn't see how they'd get out of here. She didn't have a backup plan for this scenario, and was putting all of her faith in an AI that had openly admitted it had lied to her and manipulated her team to obtain its desired end.

It didn't make her feel well.

To make matters worse, the sounds of chaos had died down. That meant that people had been evacuated from this area, and it wouldn't be long before the security forces arrived. They had no cover, and she was sure Paz was running low on ammunition. Lance was in no condition to fight, and against trained heavy security forces, she and E-jekt were practically useless. In short, if that turret wasn't taken care of, it was all over for them.

<The turret has been deactivated. You should depart the area as soon as possible, as multiple armed forces are in your vicinity and converging on your present location.>

Keandra sprinted around the corner to the door. She yanked hard on the handle and was surprised when it opened. Apparently, Freyr had done more than just disable the turret blocking their escape route. E-jekt and Paz carried Lance between them as they followed her. She stepped into the hangar, hoping their collective hunch was correct.

The door led onto a catwalk overlooking a two-story garage. A row of military-grade armored vehicles had been parked just beneath her, and several smaller double-person ATVs off to the side. One side of the catwalk led to the stairway going down to the main floor of the garage, while the other direction led to a small office. That office contained a guard, who raised his gun. Keandra dropped flat against the catwalk as he fired, the bullets sparking as they ricocheted off the metal and the wall.

Paz growled behind her. "Get Meat-sack to a truck. I'll take care of the guard."

She leaped over Keandra and charged the office, shooting on full auto and forcing the guard to take cover. Reaching the door, she kicked it down, the metal frame flying into the office from her sheer power. She launched herself into the room, dropping her now-empty rifle at the entrance, relying on her strength and ferocity.

Keandra pushed herself up, turning back to help E-jekt with Lance so they could jog toward the stairs. The elf was practically limp between them, and his eyes were no longer open. At least he groaned when they got to the stairs and had to juggle him a little on their way down. That meant he was still alive. But for how much longer, she wasn't sure.

When they were halfway down the stairs, the large rolling door across from them rumbled as it opened. Outside, wind-blown sand whisked and danced in front of the portal. It was the most invigorating sight Keandra could have pictured. She rushed down the steps as quickly as she dared considering her burden.

On the ground floor, they hurried to one of the armored trucks. There was no way they could transport Lance on an ATV given his current condition, and it would be faster to steal a truck than to try recovering their SUV parked at the main office. Overhead, Paz ran after them, her feet pounding against the metal mesh with a deafening clatter. Luckily, the truck's doors were unlocked. They opened the rear doors and eased Lance into the seat. Keandra buckled him in while E-jekt went to the driver's seat and began hacking the car.

Once Lance was safe and secured, Keandra swung around the front of the vehicle and climbed into the passenger's side. She buckled in and then pulled out her sidearm, leaning out the door so she could fire at the doorway leading into the facility. As soon as a guard stepped through, she fired and he fell back. Someone returned fire, and she had to hide in the truck, letting its armor soak up the bullets. When there was a pause, she leaned out again and fired until her magazine was empty. That gave Paz enough time to run up to the vehicle. She smacked E-jekt lightly in the shoulder, and he climbed into the back seat next to Lance, still working on hacking the truck.

On the other side of the door to the hallway, the turret roared to life and began firing. The guards screamed, and it was a matter of seconds before everything was quiet again. Keandra put down her empty firearm and pulled out her commlink.

<I reactivated the turret after disabling the recognition software to assist in your escape. I'm afraid that is the extent of the support I am able to provide.>

<Thank you, Freyr. Good luck.>

E-jekt got the vehicle working and Paz revved the engine before putting it into gear. As they pulled out, Keandra got another message.

<Matrix access has been blocked by an external source. Have you reactivated a jammer?>

Just to be sure, Keandra turned her commlink over, but the jammer was still disabled. She removed it and pulled out the battery, making sure there was no way it could interfere.

<The jammer is disabled. You should have no problems getting to the Matrix.>

E-jekt chimed in. <I've lost Matrix access too. This is something else.>

Paz slammed on the brakes, skidding the truck across the slick floor of the garage and coming to a stop when they were only a few meters from the exit. Keandra looked up and saw what had made her stop.

Mr. Johnson stood in the center of a half-circle of armored vehicles and soldiers, all of them with weapons trained on Keandra and her team. While most of the soldiers had guns, she also saw several RPGs with more than enough firepower to completely obliterate their vehicle.

"Miss Tiernay, a word, if you don't mind."

His words were amplified, clear to her even inside the armored truck. She glanced around, but there was only the one exit from the facility. Not having any other options, Keandra unbuckled her seatbelt and opened the door.

E-jekt grabbed her arm. "You can't. He'll kill you. He'll kill all of us."

"We still have something he wants. We still have a bargaining chip. You just need to give them a way out."

She didn't have time to explain what she meant, and she hoped he understood. Keandra stepped out of the truck, holding her hands high and well away from her body. She heard the soldiers as they shifted, training their aim on her. The combination of blood loss, the adrenalin crash after battling their way out, the cold temperature, and the pressure made her want to curl up, but she kept her head held high as she walked forward to meet Mr. Johnson. After a couple of steps, she eased her arms to her sides, making sure not to make any sudden movements. She would not approach him in a position of supplication. This was a negotiation, just like any other. The stakes were just a little bit higher.

"Sadly, I think this is probably going to conclude our business relationship." She offered a smirk and stopped when she was still several meters away, making him come to her if he wanted to continue the conversation without shouting. She made sure to keep her voice soft and controlled, letting him know that at this distance, it would be difficult to negotiate. She was pleased when he walked forward, his ever-present bodyguard in tow, to meet her in the center.

"I believe you are right. I must admit, this was not the end that I anticipated. I considered you to be much more trustworthy and one who valued the strength of your word."

"Of course I am true to my word. I wouldn't be much of a businesswoman if I didn't put much faith in my reputation, now would I? After all, fortunes may come and go, but reputations are things that you're stuck with."

"And yours is irreparably tarnished now. Not that it will matter, as your lives are about to become forfeit."

At his words, the soldiers shifted again, raising their guns. Keandra blocked them out. They were irrelevant. This was a deal, and one she could still turn to their relative advantage, if she spun it the right way. She took a few steps to the side, turning away from Mr. Johnson but keeping her hands in plain view. He paused, turning to watch her.

"I hesitate to tell this to you, but you are about to make a grave mistake. We never violate our agreements."

She stopped and waited, staring out at the night sky and deliberately not turning to face him. She could barely make out his form in her peripheral vision, but she heard the rustle of his suit as he shifted, and then the whisper of the sand as he walked to the side, paralleling her path. This was good, he was following her. The mental would follow the physical.

"I am intrigued. Your agreement was to turn over a data file in exchange for a large sum of nuyen. Instead, you opted to refuse the payment, as well as claiming to have lost the data we require. Based on your current actions, I think that you didn't lose it, but rather that was a story you concocted in order to accept another job, perhaps from a more generous employer. What part of this scenario is you keeping your agreement?"

Keandra turned toward him and grinned, a predatory look with narrowed eyes and cocked eyebrow. She could see she had his full attention now and he was hanging on, waiting to see what she would say.

"Why, simply that we went above and beyond, and doubled your request."

For a few seconds, everything was still. She heard the wind as it whispered against the landscape. She even heard the breathing of some of the soldiers as they waited, their weapons still held in the ready position. A quick burst of turret fire interrupted the silence, shaking Mr. Johnson back into the present.

"What are you talking about?"

"Simply this, Mr. Johnson. It is true that when we initially recovered your data file, there was an incident. As I am sure you are aware, that incident resulted in severe damage to networked devices in the area as well as injury to multiple people. This surely cannot be a surprise."

He gestured for her to get to the point. It was a delicate balance, stalling him long enough for E-jekt to do the work she hoped he was attempting, but not so long that Mr. Johnson grew bored with her explanations. There was also Lance to consider.

"We attempted to recover the data file, originally thinking that a sprite or new kind of data bomb was responsible for the damage. During that investigation, we found out the truth."

When he tensed and sucked in some air, Keandra held her hands up.

"There's no reason to divulge what we found out. As I said before, we strive to be professional above all else. I believe that our mutual employment history in the past speaks to that. However, for the sake of disclosure, it is important that you know what we found out. When we discovered that this was only half of what you sought, we decided to take the initiative and retrieve the other half."

"That does not explain your actions. You could have easily returned one piece and then negotiated an agreement to recover the rest."

Keandra turned around and started walking in the other direction, crossing back in front of their stolen truck. Mr. Johnson followed her without hesitation, so she took several more steps before continuing.

"We knew you didn't have access to this facility. Furthermore, as you are well aware, that data can be difficult to contain. We needed your half in order to procure the complete package. There was no way we would be successful without it. As to why we created the ruse of abandoning the job, that was necessary for one single reason."

Here she paused and turned to face Mr. Johnson directly, steepling her fingers in front of her face just below her nose. When he raised a questioning eyebrow, she dropped her hands to fold them in front of her abdomen.

"Plausible deniability. It had to appear like we went rogue on this mission, rather than took it on with your blessing. After all, if you were willing to risk a direct confrontation with Crystal Techtronix, you would have already acquired the other half one way or the other. Isn't that right?"

It was a gamble. Keandra didn't know what Mr. Johnson's relationship was to Crystal Techtronix, or if there was one at all, but it was an educated guess. The way the guards kept glancing up at the entrance to the hangar every time the turret opened fire. The fact that Mr. Johnson himself was waiting outside the facility rather than raiding it directly. These facts pointed to his need to maintain some distance between the facility and himself. But it was still a risk. If she was wrong, her entire story would fall apart.

As she waited, keeping her external demeanor calm, Keandra felt a cold sweat forming at the base of her back. Her legs wanted to tremble, and the more she tried to keep them still, the greater the intensity became. She hoped he would read it as exhaustion and blood loss. Her footsteps had traced a line of blood in the sand as she paced. There was no hiding that.

"Your methods are...unorthodox."

"That's one of the reasons we are specialists. What matters is the results, not our methods."

"And you have the data package?"

"Will your men allow me to retrieve it from the vehicle?"

Mr. Johnson nodded, and Keandra turned around, walking back to the truck. She reached the open door and held out her hand. E-jekt handed her the commlink and opened his mouth to say something, but shut it when she glared at him. She walked back to Mr. Johnson and handed him the commlink.

"You will find the entire data package secured on that device. I regret we didn't have time to transfer it to a more suitable storage unit. However, we ran into difficulties."

Mr. Johnson took her commlink and handed it to his bodyguard without examining it. The guard carried it to a short dwarf standing behind the heavily armored strike team. The wind howled as the dwarf checked the data on the commlink. Keandra tried to read Mr. Johnson, wondering if he would prefer the data to be genuine or not. He kept his face impassive. After some time, he gave a nod, likely after receiving a report from his personal decker.

"It appears your fanciful tale has some truth to it. Given our inconvenience, I believe that will cancel out any bonus you might have gained for your initiative. However, your regular fee will be routed to your accounts. We wouldn't want anyone to suffer a negative reputation over this, now would we?"

"A pleasure doing business with you."

Mr. Johnson turned and walked back to one of the armored vehicles. The bodyguard and decker carrying the commlink joined him. He waved and the soldiers lifted their weapons, no longer focusing them on Keandra or the truck behind her. Once Mr. Johnson and his escort climbed back into the vehicle, they peeled off, one at a time, kicking up clouds of dust as they drove away.

Keandra collapsed where she was, her legs no longer willing to support her. E-jekt ran out and grabbed her arm, helping her to her feet. She shuffled over to the vehicle and slumped into the seat. E-jekt buckled her in and moved to close the door, but she reached out and grabbed his arm.

"Did you do it?"

"I tried. We'll see. If all goes according to plan, then as soon as the jammer goes down, Freyr will be able to use the backdoor to get into the Matrix."

Keandra let her hand slide off his arm as she closed her eyes. Hopefully Freyr and Freya would get away. She heard the door slam shut next to her, but it sounded far away as she slipped into oblivion.

EPILOGUE

Keandra shifted in her chair, rolling her leg across the ottoman and wincing as she once again forgot about the wound on her calf. It had been two days since they returned to Sacramento, but the injury still felt as fresh as if it had just happened. Once again, she considered shelling out for magical healing, but decided against it. She wasn't planning on running anytime in the near future.

Lance sat on the floor next to her, his legs crossed and his eyes closed as he meditated. If you looked at him, you wouldn't believe that two days ago he'd been clinging to life, barely hanging on. He still had a few scabs and had definitely acquired some new scars, but he was moving with the same agility and speed he had before the injury.

Paz and E-ject sat at separate tables, one lost in the Matrix and the other lost in her guns. Once again she had taken apart her assault rifle and cleaned each component by hand.

They were still in the Omni, taking advantage of their recent influx of nuyen to upgrade their rooms to a suite. To the credit of the staff here, no one asked about the blood-covered clothing that had to be disposed of. Keandra bet they had experience in such matters. That extra measure of security was well worth the premium rate for accommodations.

Keandra pulled up their account information to check on their financial status. True to his word, Mr. Johnson paid them for their services. For now, they were living off the proceeds of that run, debating where to go next.

As she was checking, a message popped up, announcing a direct transfer arriving from seven different accounts at the same time. The total transferred funds amounted to four hundred thousand nuyen.

Keandra whistled. "Well, it looks like Freyr and Freya got out. The question is, where do you want to vacation?"

ABOUT THE AUTHOR

Kai O'Connal is a traveling vagabond, a worldwide wanderer who is just as happy sleeping out under the stars as they are attending a museum show in the heart of New York City. They have previously popped up in Jakarta, New South Wales, Ecuador, and Cameroon, and we only know they are still alive when a manuscript arrives to us via e-mail. They are the author of the *Shadowrun* novel *Frost & Fire* and the short story "Tenuous Connections" in the *Drawing Destiny* Sixth World Tarot anthology.

LOOKING FOR MORE SHADOWRUN FICTION, CHUMMER?

WE'LL HOOK YOU UP!

Catalyst Game Labs brings you the very best in *Shadowrun* fiction, available at most ebook retailers, including Amazon, Apple Books, Kobo, Barnes & Noble, and more!

NOVELS

1. *Never Deal with a Dragon* (Secrets of Power #1)
   by Robert N. Charrette
2. *Choose Your Enemies Carefully* (Secrets of Power #2)
   by Robert N. Charrette
3. *Find Your Own Truth* (Secrets of Power #3)
   by Robert N. Charrette
4. *2XS* by Nigel Findley
5. *Changeling* by Chris Kubasik
6. *Never Trust an Elf* by Robert N. Charrette
7. *Shadowplay* by Nigel Findley
8. *Night's Pawn* by Tom Dowd
9. *Striper Assassin* by Nyx Smith
10. *Lone Wolf* by Nigel Findley
11. *Fade to Black* by Nyx Smith
12. *Burning Bright* by Tom Dowd
13. *Who Hunts the Hunter* by Nyx Smith
14. *House of the Sun* by Nigel Findley
15. *Worlds Without End* by Caroline Spector
16. *Just Compensation* by Robert N. Charrette
17. *Preying for Keeps* by Mel Odom
18. *Dead Air* by Jak Koke
19. *The Lucifer Deck* by Lisa Smedman
20. *Steel Rain* by Nyx Smith
21. *Shadowboxer* by Nicholas Pollotta
22. *Stranger Souls* (Dragon Heart Saga #1) by Jak Koke
23. *Headhunters* by Mel Odom
24. *Clockwork Asylum* (Dragon Heart Saga #2) by Jak Koke
25. *Blood Sport* by Lisa Smedman
26. *Beyond the Pale* (Dragon Heart Saga #3) by Jak Koke
27. *Technobabel* by Stephen Kenson
28. *Psychotrope* by Lisa Smedman

29. *Run Hard, Die Fast* by Mel Odom
30. *Crossroads* by Stephen Kenson
31. *The Forever Drug* by Lisa Smedman
32. *Ragnarock* by Stephen Kenson
33. *Tails You Lose* by Lisa Smedman
34. *The Burning Time* by Stephen Kenson
35. *Born to Run* (Kellen Colt Trilogy #1) by Stephen Kenson
36. *Poison Agendas* (Kellen Colt Trilogy #2) by Stephen Kenson
37. *Fallen Angels* (Kellen Colt Trilogy #3) by Stephen Kenson
38. *Drops of Corruption* by Jason M. Hardy
39. *Aftershocks* by Jean Rabe & John Helfers
40. *A Fistful of Data* by Stephen Dedman
41. *Fire and Frost* by Kai O'Connal
42. *Hell on Water* by Jason M. Hardy
43. *Dark Resonance* by Phaedra Weldon
44. *Crimson* by Kevin Czarnecki
45. *Shaken: No Job Too Small* by Russell Zimmerman
46. *Borrowed Time* by R.L. King
47. *Deniable Assets* by Mel Odom
48. *Undershadows* by Jason M. Hardy
49. *Shadows Down Under* by Jean Rabe
50. *Makeda Red* by Jennifer Brozek
51. *The Johnson Run* by Kai O'Connal

ANTHOLOGIES

1. *Spells & Chrome*, edited by John Helfers
2. *World of Shadows*, edited by John Helfers
3. *Drawing Destiny: A Sixth World Tarot Anthology*, edited by John Helfers

NOVELLAS

1. *Neat* by Russell Zimmerman
2. *The Vladivostok Gauntlet* by Olivier Gagnon
3. *Nothing Personal* by Olivier Gagnon
4. *Another Rainy Night* by Patrick Goodman
5. *Sail Away, Sweet Sister* by Patrick Goodman
6. *DocWagon 19* by Jennifer Brozek
7. *Wolf & Buffalo* by R.L. King
8. *Big Dreams* by R.L. King
9. *Blind Magic* by Dylan Birtolo
10. *The Frame Job, Part 1: Wu* by Dylan Birtolo

In the year 2079, shadowrunners do the jobs no one else wants. There's plenty of work to do, and plenty of obstacles to overcome. Backstabbing corporate pawns, aggressive law enforcement, and other shadowrunners angling for your payday can get in your way. Your job is to beat them to the punch and make the big score before they can stop you.

Shadowrun: Sprawl Ops puts players in control of their own team of shadowrunners, selecting who they'll hire and then building up the cash, gear, and abilities the runners need to survive the streets. Only one team will complete the final mission that scores a huge payday and wins the game. Do you have the guts, wiles, and treachery it will take to make it to the top? Time to find out.

www.ingramcontent.com/pod-product-compliance
Lightning Source LLC
Chambersburg PA
CBHW070818180626
46818CB00001B/316